TORTURER'S RETURN

One of the horses stopped suddenly, and a figure turned to stare back at the cabin. It was the one-eyed leader of the group. Even across the black distance I could feel his gaze burning into my skin, and I shuddered. And at that moment I understood why his face had plagued me so. Stories came back to me, stories that my brother Sam had told me, stories that had been the substance of many nightmares for many years.

"Sam, is that . . ."

"Yes, Jim, that man is Colonel Josiah Jefferson Madison. That was the man who took delight in seeing me and my friends tortured. He's a murderer, Jim, and now he has a grudge against me. Before this is over, someone is going to be dead."

DEVIL WIRE

CAMERON JUDD

DOMAIN ™

BANTAM BOOKS
New York • Toronto • London • Sydney • Auckland

DEVIL WIRE
A Bantam Domain Book/published by arrangement with the
author

PUBLISHING HISTORY
Zebra edition published 1981
Bantam edition/February 1995

ISBN 0-553-57171-0

Published simultaneously in the United States and Canada

Bantam Books are published by Bantam Books, a division of Bantam
Doubleday Dell Publishing Group, Inc. Its trademark, consisting of the
words "Bantam Books" and the portrayal of a rooster, is Registered in
U.S. Patent and Trademark Office and in other countries. Marca Reg-
istrada. Bantam Books, 1540 Broadway, New York, New York 10036.

PRINTED IN THE UNITED STATES OF AMERICA

OPM   0 9 8 7 6 5 4 3 2 1

DEVIL WIRE

CHAPTER I

~

It's never an easy thing for a man to admit that he's been a failure, but such was the assessment I had to make of myself as I rode through the Montana night aboard the unreserved coach section of this train on the Northern Pacific rail line. I was tired to my very soul, the thrill of my first train ride long left behind me somewhere around Bismarck, the endless rumblings of the rail now a torment rather than a pleasure.

There was little I could do as I stared out through the dark windows except relive the past. And that was an unpleasant pastime, for I had few things I could recollect with pride.

I had failed. I had failed myself, my family, the memory of my father and mother. Everything I had dreamed of had crumbled away bit by bit, leaving me with the realization that it was time to give up. So here I was, a Tennessee farmer without a single success to call my own, Miles City bound and watching the Montana plains slip swiftly past my window, the land lit with the dim glow of the night sky, and my mind in such a turmoil I couldn't even appreciate the rugged beauty of it all.

Gloomily my mind moved back over the years, as steady and relentless as the rumbling, smoke-belching train on which I rode. The memories were sometimes pleasant, causing me to smile at my reflection in the dark window, but largely they were painful.

I was born a farmer and a Baptist in 1849 in the same tall oak bed in which I had been conceived the year before, and the same bed in which my brother had come into the world some five years prior to me. There was no doctor to assist my mother with either birth; the other women from further up the valley served as midwives while my father paced about in the yard, nervously puffing his pipe. In both cases his apprehensions were quickly relieved, for both my brother and I were strong, fat, healthy babies that grew to be strong young men. In those days, weakness and sickness in the family were things no hard-working Tennessee farmer could afford.

I grew up on the family homestead in Powell's Valley, a long valley that runs southwest to northeast in eastern Tennessee and western Virginia. It is a green, fertile valley that is bordered on the south by Wallen's Ridge and the Powell Mountains and on the north by the Cumberlands, and through it ran a portion of the great road that first led settlers from the hills and valleys of Virginia and the Carolinas on through Cumberland Gap and into Kentucky. Our farm lay southwest of Cumberland Gap, our home built right up against the base of the steep Cumberlands that stood in a tall, proud line, projecting gray faces of rock through the trees on their crests.

My father was typical of the breed that populated the valley in those days—few smiles and little mirth, but lots of back-breaking work. He worked from the first light of dawn, sometimes even before that, until that same light faded at dusk. And my brother and I were always with him, and together we made the farm into something of which we all were proud.

I received just enough schooling to teach me to read and write, though my mother taught me many other things as well. I developed a passion to learn, one that could not be squelched, and I read every book I could get my hands on. My mother was proud of that, as was my father to a lesser degree, for they both sensed that learning would take the place of brawn as the country grew and developed. I think that somehow they always looked on me as the one who would carry on the farm's life after they were gone. My older brother had too much of the wanderlust in him to stay in the place of his birth until the end of his days; I was a more stable fellow, not as prone to wander.

My brother went by the name of Sam, his full name being Samuel Adams Hartford. My name is James Monroe Hartford, and my callen name is Jim. My father chose the names not out of any interest in history, but simply because he had heard them and liked the ring of them. My mother would have preferred biblical names, I think, for she always called me James and my brother Samuel, rather than the Jim and Sam the rest of the world knew us by. But seemed fitting, somehow, for she had a dignity about her that didn't lend itself to slang or nicknames. It was a quiet dignity, a humble one, a very real one.

When the war came I was just a sprout of a boy, twelve years old, but fired up by the controversy of the times and the endless debates between the southern and northern sympathizers in the valley. Both factions were there, and the very air was tense in those days with dissension. When the fighting began, many local men and boys swarmed up through Cumberland Gap to join the northern forces while my father and brother decided to join with the south. It wasn't political reasons that motivated my father's decision, for he was a highly unpolitical man and could not, I think, have said just what the fighting was all about. And while his localized, almost isolated existence made it difficult for him to visualize something as big as a nation, he did have a clear concept of statehood, and he knew that his home state had joined the secession. So as a loyal Tennessean, he went with it, fighting for a cause he did not understand.

He fought with Zollicoffer in that general's last fight. My father was shot just before the near-sighted Zollicoffer was blown from his saddle while barking orders to Union troops that he took to be his own men. And the rag-tag army of farmers broke ranks after that and scurried back to their farms and families, leaving their out-dated 1812 army issue flintlocks in the mud beside the bodies of their comrades. My father's corpse was among those left behind, but my brother Sam did not leave his side, and as a result was taken prisoner by the northern troops and hauled away to a prison camp in Bryant's Fork, Illinois. The stories he told me of the atrocities heaped upon the prisoners in that camp, the cruelties engineered by the heartless, sadistic overseer of that hellish place . . . many times those stories have made me shudder.

It was after the war that my failures truly began. My mother died the year after the war ended, my brother reaching home scarcely in time to see her alive for one last time. We buried her on the grounds of the farm, near the creek and beneath an oak. Sam stayed on with me long enough to get the farm back on its feet again, then he was gone, the wanderlust claiming him, driving him west to make his fortune in the gold fields of Confederate Gulch, Montana Territory. And though he never gained the riches he hoped for, he did get enough to set himself up as a small-time rancher on the eastern Montana plains, making his living amid a growing cattle industry. And I was left alone in Tennessee, a boy not yet twenty years old, trying with all that was in me to make a success of the old Powell's Valley farm, doing my best to continue what my father had begun, working as hard as I would have if he had been looking over my shoulder. I wanted to make the farm back into a thing he would have been proud of.

And I was failing. Miserably failing. It seemed that God himself was against me, for whenever blight struck the valley, it was my crops that died first. Whenever disease ravaged the cattle, mine were the first to die. I watched my profits decrease year by year, and soon I had to begin selling portions of my farm to make up for the losses. I sold more and more, eating away at the borders of the farm, each year becoming poorer than the year before, until at last, in this year of 1884, I had sold the rest of it, even the house itself, and boarded the train with Montana as my destination.

It hurt me to have to give up on the task left to me by my father, but I tried to comfort myself with the realization that I had done my best. Yet it seemed a vague comfort, and I dreaded the prospect of having to face Sam and tell him of my failure. And the fact that I would have to ask him for work until I could somehow set myself up to make a living on my own was a cause of constant anxiety for me.

My spirits had revived somewhat as the journey progressed and my mind was overwhelmed by the new, and to me, amazing things that I was seeing. I had never in my life seen a city of any real size—I hadn't even traveled the distance south to Knoxville—and when first I set eyes on Chicago it took my breath away. I had the same reaction when I saw St. Paul, and if anyone had talked to me right then they would have found me the most enthusiastic traveler in the country, I think.

Those optimistic thoughts had come several days ago when the journey was young. But now, here in the late Montana night in the darkness just before dawn I felt quite differently. I was growing close to my destination now, my anticipated and dreaded meeting with Sam only a short time away, and my entire worldly fortune in a carpetbag at my feet. I was beginning to realize just how ignorant I was of life on the plains. I was going to cattle country, and the only experience I had with cattle was on the farm in a world utterly apart from the rolling, seemingly endless plains around me. Would Sam be able to use me, to provide me work? I felt certain he would give me a place to stay and feed me, even if there was nothing I could do to help him, but the idea of taking something without giving in return was repulsive to me, a violation of the pride of my raising.

"Good evening, sir. May I sit down?"

The speaker's voice jarred me from my thoughts, and I looked up at him sharply—and rather stupidly, I'm afraid. As soon as my mind came around to reality again, I remembered my manners and offered him the seat across from me. The unreserved coach was set up in a series of stalls, with two benches in each one set facing each other. I had been seated alone in my stall, and this fellow had been up further ahead in the car, also alone. I had noticed him earlier.

He was sharply dressed, a gold watch chain draped across his stomach, accenting the neat gray suit which he wore. On his head sat a gray derby, matching the suit, and his mustache also was gray. He was slim, tall, and distinguished, obviously a businessman, and as he sat down before me the shabbiness of my own clothing became embarrassingly apparent. But I smiled pleasantly, glad to have someone to talk to.

"Aaron P. McCuen," he said, extending his hand. "I hope I'm not intruding, but this trip is getting rather tedious, and I thought you might find a little companionship as pleasant as I would."

"I certainly would," I replied. "The name's Jim Hartford. I noticed you got on in Bismarck. You from around there?"

"No sir, though I have been there in connection with my business. Stayed about two months—meetings and all that garbage. I'm heading into Miles City now. More business."

He had a pleasant voice, smooth and clean. I wanted to get him to talk some more just to hear it. "What's your line of work, Mr. McCuen?"

"Call me Aaron—or just McCuen, if you prefer. I'm affiliated with the Washburn and Moen Manufacturing Company in Worcester. More of a salesman than anything else, and a spokesman on occasion for the company. I deal in barbed wire."

Barbed wire. Now there was something I had heard about, though indirectly. I had never actually seen the stuff, though I knew it was available in Tennessee. Most folks in the valley still used rails or stones for fencing.

But I had heard reports, second or third hand, of those who talked of the trouble the wire was causing west of the Mississippi in the cattle country, where many still wanted the ranges open. But beyond that I knew little of the matter. I wondered if Sam used the wire.

"Barbed wire, you say? I assume you're going into Miles City to make some sales. I hear the stuff has caused a little trouble at spots."

He nodded dolefully. "There's been some trouble, I'll admit, some areas worse than others. Texas has been pure hell over the matter, with wire cutting organizations and anti-wire cutting organizations, with secret signals and passwords and such things as that. There's been a good deal of violence at some spots. The wire is getting all over the country now. My company is producing not far from twenty million pounds of the wire every year. Business is booming."

"What brings you out this way? Isn't there any wire being sold here yet?"

"Oh, yes," he said, pulling out an expensive-looking cigar and offering it to me. I refused, and he paused to slowly light up. "But rail service has been in Montana only a short time—transcontinental rail service, I mean. Before last year we had to ship the wire in by freight wagon for the most part. Now we haul it by rail and most of the time just dump and sell it right beside the tracks. We sell to homesteaders and quite a few ranchers. Cattlemen are buying more and more of the wire. I guess they're starting to realize they can't really fight the stuff—it's here to stay. And it can be a real advantage to them if they use it correctly. I'm heading into Miles City to try to set up a better distribution system, maybe to try to get a few more cattlemen converted over to our side. There's been a real flurry of trouble between ranchers who use it and those who don't in the last few months. Maybe you haven't heard. The railroad tries to keep it quiet and all."

My heart sank within me. I had heard of no major trouble in the area I was going. I was suddenly fearful for Sam's safety, though I had no idea if he was involved at all in the barbed wire controversy. And I feared for myself too, for in the back of my mind was a plan to obtain some land for myself and get into the cattle business myself once I learned what I needed to know from my brother. My face must have reflected my thoughts, for McCuen frowned slightly, as if he sensed I was bothered by something.

"Well, enough talk about me and my barbed wire," he said. "What brings you out this way? And where do you call home?"

"I'm a Tennessee boy—a farmer up until now," I said. "I came out here . . . to see what my luck might be like in the cattle business." I found myself hesitant to tell the entire truth, for I was not at all proud of the way I was running for refuge to my brother.

McCuen smiled. "That's good to hear. I wish you the best of luck. Perhaps when the time comes we can talk about doing a little business about fencing."

"Maybe so. I'll admit I'm a little bothered about that trouble you mentioned. I hope I don't run into any of it."

"Oh, I doubt that you will," he said. "I intend to

see what I can do to still any unrest that seems to have
arisen over the situation."

I forced a grin at him. "I'll certainly keep you in
mind if I ever need any wire," I said.

"Thanks. By the way . . . if you plan to stay in a
hotel there, then perhaps we could share the cost of a
room. I certainly don't want to seem presumptuous,
but . . ."

"Thanks but no thanks," I said. "I have a brother
out here, and I figure to spend some time with him before I get myself set up."

"That's good. And I hope you find some good
land. A few years back you could have walked out
anywhere and made a claim, just about. But since the
government granted most of the land to the railroad
it's pretty much a matter of buying whatever half-
decent places you can find. The old-timers have all the
land near town. New settlers have to range further
out."

I felt a growing depression. It seemed every piece
of news I was hearing made me wonder more and
more if I had done the right thing in selling the
Powell's Valley farm. I turned toward the dark window, brooding.

Outside the plains were bathed in a soft light, and
the distant horizon was a lightening shade of purple
and lavender. The newly rising sun was invisible to me
as I stared southward, but I could follow its course
as the shadows stretched black and long toward the
west, then shortened rapidly as the sun rose higher. I
heard the noise of the train's brakes, and we pulled to
a halt in front of a station platform marked "Glen-
dive."

Passengers rose and moved off while others got
on. McCuen had been dozing, and a man brushed
roughly past him, his jacket knocking McCuen's hat
off and waking him up. My companion stirred,
frowned at the man's back, and picked up his hat.

"I didn't realize I had gone to sleep," he said. "I

couldn't even think of sleeping all night, and now that daylight is here I'm getting drowsy." He looked at his cigar and frowned to see it had gone out. He began to dig in his pocket for a match, then murmured something and cast the smoke to the floor. He leaned back, pulled his hat low over his eyes, and dozed off again as the train began pulling forward again. He lay with his supple fingers folded across his stomach, snoring faintly. I had to smile. This elegant man could even snore elegantly.

I turned and looked out again over the Montana plains, my stomach tying itself in knots inside me. Could I do it? Could I really make a success of myself here in this unknown land, or would I be simply a burden to Sam?

I looked around me at the other passengers. Some sat sleeping; others were staring out the windows. How many of these were other men bringing their families to the Montana Territory to try to make up for past failures? Children roamed the aisle. Many larger families were traveling together, probably hoping to buy or claim enough land to make some sort of living. From what I had heard, many were predicting a great influx of settlers to Montana within the next twenty years. The railroad literature promoting the land showed pictures of neat cottages surrounded by flowers in a land that looked like a depiction of paradise. As I looked out the window I saw a land that was unlike that in the pictures, and felt certain many other men in the train were just beginning to realize that the land was not the promised country they had dreamed about. The train stopped again, and again. More passengers.

Like me, many new settlers were southerners, I guessed, probably trying to remake fortunes lost during the war. It was a standing joke that the Confederacy was not dead—it had just moved to Montana. Broken men, shattered families that had lost a lifetime's worth of homebuilding and hard labor when the war swept through the south ... many were surely desperate, with only a few dollars and a bagful of dreams between themselves and starvation.

At least I had some money from the sale of my land—enough to take care of me for a time, and hopefully enough to buy a good piece of railroad property. I reached down to pat the side of my carpetbag.

It was gone.

The shock spread over me like the touch of death, chilling me, filling me with an overwhelming panic. Gone! Suddenly I stood, a violent gasp breaking from my lips. McCuen stirred but did not wake. I looked about the car in desperation.

There ... there it was, in the hands of a tousleheaded boy, a lad that could not be more than ten years old, lugging it as fast as he could toward the rear of the car. Apparently he had only just now slipped the bag from beneath my feet while I was lost in contemplation.

But now I had him. He couldn't get away. I ran from the stall where I had been seated and headed after him just as he made it out the car's rear door. The other passengers looked at me with dull eyes, not concerned about what I was doing.

I caught the little devil on the platform at the rear of the car. My hand grasped his shoulder and the other reached for the bag.

"Give it back, you little beggar! Give it back, or I'll box your ears until your jaws ring!"

I've heard plenty of cussing in my day, but none to match in vigor and vileness the language that burst from that young throat. And as his words damned me, his hands pushed me with unexpected force, upsetting me, sending me back against the platform railing as the bag slipped from my grasp.

And then I was over, falling, striking the embankment beside the tracks and rolling down it, landing at last almost twenty feet from the fast-moving train, the morning dew soaking my pants and a dazed expression shaping my features as the train moved past me, the young devil waving my bag at me with a taunting look on his face.

For several long minutes I sat there, my dulled brain unable to take it all in. I was stranded, without a horse or weapon, here on the Montana plains, every cent I had in the world being carried away from me by a young thief who was probably anticipating an orgy of candy and licorice water. I was stuck, alone and isolated. Miles City was on down the track, a long walk. Maybe I could find that young robber there and recover my cash, but I wasn't sure Miles City was where he would get off. I was broke, unarmed, and alone in a place where I knew no one. Sam's spread was out there somewhere, but I had no idea of its exact location.

So I got up, brushed myself off, and started walking.

CHAPTER II

I followed the tracks closely, taking the opportunity to view the country to which I had come. For the most part it was grasslands, generally flat but with low hills that stretched far in all directions. There were larger hills, too, and cottonwoods that grew tall and lonesome out on the grasslands. More cottonwoods grew along the course of a meandering brook. I debated whether or not to take a drink from the brook, but the brown tint of the water killed the idea.

Occasionally I saw cattle roaming lazily in the distance, and I could see why Montana had perhaps the biggest cattle industry in the west. I could also understand the hesitancy of some ranchers to have the land fenced in. Many of them had come to the Montana Territory many years before, riding a weary gelding and leading a handful of scrawny cattle. Many with just such a humble beginning were rich today, for on the open range many calves were born who were the fair and legal property of whoever first managed to get a rope around their necks. A good active rope could make a cattleman successful back in those old days even if he had little money to invest in stock. Those days were ending now, being killed by fences and railroads. No wonder many were sad to see the coming of the new settlers. The whistle of the railroad engines marked the beginning of the end of the west that was. Civilization was reaching across the plains on a track of steel.

I noted the irony of having to walk slowly beneath the sun along the railroad, the modern miracle that could move a man from one end of the nation to the other in a fraction of the time it took to travel by river or horseback. The passenger car in which I had been riding had hardly qualified as luxurious, but now I wished fervently that I was back on it. Into my mind flashed a report I had read some months back of how the people of Bozeman, a town west of Miles City, had greeted the arrival of the first passenger train last March with a huge banquet. When I arrived in Miles City there would be no such welcome for me. I didn't even know how I could get in touch with my brother.

I spotted a small dwelling nearby a creek that was hardly more than a trickle. Though I wasn't certain, I thought myself about fifteen miles from Miles City, also called Milestown by some of the older residents of the area. It was still early, and I knew I could easily reach my destination on foot, but I hoped I could hitch a ride on a passing wagon. I walked toward the isolated little dwelling, noting a narrow wagon road leading from it and roughly paralleling the railroad.

As I drew near I looked for some sign of life about the place, but there was none save for a lone horse in a split-rail corral near the house.

The place was small, one of the sort of houses I later learned was almost standard in the territory. It was a log house, obviously well constructed, with evenly sized, tight-fitting logs. I looked the place over very carefully. I had gained some limited experience with log buildings in Tennessee, and always I found them fascinating. Whoever had built this one was a craftsman. This was no loosely chinked dirt-roofed structure; the roof was made of hand-split shingles, and the chinking was tight. The builder had put real glass into the windows, as well as store-bought shutters. It was an appealing spot, with a restful and calm atmosphere about it. I noticed an extensive garden behind the house, beside which the small stream widened into a large pond of the sort that was good for watering animals. I found myself envious of whoever owned this little spread, for although it didn't appear to be a ranch as such, it was obviously a well-kept and productive little spot. I assumed whoever lived here was a self-sufficient individual who lived on what he raised and hunted, for I could figure no other way he could survive out here unless he was a rancher. Large-scale farms were a rarity in these parts, and I saw no signs of extensive cultivation.

"That's far enough, buddy. You just reach good and high and turn around real slow."

The voice was gentle, its tone belying the threatening content of the words. But I wasn't about to call the bluff, if bluff it was, and very quickly I obeyed. I thrust my hands straight up and turned completely around.

It was a gray-bearded fellow that I saw step from behind a cottonwood, a Spencer rifle aimed at my gut. His voice may have sounded calm, but the look in his eye sent a chill through me, and I had the unnerving sensation that this fellow would not hesitate to put a bullet through my gut. I wondered just what I had walked into.

"Easy, mister . . . I meant no harm. I got thrown off the train a ways back, and thought maybe you might have a cup of water. I was just about to holler for you."

"Good thing you didn't," he said. "I might have blowed your head off. I been right skittish lately. I reckon you must be new to these parts. A man don't just walk up on somebody else with no warnin', especially the way things is right now."

I wasn't sure what he meant by that last comment, but I was in no mood to quiz him. The gun was still aimed at my abdomen, and my hands still reached for the clouds. And as long as that big Spencer's muzzle was giving me its one-eyed stare, I wasn't about to lower them. My father had carried a Spencer, and I knew of the tendency of that sort of weapon to go off with only a slight bump to the stock, and I prayed that he wouldn't bump the butt end of that cannon against one of those cottonwoods.

He was looking me over, obviously in no hurry to make any changes in the present situation. I felt I was being sized up. And with my sweat-soaked condition, along with the dirt that had smeared on my trousers when I fell from the train, I wasn't sure I would pass whatever mental test he was putting me through. But apparently I looked more pitiful than threatening, for slowly he let the muzzle of his weapon drop and he looked at me with almost a disdainful expression.

"Well, you don't look any too dangerous. But with the trouble we've been havin' the last few months I ain't about to be careless 'bout no one that comes up unexpected. But you're on foot, so I reckon you ain't one of them riders."

I let out a sigh as the gun's barrel dropped, and slowly I lowered my hands. "Thanks for dropping that gun, mister. I had no intention of disturbing you. I'll be on my way."

"No—not until you've had that water you wanted," he said, now just as amiable as he had been hostile moments before. "I ain't gonna have it said that Jasper Maddux sent anybody away thirsty."

He supplied me with a dipper of ice-cold water fresh from the well. It was a luxury, cool and refreshing, filling me with vigor and clearing my mind even as I drank it. When I had finished I had another, then another. The old fellow grinned at me all the while.

"I reckon you were right thirsty, feller," he laughed. "What can I call you?"

"Jim Hartford," I said. "I'm from Tennessee. I just got into the territory this morning."

"You say you fell off the train?"

I flushed, ashamed to tell him what had happened, but I managed to get my story out, and actually felt grateful when the old fellow didn't laugh. I omitted any reference to my brother, for still it filled me with shame to have to come crawling to him, and I had no desire to talk about it.

"What is it you aim on doin', now that your cash is gone?" he asked. "I wish I could help you out, but I'm about as busted as you are."

I found I couldn't answer him. I had no desire to face Sam until I had at least tried to regain my cash. I shook my head.

"I don't really know, Mr. Maddux. I reckon I'll go into Miles City and try to get a little work somewhere and maybe find that little jackass that took my money. Right now I just need to get on into town."

"You came by at a good time, then. I'm headin' in that direction, though I ain't goin' but within about five miles of town. You can probably hitch a ride with somebody from there who'll take you the rest of the way."

Within ten minutes we were bumping along in an old flatbed, following a wagon trail with the deepest ruts I had ever seen. It was ten times rougher than any wagon ride I had ever taken, but Maddux didn't seem to notice. The vague references to trouble that I had heard both from him and McCuen came to my mind, and I inquired about the matter.

"It's been a real problem lately," he said. "Worse than any I've ever seen. Riders are what are causin' it all, night riders that cut wires and threaten folks that fence in their land. They gave me a bit of trouble the other night, tryin' to cut the fence I got around my waterin' hole. I ran 'em off, though. That Spencer roars good and loud." He grinned and displayed red gums with two yellow teeth in the front worn down to nubs.

I hadn't noticed the fence around the water hole. And though I was grateful to Maddux for the help he was giving me, I couldn't help but feel he had done the wrong thing to fence in his watering hole. No wonder ranchers were angry at fence-stringers! Water holes were precious in cattle country.

"Does anybody know who these riders are?" I asked. "Whose men are they?"

"Nobody knows. They're all strangers to these parts, best anybody can tell. I figger somebody has hired 'em, moved 'em in from somewheres to cause trouble. Cattlemen, probably . . . maybe several of 'em together. So far there ain't no proof that they're tied in with anybody in particular, and all the ranchers say they don't know a thing about it. But I figure somebody has hired 'em. We'll find out sooner or later."

We rode the remainder of the distance with few words. When we reached an area where an even rougher road led southward off the one we were on, Maddux stopped the wagon and I climbed down.

I gave him my thanks and he headed down the side road. I waved at him until he disappeared from view, then I started walking again, moving west toward Miles City.

The sun was high in the east, beaming down much hotter than before. But the air was pleasant, and though I was hungry I felt quite vigorous, and walked with a fast and firm stride. I felt fortunate in one way to have no burden to carry, but I also missed the feeling of my carpetbag in my hand. I refused to let myself worry excessively about my loss, for I knew that worry would do nothing to help me replace my lost money or get started as a rancher.

I had it in mind to find work somewhere around Miles City. I had no idea what sort of jobs were available, but I was confident enough of my abilities to give me the assurance that I would find something. And in the time I was not working I could scout around and see if there was any sign of that young thief who stole my bag.

I turned when I heard the noise of a buggy on the road behind me. A one-horse buckboard approached me at a good clip, raising a sizeable cloud of dust on the road. It was a fine vehicle, a very expensive model, I could tell, but the driver was of far more interest than the buckboard itself.

It was a young lady, pretty and auburn-haired. She was steering the buckboard like an expert, and her bearing and confidence in her task caused me to sense immediately that this was a lady of strength and pride. And if the expensive buggy was any indication, she was also a lady of some wealth.

I smiled at her and nodded as she approached. She slowed the buggy down and pulled up beside me, looking down at me from her perch like a queen from her coach. My lands, she was pretty!

"Hello, ma'am. How are you today?"

"Fine, sir. And yourself?"

"Very well, thank you. I couldn't be better." It was a lie, of course, but I had learned long ago that people making polite conversation weren't interested in hearing honest answers.

"What puts you on foot, sir? Has your horse had some trouble?" Her voice was clear and bell-like, perfectly suiting her appearance. I felt warmth steal over me.

"No ma'am. You might say I had the misfortune to fall off the Northern Pacific back some ways up the track. I hitched a ride with an old fellow just this far. I'm heading for Miles City."

She looked at me carefully, curling her lip in a way that made my heart beat faster. She sighed loudly.

"My father would thrash me if he knew I picked up a stranger on the road," she said. "But I'm going into Miles City and would be glad to have some company. Hop in. My name's Jennifer Guthrie."

"Jim Hartford, ma'am. I appreciate the ride."

The buggy rode a lot smoother than Maddux's wagon. I settled back on the soft upholstery and enjoyed the scent of her perfume as it wafted over to me.

"Miss Guthrie, I can't tell you how grateful I am for the ride. I was getting a bit weary out there."

"I imagine so. How did you manage to fall off the train?"

There it was . . . the same embarrassing question Maddux had asked. I gave her an abbreviated version of the story, again omitting any mention of my brother. It crossed my mind that she might be from a ranching family, and should she and Sam be on opposite sides of the barbed wire struggle it might be the end of my free ride. She didn't react with the same reserve Maddux had shown toward my story; she laughed, and I blushed crimson. It was very difficult to admit to a pretty young lady like this that a child had outwitted me.

She apologized profusely for her laughter. "I'm sorry . . . I guess it isn't funny to you at all. Please forgive me." She smiled silently to herself for a time, and I could almost see the pictures flashing through her mind—pictures of me falling off the platform of that passenger car while a five-foot devil laughed at me. I had to admit there was a certain comical element in it.

She asked me about myself, my background, my plans. I told her a little, though very little, and in the process learned much about her.

Her father was Luther Guthrie, she said—a man whose name was known even in Tennessee as the owner of the fantastically successful Muster Creek Cattle Company, one of the biggest dealers in beef in the territory. I had heard of him and his company through talk back home and in my reading in preparation for the trip. From what I gathered, Luther Guthrie owned millions of dollars and had almost complete control over huge tracts of the best grazing land to be found in hundreds of miles. It astounded me to realize that I was sitting beside his daughter, smiling and talking with her almost as if we were old friends.

"You're needing a job," she said. "Have you ever done any cooking? I mean for large groups of people."

It was an unexpected query, but I managed to bluff my way through it. "Yes," I lied. "I was a cook in the army a few years after the war. I cooked for dozens at a time." There wasn't a trace of truth in it, but I sensed a job offer coming on, and I intended to take advantage of it. Working for Luther Guthrie could be a very lucrative job, just what I needed right now.

"I'm glad to hear that. You see, our cook died just two weeks ago, and we've been just scraping by since then. You'll need to work to make up for that money you lost. Would you consider coming to work for us?"

I had assented to the offer scarcely after the words had left her lips. She smiled, apparently sincerely pleased that I would be working for them, and I sat back with a sense of gratification. I had managed to bluff my way into a job . . . now if only I could bluff my way through a few meals, maybe I would have some money.

We talked casually until we reached Miles City. Miles City! The very place I had dreamed of, the place where I hoped to rebuild my life. Miles City of the Montana Territory—several hundred people, over twenty saloons, and several businesses of the type a man doesn't mention in polite society. I felt a thrill of excitement as the buckboard entered the wide dirt street.

There were a goodly number of people walking about in the street, and many of the men paused to politely tip their hats to Jennifer, and she smiled and nodded back. I could feel them looking me over, wondering who I was and what I was doing in the company of Miss Jennifer Guthrie. I felt a little like a plucked chicken hung for display in a butcher's window.

Miles City was not an exceptionally large town, though the coming of the railroad had started a spurt of growth. Many of the town's retail establishments were lined up in two facing rows on either side of the wide street. I looked over some of the signs. Ringer and Johnson Livery ... Lodging-Rooms ... Chinese Laundry ... The owner of the laundry smiled and gave a curt bow as we passed his business. Leaning up against the wall of the building beside him was a slender young man with a neatly-trimmed mustache and sideburns. He too waved at the lady and stepped back inside the building sporting the sign that read Huffman's Portraits.

"It seems that you're pretty well-known in this town," I said as she pulled the buggy to a stop. I leaped down to circle the buggy and give her a hand as she stepped out.

"Oh, I guess my family has been around these parts for quite some time," she said. "My father has done well with cattle, and the family name has spread pretty far."

"Ma'am, I think I'll walk over to the livery and enjoy the shade while you take care of your business. Maybe I'll explore the town a bit. If you would like I would be happy to take over the driving when it's time to head back to your ranch."

"Why, thank you, Mr. Hartford. I would appreciate that."

She turned and moved on down the boardwalk, entering a textile and general merchandise store. I looked after her, unable to take my eyes from her until she was gone. Sitting in the buggy with her had made me forget my troubles very quickly. I think if that little railroad thief had popped up before me right then I would have patted him on the head.

I loitered about for awhile, finally heading across to the nearest saloon for a glass of water, the only drink that didn't cost any money. I was halfway across the street when I heard a voice calling my name.

I turned to see Aaron McCuen approaching me. In his hand was my bag.

"Thank heaven!" I exclaimed, opening the bag to find all my money intact where I had stowed it in a side pocket. "How did you come by this?"

"Oh, I took it from that little fellow that had it. I knew it was yours, but I couldn't figure out where you had gone."

And so again I had the humiliating experience of telling my story, and again it was greeted with laughter. I didn't really mind this time—I was growing used to it.

"Come in and join me for a bite," he said, gesturing toward a cafe. I accepted the invitation.

We sat in a cool, dark corner of the cafe with our meals before us, and into my mind came the tale of the wire-cutting night riders Maddux had told me about. I related it to McCuen, and he seemed upset by the news.

"This is bad . . . bad," he said, shaking his head. "I don't know what kind of effect this will have on my business. It isn't good at all for people to associate barbed wire with violence and threats. Something is going to have to be done."

He sat brooding for awhile, and I stayed with him until I saw Jennifer Guthrie emerge from the store across the street, a full basket in her arms. She headed back toward the buggy, and I took my leave of McCuen, again thanking him for the safe return of my bag.

She was pleased to see my bag had been returned. I told her about McCuen, not mentioning his business for fear she would not be pleased if the subject of barbed wire came up.

"Was your money in the bag?" she asked.

I started to answer, then caught my breath. If I said yes, she might assume that I would not be interested anymore in her offer of work at the Guthrie ranch. And I suddenly realized that money or no money, I wanted that job. I wanted to be near her.

"No . . . the money was gone," I said. She shook her head sympathetically.

"I'm sorry. I guess you'll be coming to work for us then. Will you watch my things for me? I have a bit more to do before I'm ready to leave."

The "bit more" took the rest of the day. By the time we at last climbed aboard and headed for the Guthrie ranch on Muster Creek it was late afternoon.

CHAPTER III

It was getting dark when we made the turn north off the main road toward the Guthrie ranch near Muster Creek. The horse was slow—hungry, I suspected, for it had not grazed for quite some time—but Miss Guthrie assured me the ranch was not far.

I noticed as we drew nearer the ranch that Jennifer Guthrie was growing nervous. Her face appeared slightly pale, and she clenched her fists in her lap, responding to my attempts at conversation with a minimum of words, staring ahead into the growing darkness.

At last I asked her what was bothering her, and she began to deny that anything was on her mind. But she paused, smiled sadly, and said, "I'm a bit worried about how my father will react when I get back. You see, I stayed much longer in town than I thought I would, and he always likes to know where I am at every minute. He's very protective, you know—still thinks of me as a child."

I sighed. That didn't sound good. If Luther

Guthrie was the type to grow angry just because his daughter came in late from town, then he probably would be even more upset to meet a fellow she picked up on the road. I grew apprehensive. I suspected that my greeting at the Guthrie ranch might be something less than cordial.

We came upon the ranch quickly, and in the moonlight it was an impressive sight. The house was one story tall, built of logs, and spread out long and narrow. I could tell that the place had been expanded several times, and as we rounded a turn in the road I could see that there was another large extension on the rear of the house, making the structure into something like a large L.

Light streamed from the windows, making a soft glow about the front of the house. It looked friendly, somehow, like a place where a traveler would be welcome. My fears eased a little. After all, I had been assured a job at the place, so what was there to worry about?

There were several outbuildings, also log structures, and a few smaller sod buildings set further off. A hill covered with scraggly brush rose up behind the ranch, and in a pen built on the hillside I saw the faint white forms of chickens. There was a corral built alongside one of the larger outbuildings, and several horses were inside. The moon was growing brighter as it climbed through the sky, and the whole scene was bathed in dim light, giving it all a sort of dream-like quality.

We pulled the buggy up right before the house, and the dream became a nightmare.

The front door burst open suddenly, and a big figure stalked out, approaching us with obvious anger. My self-confidence vanished like a drop of water on a hot rock. I had no doubt that this was Luther Guthrie.

"Jennifer, where have you been? Do you think that I haven't been worried about you?" Then he looked at me. "And who is this melon head?"

I glanced over at the young lady. Even in the darkness I could see that she was pale. It was a long moment before she could speak, and I suddenly realized that she was afraid, terrified of her own father.

"I . . . I'm sorry, Pa . . . I just stayed longer than I meant . . . I'm sorry . . ."

Her voice was quaking, making her sound like a small child. Yet she was at least twenty-five years old, I estimated. It seemed incongruous. What kind of man was this Luther Guthrie, to raise a daughter in such a manner that even as a grown woman she was terrified of him?

"Stayed longer than you meant, did you? Well, that's a blamed fine reason!" He snorted, then looked again at me. "I asked you who this joker was. What do you mean riding home after dark with a stranger, like some brothel girl? Mister, you better have an awful convincin' explanation as to why you're here, or else . . ."

Hot anger flashed through me, and my voice spoke before my mind did. "My name is Jim Hartford, sir," I said with mock respect. "Your daughter was kind enough to let me ride with her into Miles City. I wanted to return the favor by driving her back. I planned to discuss the possibility of working as a cook for you, but I think that would be pointless now." I turned to Miss Guthrie. "Thank you for the job offer, but I don't think it's going to work out." Then I immediately regretted my words, for they were new fuel to the fire of wrath which the rancher heaped upon his daughter.

"Jennifer, do you mean to tell me you offered this man a job?" he exclaimed. "Without even checking with me? If you were a few years younger, I'd turn you over and . . ." He glowered at her with an expression that looked very much like one of hate. It disturbed me, and I felt an instinctive urge to protect the young lady. "Get out of that buggy, Jennifer! And you too, whoever you are."

Jennifer Guthrie obeyed, her cheeks now wet with tears. I too climbed down, but my face was calm, for this loud man had stirred up my pride. I stood to my full height, better than six feet, and looked down on his face. I would not cower before him.

His eyes looked up into mine, and he spoke through gritted teeth. "Get out of here, mister ... get out before I turn the dogs loose on you! And if I ever see you near my daughter again I'll kill you. Is that clear? Now hit the trail!"

Jennifer Guthrie was sobbing, pleading. "But Pa, he did nothing! He helped me! Please ... he doesn't even have a horse."

"He's got his legs. Get inside, girl. I'll deal with you in a moment. And as for you, mister, you'd best be movin' on right now!"

I was bitter angry, deadly angry. But I kept my temper and looked at him without losing one bit of my calm. And then I smiled, deliberately and slowly, purposely showing that he could not make me run. When I walked away, it would be under my own power and by my own will.

"Good evening to you, sir," I said. "Perhaps we will meet again."

And then I picked up my bag from the floor of the buggy and started walking away. I didn't look back once, but I could feel his gaze like a prickle in the back of my neck. I walked proud and firm, like a king.

I was almost back to the main road before my anger had cooled to the point that I could think clearly again. I was still mad over the way I had been treated, but in that small portion of the mind where cold objectivity is often at odds with self-pride, I sensed that the rancher's reaction to my presence was understandable. This was not a country where strangers were to be trusted, and Jennifer Guthrie's willingness to pick me up without question on the road this morning told me that she was a bit naive about her own safety. No wonder her father was protective. If I had a daughter like that I would be protective too.

But still, he had treated her quite rudely, and for some reason I could not understand I felt that his rudeness to her was also a personal affront to me. And I knew that I had to see her again. Not only in contempt for her father's demand that I not do so, but for another reason as well, though I couldn't put it into words. But I had to see her, somehow. And I knew that I would.

I reached Miles City again at about midnight. I slipped into the livery and spent the night on a scratchy mound of hay, my bag as my pillow. All night my nostrils were choked with the smell of hay, dust, and manure.

I woke up with the sun, more refreshed than I would have expected. I stretched, straightened my rumpled clothes, and pulled loose hay from my collar. Today I would buy a horse, and a gun. Out on the plains, a man had to have a gun.

But first he had to have breakfast, so I headed across to the cafe to wait for it to open.

On the boardwalk I found the little varmint who had taken my bag on the train. He had his back to me, and he was puffing a huge cigar. I grabbed him by the collar and yanked the cigar from his mouth and crushed it beneath my boot.

"You're too young to smoke," I said, giving him three or four smacks on the rump that sent him wailing down the street. It was all very satisfying.

I bought a good breakfast of steak and fried eggs, along with several large hunks of good wheat bread and three big mugs of strong black coffee. It was by far the best meal I had enjoyed since I left Tennessee, and I exulted in the satisfaction of having a full belly. I praised the meal as I paid my bill, and the lady who took the money smiled proudly. I left feeling very good.

The gun shop was just opening across the street,

and I walked over and looked over the stock. There were many good weapons for sale here, most at good prices. I had owned a rifle back in Tennessee, as well as a pistol, but both were now outdated weapons and I had sold them before I began my westward trip. I had it in mind to buy a '73 Winchester, along with a Colt Peacemaker. I had read of these guns, and seen a Peacemaker in action once, and I admired them as fine weapons. The fact that they fired the same ammunition was a real advantage, too, for it eliminated the possibility of confusion in a pinch and generally simplified things all around. It was a mark of distinction to carry a '73.

There were cheaper guns for sale, and the temptation to save some money was strong, but my desire for the Colt and Winchester was stronger. I yielded, and walked out of the store the proud owner of two fine firearms. I felt like a true westerner.

I set out in search of a horse dealer, and found one bending his elbow in a saloon at the end of the street. Horses and horse dealers were as numerous as bedbugs around Miles City, and many local ranchers ran almost as many horses as cattle out on the range. I knew I would have to deal carefully, though, for many of these dealers were very adept at passing off a bad deal to a greenhorn. And unflattering though the thought was, I had to admit that I was a greenhorn. But it didn't necessarily follow that I was gullible, for I knew horses.

The horse dealer smelled of his trade, mixed with the odor of earthy sweat and not a little alcohol. He led me to the area where he ran his stock. It didn't take me long to spot a bay that looked like a good mount, but I took my time in bringing it up, discussing with him the merits and disadvantages of many of the other animals before at last getting around to it. I had already haggled down to a more reasonable price than he had first named by the time I brought up the horse I wanted, and after further argument I got him down to a figure that I could afford. I bought the horse.

making him throw a halter and bridle in the deal, and headed for the livery.

There was an old saddle for sale there; I had seen it the night before. It was in pretty poor shape, but the price was low, and I was confident that with a little work I could turn it into a saddle worth owning. I also purchased a blanket and a scabbard for my rifle. I was pleased with the fit of the saddle on the horse, and when I mounted a new sense of confidence swept through me. Now I had transportation, a means of getting around to look over available land. And still I had spent only a small portion of my cash. I felt that all around I had made a good deal.

All my dealings had worn away the morning very quickly, and my big breakfast was feeling ever smaller in my stomach. I rode back over to the same cafe once more, proudly tethering my horse outside at the hitching post. A burly fellow dressed in skin clothing sat outside in the shade, looking with an expert eye at my horse.

"That's a good hoss," he commented as I came up beside him on the shaded porch. "It ain't no puddin' foot."

"I think I got a good deal," I said. "You know horses pretty well?"

"I know 'em right well," he said. "A man can get cheated pretty quick if he don't. I got me a good hoss, a sorrel, but it's got a pretty bad turn of the ankle right now. There's a hoss doctor here in town—he ain't no official doctor or nothin', just an old boozer who has a good way with an animal—and he's takin' a look right now. That's why I'm here instead of out on the plains shootin' buffalo."

He talked in a fast flurry, and I was rather surprised, for men of the plains rarely tell much about themselves to a stranger. But as I looked at him closely I could see why he was so verbose. His eyes refused to turn to mine, and in them was a faint mist of tears. This man was grieving, worrying over his hurt horse. It was strangely touching, and told me much about the feeling of a plainsman for his horse. Over the years a man's mount became more than a means of transportation; it was a companion, a partner. To lose it was like losing a part of one's self. If this buffalo hunter's horse was injured to any great extent, he would be forced to shoot it. And from looking into the sad eyes of this man I could tell that he would sooner shoot himself.

I felt a strong compassion for this fellow, and I invited him to share a meal with me. He seemed glad to accept, and we moved quickly into the coolness of the cafe.

I ate less than I had earlier in the morning, and while my companion, whose name was Jack Tatum, ordered a huge meal, he ate little of it. I tried to turn the conversation to pleasant topics, hoping to relieve my partner's melancholy.

He told me of buffalo hunting, of how the animals were almost gone now, wiped out with such speed that at times the ground north of town had been littered with dead carcasses like leaves under a tree in late fall. The railroad had brought an increase in the hunting of the buffalo, he said, and Miles City was becoming a center for the trade of hides of the disappearing animals.

"There's a lot of new things springin' up all over these days," he said. "And I figure it's only the start. The railroad is the biggest change—some call it improvement, but I ain't sure—and in the next few years folks will start pourin' in thick as sorghum. That ain't the only changes, neither. The sheep herders are movin' their woolies in from the west more and more lately. The cattlemen don't like it for the most part, but there ain't been too much trouble. The main trouble is between the cattlemen themselves. I reckon you've heard about the riders that have been cuttin' fences. Well, they hit again last night, at several places, or so I heard. They really hate that 'devil wire,' as the ranchers have took to callin' it."

"Where did they hit?" I asked absently.

"I don't know all the places, but I seen 'em myself headin' over toward Sam Hartford's spread near South Sunday Creek . . ."

My glass dropped from my hand, and Tatum's words were suddenly interrupted. He looked at me strangely, and I was embarrassed.

"Did you say Sam Hartford?"

"Yes . . . you know him? He's a good one—a good feller."

I looked straight into Tatum's eyes. "He's my brother, Mr. Tatum. I'm Jim Hartford."

I don't know just why I revealed myself to him, for I didn't want Sam to hear of my presence here until I had seen him myself. But the mention of the night riders sent a chill through me. I had the sudden gripping fear that perhaps Sam had been hurt, or was in some sort of danger.

"You . . . you're Sam's brother? Why, he's spoken of you, lots of times!" He leaned back and looked at me as if I had suddenly become a new person. "Land o' goshen, I never would have figured! Does Sam know you're about these parts? Last he said you was in Tennessee."

"No, Mr. Tatum, he doesn't know, and to tell you the truth, I hadn't aimed on telling him 'til a little later. But these riders . . . you say they were heading for Sam's place? Do you think . . ."

Tatum shook his head. "Don't you worry. Sam's alright. I heard from a friend that nobody was hurt nowheres last night. Sam's been usin' fencin' the last year or so, keepin' his stock confined instead of runnin' over the range. Probably those riders cut that fence in a lot of places. It'll cost Sam to replace it. But he'll do it, I reckon. He's done it before."

I frowned. The idea of Sam being harassed by those riders bothered me, for my family had always been a close and protective one, every member standing up to fight if any one of us was threatened. And

Sam had a temper, which was another thing that worried me. He wouldn't long stand for anyone damaging his property, if he was the same Sam that I knew from years back. I felt a sudden strong impulse to see him. If he needed help I intended to give it to him.

"Mr. Tatum, where is this South Sunday Creek? I think I'll ride out to see my brother."

He gave me quick directions. I could reach Sam's spread by riding up the Fort Buford road for a short distance, then cutting northwest until I reached a creek. If I followed that creek northwest I would come to Sam's spread.

I didn't tarry long after that. The desire to see my brother was overwhelming. I gave Tatum best wishes for the recovery of his horse, thanked him for the directions, and walked out into the sunlight. I mounted my newly purchased horse, and headed off to find my brother. It felt good to be in the saddle, but I was nervous about the task before me.

As I rode I thought of the years that had passed since we had last seen each other. How would he be? Would he seem much older? He had married many years before. Whether he had children I didn't know. We had been boys when last we saw each other, and now we were both far into manhood. It seemed like only days since I had watched him leave for Montana, yet in a paradoxical way it seemed an eternity ago at the same time.

The passing of time had brought changes not only to the west but also to our own lives. I would soon be faced with the torment of telling Sam of my failure to sustain the old Tennessee homestead. How would he react? Would he be pleased to see me? I didn't know, and the realization of the momentous nature of this occasion sank further into my mind as I plodded along.

I reached the South Sunday and began riding northwest. It was then that I saw my first barbed-wire fence.

CHAPTER IV

It was a fearsome-looking stuff, this barbed wire. I stopped long enough to examine it.

This wire could be pretty rough on a fellow's leg should he allow his horse to brush him up against it. The barbs looked more like miniature daggers than anything else, at least a half inch long. It wasn't what I had expected, somehow. No wonder this stuff kept such good control over cattle.

This wire was rusted, reminding me that the prickly wire had been available for about ten years now. The railroads were of course carrying it across in greater quantities than before, but there was nothing really new about barbed wire. Just why there was so much trouble right now over the stuff I couldn't really say; apparently something had set off hard feelings about it—the coming of a larger number of settlers with more fences, maybe.

I continued on, following the course of the creek. I found myself repeatedly swallowing an unrelenting lump in my throat, and my mouth was dry. I could feel my chest throbbing with the continual beating of my heart. Soon I would see my brother for the first time in many years. It was a frightening thought, making me anxious and full of a sort of dread.

I don't know with what instinct I realized that the spread I next encountered was Sam's, but somehow I knew it at first glance. There was certainly nothing glorious about the place. I recalled the literature of the railroad and its promise of neat, white cottages. No neat cottage this dwelling! Just a low, dirt-roofed cabin with a couple of outbuildings and a sprouting garden behind it. Grass grew on the roof, which seemed to be so low that I wondered how Sam managed to stand upright without bumping his head. I felt a kind of sadness steal over me. Back in Tennessee I had talked proudly of my pioneering brother and the beautiful spread he worked in the Montana Territory. Somehow actually seeing the place let me know just how rough this sort of life could be. This was the life my brother had chosen. And now, it was also to be mine.

My horse plodded steadily toward the little dwelling, and I found my hands trembling as they held the reins. My eyes darted about the place, looking for Sam, scanning the entire area. I couldn't see him.

The door was standing open, though I could not see into the dark interior of the cabin. But then a figure filled that door, and a Sharps aimed its fearsome muzzle at me.

"Who are you and what do you want?" It was Sam all right. The gravelly voice was just the same as it had always been.

"Sam, don't you know me?"

There was only long silence. I couldn't see his face because of the shadows in the doorway, but I could guess at his expression as the realization of who I was stole over him. The muzzle of the gun dropped slowly, then the weapon was leaned against the doorpost. Sam's voice came, scarcely audible, its query tentative in tone.

"Jim?" Then again, more loudly and with assurance, "Jim!"

I was down off my horse and moving toward him as he came out of the doorway. I recognized his face immediately, those same blue eyes, the sandy hair, thinner now. I threw my arms around him, and he did the same to me, and he gave me a bone-crushing hug of the sort that only a brother can inflict. Then he backed away, his hands on my shoulders pushing me back so he could study my face.

"My Lord, boy, I never thought I would lay eyes on you for a long, long time—maybe never. But you ain't a boy no more, are you? My gosh, you're a man, a full grown man!" He beamed at me, shaking his head at the wonder of it all, thrilled to his soul to see me and making no effort to hide the fact.

"Jim . . . Jim!" He sounded my name with satisfaction. Then a sudden look of trouble came over his face, and he said, "I'm sorry about the gun . . . I didn't know who you were. There's been some trouble here just last night, and I thought maybe . . ."

"I know, Sam. That's part of the reason I came out here. I didn't plan on seeing you until . . . well, I have a long story to tell, and I'd rather not start it here."

"Then come inside, brother, and meet my wife. Becky! We've got a guest . . . my brother! It's Jim, Becky, come from Tennessee!"

He hustled me inside, and I saw Becky. It was a strange feeling, looking at a woman I knew was my sister-in-law, and had been for years, but who I was just now seeing for the first time.

I shook her hand and noted the calluses. Her face was like that of many ranchers' wives I was later to meet. It was neither young nor old, unattractive nor pretty. Her eyes were brown and limpid, and her features told of a beauty that had long ago faded from toil and hot sun. She smiled, but her smile was weary, and her mouth had something which I can only describe as a hardness, a firmness molded forever into her face from years of wind, sweat, labor, and more labor. But she was a pleasant enough woman, and it was with real happiness that I greeted her.

Minutes later I was seated at a rough, hand-made table, my hands around a mug of coffee, telling my story. It was, as I had promised, a long story, one which spanned all the time since Sam and I had separated sixteen years before. And it was not a pleasant story, and when at last I had to tell Sam the thing I dreaded most—the fact that I had been forced to sell the family homestead—it was all I could do to force out the words. But he looked at me with no trace of condemnation in his gaze and with no tone of accusation in his voice.

"You tried, Jim. That's what counts. Some of us try to farm in Tennessee and don't quite make it, and some of us head to Montana to strike it rich and don't quite do that either. There ain't no hard feelings, in case you were worried about that. You did your best."

I can't describe the relief that swept over me with those words. Like Bunyan's Christian before the cross I felt a burden fall from my shoulders to never return. I looked down at my coffee mug, hoping not to blubber like some woman.

Sam told then of all that had happened to him, and I found myself fascinated by the tale. It had been a far rougher life than the one he had anticipated when he left Tennessee, and things had not worked out quite as he had planned. But he had lived, managing to get a good piece of land not far from town, a real asset in these days, for he could easily afford to make several trips to town each year, while most dwellers of the plains were more limited in the extent to which they could travel.

For two hours we sat at that table, squeezing in the events of sixteen years, feeling the same sense of family unity which we had known back in Powell's Valley growing between us again. Sam was older, much older, and his face showed it, but still he was Sam, my brother and companion. It was good to be close to him again.

Becky refilled my cup and I looked down at the table. "Sam," I said, "I've heard talk in town of trouble with fence cutters, and I heard they hit here last night. Is that right?"

Sam's face clouded. "You'd better believe it's right. They cut my fence last night, five places. And it ain't the first time, and I ain't the only victim. This situation is getting bad, Jim, real bad. There's gonna be blood before this is over."

To hear my own brother saying those words chilled me. He had an air of morbid certainty about what he was saying, and Sam had never been one for idle or unfounded talk. Something was brewing around here; I had felt it from the first time McCuen had mentioned the subject on the train. And apparently my own brother was going to be involved in whatever trouble erupted.

"How can you be so sure things will get that bad, Sam?" I asked. He was silent. Becky looked at him inquisitively.

"Sam, should I show him . . ."

He nodded. She moved over to the opposite side of the cabin and delved into a trunk. She returned with a crumpled paper in her hand. Without a word Sam took it and handed it to me.

The words on it were scribbled in large, crude letters, and to read them sent a spasm of fear through me.

"We have given our warning—the devil wire must go, else there will be blood on the land—no home, no wife, no child will escape—the land shall run red with fence-stringer blood."

I looked up into Sam's cold blue eyes. "Where . . ."
"Tied on a rock, tossed through my window last

night," he said. He gestured over toward the front window. A pane of glass was broken, the hole temporarily covered with a piece of muslin. My numb hands let the paper fall from my fingers back onto the table.

"Do you have any idea who is behind all of this, Sam?" I asked. "Any clue at all?"

Sam stood and paced toward the center of the cabin. "I have no proof, only the rumors that I've heard," he said. "And because of that I've been slow to put the blame on anyone. But there's been those who say they've seen the riders mostly around one place, a ranch not too far from here. Have you heard of Luther Guthrie?"

I felt a sudden redness come to my face, and my breath quickened. Sam noted my sudden start, and eyed me curiously.

"Yes, I've heard of him," I said. "Do you think that he's the one behind this?"

"The riders have been spotted several times. Always they move back toward the Guthrie spread. I have friends around here, other ranchers, shepherds, buffalo hunters. Many of them feel there's no doubt that Guthrie has hired the riders. I know from meeting him on a couple of occasions that he is a totally unreasonable man. It goes beyond what you might think. A lot of cattlemen have a dislike for 'devil wire,' as they call it, but most of 'em manage to tolerate it, or so it appears. But this Guthrie . . . I can't figure him out. He literally gets red with rage anytime anybody even thinks of fencing in the range, and on occasion he's even threatened lives. If anybody around here would hire those riders, it would be him."

Although I knew nothing of Guthrie's hate for fences, I knew quite well of his personality. He was obviously a man easily angered, especially concerning anything that was his—his daughter, for example, I thought ruefully. I could easily imagine him being much the same way toward his land, his cattle, his profession. There was a logic in what Sam was saying. It was quite possible that Guthrie was the culprit.

But why did that bother me so? Why did I feel the sudden panic that was overwhelming me? I didn't want to admit the answer, but I knew it full well.

It was because of her—because of Jennifer Guthrie. If her father was involved in this, and if in fact it did come down to open conflict and bloodshed, then she could be hurt. If not physically, at least mentally through seeing her father fighting, maybe even injured or killed, if things went that far. I had no love for Luther Guthrie, but I did not want to see him hurt, for that would in turn hurt Jennifer. Jennifer ... in my mind she was no longer "Miss Guthrie" ... she was Jennifer. I frowned. What was coming over me?

If there was a conflict between the angry cattlemen, then I would have no choice but to support Sam's side. And then in a sense, Jennifer would become my enemy. And that was a surprisingly painful thought.

I stood. "Sam, you have no plans to make some sort of move against Guthrie, do you? Do I sense that kind of notion rolling around in your mind?"

Sam said nothing. The silence was a ringing affirmative.

I moved toward him. "Sam! What could you do? Guthrie has men, cowboys. And if he is the guilty one, which he well might not be, he would have the riders, too. What chance would you have against him? What would you do?"

"I wouldn't have to go alone. There're others like me."

"But they're spread all over the plains."

"We could unify. It's been done in other places."

"But ... violence, Sam? Violence? Would it be worth it?"

He looked at me coldly. "I'll not see my land ruined, my fences cut, my wife hurt ... or my baby."

"Baby? You have children, Sam?"

"I will soon. Becky's with child."

I turned to look at her. She gazed modestly at the floor as I took note of the slight swell of her belly. I hadn't noticed it before.

I turned again to Sam, silent. He looked at me with the same cold, dogmatic expression. "It's something we have to do, Jim. You'll be ranching yourself before too long, and then you'll see. You'll be ready to stand up to Luther Guthrie. You'll understand."

But you don't understand, I thought silently. You don't understand the way I'm beginning to feel about the pretty young lady who would certainly be caught up in the middle of the fight. You don't understand at all, Sam. I turned away.

"I have a few things to do, Jim. I'm heading into town to buy some new fence. I'd appreciate it if you stayed around here to look out for Becky. After last night I don't feel like this is a safe place."

I smiled. "I'll be glad to stay, Sam." Then he was gone.

"More coffee, Jim?" Becky asked. I shook my head. "I think I'll just look around your place awhile. I've got a lot I need to learn about setting up a spread."

I looked closely at the cabin Sam had built. It looked rough from the outside, but the interior was actually pleasant. The table at which we had sat was rough, but well constructed and large. Around it sat several three-legged stools, not pretty but very serviceable.

The kitchen occupied one corner of the main room, consisting of a box like one might find on the back of a chuckwagon, with shelves and little nooks where cooking utensils could be stored. There was a cover on the box, which when folded down could serve as a kind of counter. Beside it sat a three-legged stove of black iron, with a large supply of wood stacked behind it.

The furniture was sparse, much of it homemade, but there was a large oak cabinet against the opposite

wall that Sam had hauled in from who knows where
that added a real domestic touch to the place. I felt
sure that Becky was proud to own it.

The inside walls were white, the logs hewed off
flat and covered with muslin. The muslin was white-
washed with a substance I couldn't identify. Becky told
me it was a mixture of crushed white shale and water.
The south end of the cabin was papered with old
newspapers, several layers thick.

There was a narrow straw mattress on a hand-
made bed against that wall. It looked new. Becky saw
me looking at it and smiled.

"When Sam heard we were going to have a child
he got so excited that he started building all sorts of
things for the baby. He made that bed and tick just last
week. Of course when the baby comes we'll have to re-
stuff that mattress, it will be so old, but Sam was too
happy to listen to reason. Of course it worked out
good that he made it, 'cause now you'll have a place to
sleep tonight."

I moved outside, looking over the structure of the
cabin. Sam had done a good job, hewing the logs to
uniform size. I checked out the notches. They were of
the dovetail variety, tight-fitting and strong. He had
chinked the cabin with clay. Some in this area used
cow manure.

There was an outbuilding made of sod not far
away, and I walked over to it. It was the first time I
had had a chance to look closely at a sod building. I
pecked on the wall with my fist. It was rock hard, with
a hollow sound to it. After closer examination I understood the reason for that sound. Sam had built this
house with two layers of sod, leaving a foot-wide air-
space between the walls. That foot of dead air would
keep this building snug and warm all winter and cool
in the summer. Sam had done good work.

I entered and looked at the shelves that lined the
walls. They were filled with jars, sacks, cans. Becky
had done a lot of canning, it seemed, for there was a

good supply of jelly, apparently made from wild plums. There was dried fruit, two large sacks of beans, and a huge can of molasses. There were storebought cans of different foods, along with a can of syrup. A side of bacon hung from the ceiling, and a tarpaulin was slung across the room with something bulky and heavy inside. I looked in it—there was a young beef, slaughtered and slung inside the tarpaulin. I had heard of this procedure before. Beef would not spoil very quickly when stored this way, unless it was left for a great length of time. Hot weather could turn such a system into a disaster, though.

I moved back outside and shut the door. Sam's garden stretched away behind the sod house and filled most of the area between it and the cabin. I walked toward the garden, frightening a jackrabbit from its hiding place and sending it scurrying away at top speed.

I stood in the shade of the cabin and thought about my own home. Where would it be? I hoped I could find a place not too far from Sam, but that might be difficult. With new settlers beginning to come in, the land was being taken up. The railroad had control of alternate tracts of land in a checkerboard pattern for miles on either side of the rails, and it even managed to control many of the tracts not specifically granted to it because of various legal questions which made it uncertain just who owned them. The railroad was in no hurry to resolve the questions, for as long as there was doubt most folks just assumed the railroad was the owner and left it at that. So rather than try to claim free land I would have to go to the railroad land office and buy my spread, using the money from the sale of the farm back in Tennessee.

It would be lonely when I moved out alone to my new home, wherever it would be. I was used to loneliness, so it didn't frighten me, but still I couldn't help but think it would be so much nicer if I had a wife to share it all with me, somebody like Jennifer Guthrie . . .

I cut the thought short, amazed that it had even risen in my mind. I hardly knew Jennifer Guthrie, and after my very undignified exit from her home it was unlikely I would see her again for quite a long time. It was absurd to even think of such a thing as marriage to the daughter of a man as wealthy as Luther Guthrie—a man who just happened to dislike me, too.

I smiled ironically. What would be Luther Guthrie's reaction if his daughter married an upstart like me? Likely he would go off like a box of dynamite. He would probably sooner have his girl elope with a grizzly as to marry Jim Hartford.

Sam got back about sunset with a load of wire. I helped him unload the rolls and stack them inside one of his outbuildings. We went back inside the cabin and sat down to a delicious supper of beef and sourdough bread, along with more coffee, then we sat talking of old times until Sam and Becky retired to the single bedroom built off the back of the cabin, and I laid down in the narrow bed in the front room. The fresh hay smelled sweet.

It was later that night that the riders came.

CHAPTER V

ike ghosts through the night they came, the faint noise of their horses' hooves being my first indication of their approach. As the quiet noise became louder, I first sat up in my bed, then rose and went for my Winchester that sat against the wall beside the door. Sam came up behind me, his face fearful and his Sharps in his hands. Neither of us spoke.

Directly in front of the cabin they rode, then there was the sudden blasting of rifles in tandem with the crashing of a glass pane. Sam gave a low cry in his throat and moved to the front door, throwing it open and sending a quick and useless shot out into the darkness. Then they were gone, riding into the thick, black night. Above us the moon swam in a pool of murky clouds.

Still neither my brother nor I spoke. Sam stood in the doorway, staring after the riders, his face invisible to me but his rage and tension filling the air like electricity. I moved over to where a stone, wrapped in paper, lay on the dirt floor. I picked it up, noting with irritation the trembling of my fingers, and removed the wadded paper.

Another threat, another warning of "death for fence-stringers" if the fences weren't removed. I handed it to Sam; he read it and tossed it aside.

"I can't understand it, Jim. It makes no sense. If I were fencing in a water hole, if I were blocking good grazing land, then I might understand. But I've been here for years, Jim, and I've hardly had any trouble with anyone in all that time. Now, all at once, it seems like someone around here has got it in for settlers. But why . . . why now, like this?"

I couldn't answer him. I pulled on my pants and threw on my shirt. He looked at me curiously, then Becky slowly walked into the room and put her arm around her husband's waist. I could see the fear in her eyes. She too eyed my preparations inquisitively.

"I'm going after them, Sam. Don't worry . . . I'm not planning to try anything—I'm not such a fool as that—but if I can get their trail, then maybe we can find out once and for all who is behind all of this. Hand me my gun . . . I'll be careful. I expect I'll see you around sunup."

And then I was gone, moving out to saddle my horse. Then into the blackness I rode, looking far ahead of me on the trail for some sign of them. My eyes scanned the trail. It was no use—in the darkness I could not make out any tracks. I would have to come within eyeshot of them if I planned to follow them. It would be dangerous, but I felt a reckless courage in me, from what source I do not know, and I plunged on fearlessly. This was to be my home, this territory, and I had no intention of beginning my life as a plainsman in a land terrorized by such trash as this.

They had gained a good lead on me, and to be honest I was riding blind, guessing at what direction they might have taken. I followed the road, assuming they had done the same, though they might have turned off it to cut across the plains at almost any point. I realized that my rapid pace was tiring my mount, so with reluctance I slowed down, then stopped. I listened, hoping my ears could do what my eyes could not.

Faint in the distance, it seemed, I could hear the noise of horses running—a muffled sound, as if they were on grassland. I looked to my left, scanning the open plain. The moon emerged from a bank of clouds for one moment, but in that moment I saw them.

How many there were I could not tell, but they were moving away from me, heading east. East . . . in the direction of Muster Creek and the Guthrie ranch. I felt a sharp pain inside me. Maybe Sam was right. Maybe Guthrie was the one behind this. Again I thought of Jennifer.

I moved off after them, aware that I would have to keep a good distance if I wanted to avoid detection. That would be fatal beyond any doubt. Intermittently the moon moved into clear areas in the sky, flooding the land with light. In those periods I could see them, moving slower now, still heading east. There appeared to be eight or nine of them, riding abreast of each other.

I do not know how long we continued moving, for it seemed endless, but in a short while I realized that they did not have the look of men bent on doing any more of their destructive work tonight. They were finished, and obviously felt safe, for they moved slowly but steadily, heading for what I hoped would be their camp and base of operations. Still we moved toward Muster Creek.

The land was flat, seeming almost barren in the sporadic moonlight. But before us rose up a large bank of hills—large at least for the flatlands of Montana—and something like recognition played at the corners of my mind. There was something familiar about those hills. And then I remembered.

There were hills directly behind the Guthrie spread. Barren hills, like the ones before us. And judg-

ing from the direction we had come and the time we
had ridden, I guessed that what I saw before me was
the backside of the same hills I had seen before my un-
fortunate run-in with Luther Guthrie. On the other
side of that bank of hills was his ranch. It had to be.

I stopped. The riders far ahead of me had reached
the hills and were moving into them. It was there, I
guessed, that they made their camp. Sam had been
right. It was Luther Guthrie who was leading this reign
of terror. I felt deeply sad and faintly sick.

I sat in indecision for a long moment. Somehow I
wanted to get closer to those men, maybe even see a
few faces. But the danger of that would be overwhelming, and I doubted whether anything I could learn
would be worth the risk. For a full five minutes I debated with myself. Finally the decision was made. Better to be alive with what little information I had than
to gain more and quite possibly be killed in the process. I would be of more service to myself and the other
terrorized ranchers if I proceeded carefully in all of
this. I turned my horse and headed back toward Sam's
ranch house.

In a few moments I realized the wisdom of my decision, for I detected a faint light about me. Then
sometime later the sun rose in full glory behind me. I
turned and looked back at the hills.

Streams of light poured over their slopes, silhou-
etting them against a blue and gold background, shining out across the wide grasslands, the misty scent of
morning all around. Beautiful, this land . . . very beautiful. Even with the threat of the night riders, the danger in which all of the settlers now lived, I realized that
I was glad I had come to this place. I had made the
right decision. Since the beginning of my journey I had
been plagued with occasional doubts about the wisdom of risking what little I had left and coming to the
Montana Territory, but at this moment in the glorious
light of morning, those doubts faded away, never to return. It was here that my destiny lay. It was here I

would live and die, right here on these plains. The sunlight beamed against my face, warming it, and I smiled.

I did not tarry long, for I had promised Sam that I would return at sunrise. Already I was a little late, and it would not have surprised me in the least to see him come galloping across the plains in search of me. I goaded my horse to greater speed. This had been my first real chance to test the capabilities of the animal, and I was pleased with the purchase I had made.

I found Sam waiting on the front step of the cabin, his rifle across his knees. His face looked ashen. I could tell that the torment the riders were putting him through was beginning to wear on his nerves. I felt a strong pang of concern not only for his safety but also for his health.

He looked up at me. "Well?"

Something in me rebelled at telling him what I had seen. I had actually prayed that Guthrie had not been the mastermind of the night riders, hoped with all my soul that he was not involved simply for the sake of Jennifer. It was painful to have to admit that those prayers and hopes had been in vain. But Sam had a right to know, and I told him all I had seen.

He nodded grimly. "I thought so. It makes sense. I still can't understand why I'm being threatened, for I've never caused a bit of trouble for Luther Guthrie or any other cattlemen. But I'm getting tired of this . . . really tired. This just can't go on without something being done."

We went inside the cabin and had a breakfast of bacon, bread, jelly, and coffee. Although I was hungry, I could eat little, for my stomach was in a knot of tension. Sam apparently suffered from the same affliction, for he merely played with his food, hardly eating a bite. Becky was silent, but from the hurried glances she sent toward her husband, I could tell that she was worried about him. I didn't blame her. Sam's eyes were flashing with a strange anger that at times made him appear almost a madman deep in contemplation. I had seen his temper exploding at full force only a few times before, but from the looks of things it would not be long before that storm of fury erupted again.

Sam and I spent the morning in work, half-heartedly going through the motions of running the ranch. Close to noon we heard the sound of a horseman approaching, and with some apprehension we moved out to meet him.

I didn't know the fellow, though Sam apparently did, for he greeted him cordially and with some relief. I think he had expected more trouble.

The rider was young, hardly more than a boy. He had obviously been in the saddle all morning, for he seemed very weary. Sam invited him inside for a cup of coffee, and the breathless youth accepted gratefully.

Seated at the table with the mug of steaming coffee before him, he looked more relaxed. But the news he carried did nothing to calm the nerves of the rest of us.

"There was a man killed last night," he said. "And from the looks of it all it was them riders that done it. He was shot through the head and the chest, and all his fences was cut."

Sam tensed, his fist closing until the knuckles were white against the bone. "Who?"

"Jasper Maddux, from southeast of town."

I cried out without warning, and the youth jumped, startled. Sam said nothing, but his ashen face clouded with despair and he looked down at the table. Then he shook his head and said:

"Jasper . . . he's been here as long as I have. I've hardly seen him in the last year or so. The old fool . . . he wasn't even a legitimate rancher and had no need for fencing, but he strung some up anyway when the trouble started just to spite the riders. Old fool . . ."

The boy spoke quietly. "He didn't even have his gun on him when they found him. And he was tied up. It was murder outright."

Sam looked at the boy. "How far have you spread the news? Do all the ranchers know?"

"I've hit every spread I could reach this mornin'," he said. "And there's plans for a big meetin' in town tomorrow at noon. All the ranchers that can get there are gonna come, ones that have been bothered by them riders. We'll meet in Shorty Myers' big barn there in town. Luke McDonald is the man behind the meetin', and he's talked of everybody takin' up arms against whoever had hired them riders."

Sam nodded, his mouth set firmly. "Good. It might be necessary for us to do that. I had my house shot on last night, and got another threat. I'll not sit by anymore. And you can count on me being at that meeting."

After the boy left I approached Sam. "Do you think people are ready to take up arms about this? If it finally comes down to a range war, there might be a lot more people killed than it's worth."

Sam looked at me sharply. "Better to be killed fighting for something that is rightfully yours than to be murdered in the night like some dog," he said. "Jasper's murder shows that those threats aren't something to be scoffed at. It's not a matter of us starting a war—the war has already begun."

We passed the rest of the day in silence, working on replacing the fences that had been cut. All through the afternoon I thought of Jennifer, and it made me feel sad. What would be her place in all of this? How badly would she be hurt?

We were up before dawn the next morning and on the road to Miles City shortly after that. Sam carried his Sharps, I had my Colt and shining new Winchester. It was a strange thought, realizing that the gun I had bought to kill game might end up being used against a man. I had never killed a man before, nor even aimed a gun at another human being. I didn't feel any desire to do so now.

On the trail we met others heading for town, all

of them armed, the same light of fear burning in every eye. All words spoken sounded like those of men under siege.

"Did you leave your wife with a gun?"

"She's with Mrs. Ford on down the creek. Both of 'em have rifles. The children are there too."

"You had any fences cut?"

"Several times. The other night they even shot my milk cow. Don't know why."

"You think there's some big-time cattleman behind this?"

"Who else?"

By the time we reached Miles City there was a large band of us, some fifteen altogether. We drew a lot of attention when we rode down the main street. I could see faces peering around lacy curtains from the houses and merchants watching us from the porches of their businesses. No one asked us what we were doing. Everyone knew.

Some of the horsemen made a real show of their weapons, as if they were a gang of outlaws riding in to take over the town. It bothered me, for I sensed the beginning of that kind of unbridled rage that always injures more than it helps. There would be fighting before this affair was settled. I felt almost ashamed to be riding in the midst of the crowd of angry men, their rifles drawn and their handguns slung high on their hips. I realized why they were so angry, and I sympathized with their plight, but still I felt that our group had almost a pitiful quality to it, and I felt like hanging my head. I didn't want any part of mass hysteria, for a clear mind was something which I prized highly.

We found some men already there and waiting for us. Sam pointed out Luke McDonald, the organizer of this meeting. He was a hefty man with a belly that hung out like a sack of lard over his belt, and his pants hung low about his hips. It was beyond me what kind of magic kept them from falling around his feet. He stood in the street before the barn where we were to meet, his hands on his hips and his jaw jutted out in a pseudo-military fashion. I didn't like the look of him. There was too much of the glory-seeker about him, and he had the air of a man with more pride than brain.

It was still some time before the meeting was to begin, and I left my rifle with Sam and walked down the street, hoping to pass the time by loitering in the stores. I went into the same general merchandise business that Jennifer had entered the other day and began poking about, examining items, trying to think of things that I might need when I set up my own spread. I found it hard to concentrate, though, for I was worried about what might come out of this meeting. Suddenly I felt a hand on my shoulder.

I turned to see McCuen standing there, a troubled look about him. I greeted him and shook his hand.

"Mr. Hartford, just what is this all about?" he said. "I saw your group riding in. Is this about the wire cutting?"

I nodded. Briefly I told him what had occurred, of the death of Jasper Maddux and the hysteria that was gripping the angry men. I told him of my fears about what might occur.

He shook his head slowly. "I was afraid of this. It has happened all over the west, and now it's happening here. If only we could get this thing stopped before there's violence! But I don't know who to go to, nor what to do . . ."

I looked at him closely. He looked trustworthy, and I had personal evidence of his honesty based on my experience with my stolen bag. I needed a good, clear-headed man like him to help me if I was going to do anything to stop the carnage that seemed so inevitable.

"Mr. McCuen, I think I might know who we need to talk to about this," I said. "I think I know who is behind this wire cutting business."

He looked at me with sudden interest. "Who? How do you know?"

I told him about having followed the riders during the night, and of where they had gone. He nodded all the while.

"Luther Guthrie, you say? You know, it makes sense. From what I've heard of him he's just the type of fellow that would do something like this. If we could only talk to him, reason with him . . ." Suddenly he stopped short, and a grin spread slowly over his face. "You know, I think I might know just the thing to do. I think I might know someone who can go with us to talk to Guthrie. Would you be willing to go along with me on this?"

"I'll do anything to keep a range war from beginning," I said. "What do you have in mind?"

"I know a rancher by the name of Jedediah Bacon, a younger rancher than most, and a good man. I was acquainted with him in the east—Boston—and I've had every intention of going to see him now that I'm here where he settled. He's a far thinking fellow, one that doesn't cling to something just because it's old. And he's been using barbed wire for years, holding his cattle where he wants them, breeding them for weight. He's living proof of what the proper use of the wire can lead to. Maybe he can talk some sense into Guthrie's head and get him to call off his men before this thing gets out of hand."

If he could do a thing like that, I thought, then he must be a remarkable fellow indeed. But I wanted to try, for obviously the approach now being taken by the men in town was bound to end in tragedy for many families. I assented to McCuen's idea.

"Let's not waste any time about it," I said. "Let Sam stay for the meeting—I'm going with you. Once those folks get themselves worked up into a frenzy there's no telling what might happen."

We moved back into the sun-lit street. More

armed men approached. The sun was climbing toward the center of the sky. Soon the meeting would begin.

I didn't bother to tell Sam of my plans, for I feared he would only try to talk me out of it. I mounted my horse, and McCuen headed to the livery to get his own mount. When he returned we headed out of town and toward the south. McCuen talked further about his friend all the while.

"I've written to Jed over the years," he said, "and he's sent back some good reports about his use of barbed wire. Of course a lot of the really successful ranchers are slow to change their ways, at least in these parts. But he's a persuasive young fellow, and if anyone can knock some sense into Guthrie it will be him."

McCuen talked on, but I didn't listen. I was thinking of someone else, someone with beautiful eyes and auburn hair that shimmered like nothing I had ever seen. Jennifer . . . she would be there, at the Guthrie ranch. And when we went to reason with her father, perhaps I would see her . . .

I cut short the thought. I knew it would be impossible for me to accompany McCuen and his friend to the ranch, for Guthrie would throw us off as soon as he saw me. I couldn't let my bad standing with Guthrie thwart McCuen's mission and perhaps end up costing lives. I would have to stay behind when they went to the Guthrie ranch.

And so at least this time I would not see Jennifer. Not this time. But later . . .

CHAPTER VI

⌇

Jedediah Bacon's spread was typical in many ways, yet it was more orderly than most of the ranches I had seen before. It was obviously set up in a logical fashion, every fence and building in just the proper place. And so I wasn't surprised to find that Bacon himself was a neat man, not fancily dressed but nevertheless well groomed and clean. And he was young, obviously not much more than thirty. He greeted McCuen warmly and seemed quite glad to meet me. He was a jolly fellow, and very likeable. I felt relaxed in his presence and impressed by his calm and self-confident bearing.

McCuen wasted little time in telling Bacon why we had come. The young rancher had heard of the riders and their terrorist actions, but the murder of Jasper Maddux was news to him. He seemed troubled when McCuen told him of it.

"It's ridiculous, this business of riders and murder. Why can't some cattlemen accept the fact that the plains are changing, and we're going to have to adapt to those changes? The old ways aren't necessarily the best ways, but still people seem to want to cling to them no matter what the consequences. I'm acquainted with Guthrie through the cattlemen's association—and a more stubborn old fellow you couldn't find within five hundred miles. He's opposed every new idea, every hint of acceptance of the fact that new times are here to stay. A lot of ranchers are becoming convinced that running cattle on enclosed pasture rather than open range is the best way, but Guthrie is among the old school, those who still think the long drives and open land are the only way to raise cattle. But I'm surprised that he would go so far as to hire fence cutters. And murder . . . well, I think that's unbelievable. I'll be glad to go with you and talk to him, though I figure he won't really listen. And Mr. Hartford, I don't think Guthrie would take too kindly to a Tennessee farmer new to the territory coming into his home to tell him what to do. I suggest you stay off the ranch itself. No offense intended—I just think it would be the best way."

That was a suggestion I readily consented to. There would be no quicker way for us to find ourselves kicked off Guthrie's land than for me to waltz into his house. It was almost comical to think of how the rancher would react to such brashness.

We headed toward the Guthrie ranch without hesitation. McCuen and Bacon talked of the old times they had spent together, and I discovered the surprising fact that Bacon had attended Yale. I asked him about that, and why he had come from a career as a lawyer to raise cattle in Montana. He laughed at the question.

"I started reading every book I could on striking it rich on the plains through the cattle business. Believe me, there was plenty of that kind of propaganda floating around! I couldn't resist the idea of quick wealth. It didn't work out like I planned—I'm a long way from being rich—but still I haven't been a failure, either. I don't regret coming out here. I wouldn't be elsewhere, now."

I was impressed with Bacon, and hoped Guthrie would be as well. After all, he was proof that ranching by new methods could be a success. I asked Bacon how his method of ranching differed from Guthrie's.

"Well, there's several things I do differently," he said. "Not all of them are in any way easier than Guthrie's methods, but as the land changes I'll be able to continue with my style of ranching while he will have to adapt his.

"Guthrie still runs his cattle on the unfenced range for the most part. Some of the land is his, most is still public domain. With every new settler a little more of that land is taken from him. Someday it will be gone, and then where will Luther Guthrie be?

"I use less land, all legally mine, and I have it fenced in with plenty of Aaron's barbed wire. My cattle aren't the hit-and-miss type of breed that results from free-roaming and interbreeding cattle out on the plains. My stock is fatter, with more meat, and while I'll admit that my stock isn't as hardy as those running on the open range, they'll bring a better price at market. And there's not really as much need for them to be hardy, 'cause they're confined where I can keep a close eye on them for disease and so on. Of course, I have to raise hay to get them through the winter and sink wells for water, but I think it's definitely worth the trouble. I don't know if you noticed the windmill out on my spread—that's how I pump water for my cattle. Guthrie's system is dying; mine is just being born."

It made sense. Guthrie's method had definite advantages, I was sure, but obviously Bacon would be able to run his business over the years without the major changes that Guthrie would have to make. I knew that raising cattle in fenced-in pastures had its disadvantages, too, for I had read of cattle freezing in blizzards when fences kept them from getting to shelter. I had heard of the huge piles of rotting corpses found piled up against fences when the spring thaw came. But all in all, it seemed to me that Bacon was operating the system of the future. Just as cattle on the open plains had to adapt to changes in their environment or die, so also would the cattlemen have to adapt to the changing west. Luther Guthrie was fighting a war doomed to fail for methods that were outdated.

When at last we reached the Guthrie spread, I hung back just within view of the house. My humiliation of my only encounter with Guthrie came back to me, and I sat glumly in the saddle, biting my lip in anger. But thoughts of that embarrassment were quickly replaced by thoughts of Jennifer Guthrie, who was no doubt somewhere down there in that ranch house. I wished I could see her.

As McCuen and Bacon rode on down to the house, I dismounted and tethered my horse to a low bush in a grassy area. I began to roam about the general vicinity, realizing my wait might be a long one. I worried a bit about my not telling Sam of my plans, for he might well be concerned about my absence from the meeting. But I couldn't let that bother me—I was a grown man, in control of my own actions, and I felt that the course being followed by me and my two companions down there in Guthrie's house was by far a superior one to the hot-headed reactions of angry ranchers. Better to fight long and hard with words and logic than to turn to bullets. I hoped that the angry men in town would not be such fools as to ride in on Guthrie's ranch like an army and perhaps wind up filling graves.

"Mr. Hartford?" The voice was unmistakable. I wheeled around.

"Jenni . . . Miss Guthrie!" I'm afraid my excitement to see her so unexpectedly was clearly evident in my tone. I couldn't believe that she was actually here; I had convinced myself that I would not see her today.

"Don't worry about the 'Miss Guthrie,' Jennifer is fine," she said. "I was walking around the place—it's a habit I have—and I saw you and your friends riding up. That was Jed Bacon with you, wasn't it?"

"Yes . . . and Aaron McCuen, the man who returned the bag that was stolen from me on the train."

"Is it some sort of business visit?"

"Yes." I said nothing more about it, for I didn't want her to know the exact nature of what my two companions were even now discussing with her father. For a moment after that there was a rather uncomfortable silence, and I smiled at her in a way which I later realized probably made me look like a half-wit.

Jennifer paced about nervously, obviously looking for words.

"I'm very sorry about the reception my father gave you the other evening," she said. "He's very protective of me, and his temper often gets the best of him. I hope you weren't too insulted."

I shook my head. "Don't worry about it. I'm just sorry he treated you like he did." I realized that the last part of my comment might have been offensive to her, and I quickly added: "I'm sorry if I shouldn't have said that . . . your family business is none of my affair. I could tell you were unhappy, though."

"I have to admit you're right about that. Father often forgets that I'm a grown woman. To him I'm still the same little girl that he trotted on his knee years ago. I think that he will always feel that way."

"I'm sure you were a very pretty little girl, if your appearance now is any indication," I said. She blushed and smiled.

"Thank you, Mr. Hartford. You're very flattering."

"If I'm to call you Jennifer, then it only seems appropriate that you call me Jim," I said. "And I hope that in spite of the rather uncomfortable experience we had the other night that you will consider me your friend. Lord knows, as new as I am to this territory, I need all the friends I can get."

She laughed—a beautiful, ringing, musical sound—

and I felt a warmth steal over me. "Of course I consider you my friend," she said. "I certainly don't give buggy rides to strangers unless I feel they are the kind of people that can be trusted. I guess that I was rather careless to pick you up like that, but you certainly didn't look threatening with that big spot of mud and grass stain on the seat of your pants." It was now my turn to blush. I guessed that I had picked up the stain when I fell off the railroad car.

"I suppose I was a long way from being a dashing figure," I conceded. "You can't imagine how much I appreciated the ride."

For quite some time we talked, chatting of trivial matters, and yet I hung on her every word as if our discussion was of profound importance. And, wonder of wonders, she seemed to be doing the same with me, as if my presence gave her pleasure. I felt as if I were floating in a dream world, a kind of paradise. Our time together was at most fifteen minutes, but when at last I saw my two companions emerge from the house on down the road, it seemed that those short minutes were even shorter, reduced to mere moments. I was deeply sorry when she turned to see McCuen and Bacon approaching.

"Your friends are coming back," she said. "I'll slip on away. It's been very good to talk to you. Perhaps I'll see you again soon."

"I would like that very much," I said.

She turned to leave, and from some untapped reserve of courage I suddenly found the power to speak words which surprised even me as soon as I had said them. "Jennifer . . . if you take another walk tomorrow, do . . . do you think I might accompany you?"

She looked first surprised, then pleased. "Why, I would find that very pleasant, Jim. I'll meet you here at one sharp." Then she turned and was gone, moments before McCuen and Bacon came riding up. Such was my elation that I actually forgot for a moment the purpose of our trip, and it was a long wait before I gathered my wits enough to ask them how things had gone with Guthrie.

McCuen looked a bit disgusted. "As well as could be expected, I imagine, but not nearly as well as I would have liked. He listened to us, then got indignant when we hinted that he was the man behind the riders. He scoffed at the meeting going on in town, calling it a convention of 'fools and idiots.' But when Bacon mentioned the murder of Jasper Maddux he looked sincerely shocked. It was obvious that it was the first he had heard of it. After that he told us to leave— that's why we're back so quickly."

"So things are standing pretty much as they were," I said. "At least we tried. Maybe your talk to him did more good than he would lead you to think. Maybe he'll call off his hounds for awhile."

"I hope so," said Bacon. "One thing I believe for certain: Guthrie didn't order the death of Jasper Maddux. Apparently that was something his riders did on their own, 'cause that was sure no pretended shock that he put on. He really didn't know about it until we told him. It really threw him, too."

McCuen accompanied Bacon back to his ranch, and I left them in Miles City. I found Sam waiting for me on the boardwalk in front of the Chinese laundry.

"Where have you been? Why didn't you come to the meeting?"

I saw no harm in telling him what we had done, so I did just that. He didn't react except to nod when I told him that our trip had apparently done little good.

"It was a good idea," he said, "but trying to argue with someone like Luther Guthrie is about as useless as telling a dog not to scratch his fleas."

I was anxious to hear the outcome of the meeting. Sam didn't look too happy when I asked him about it.

"It was a joke, Jim, a joke. Nobody could get together on anything, it seemed. There were those like Luke McDonald who were ready to go in and shoot whoever is behind those riders—they didn't know that it's Guthrie, and I didn't tell 'em for fear that they would do something drastic and get themselves killed. The rest of us were more moderate and wanted to stay on the defensive awhile longer before we switch to the offensive. Some of 'em were talking lynching or shooting for any rancher that made any kind of threatening move against any of us. It was all complete tomfoolery, all of it. The only thing good that came out of the whole thing was that all of us are more organized now, in case there's more trouble."

I was pleased at the moderate stance Sam was taking about the riders. From the look in his eye the last couple of days, and from the way he had talked, I had expected him to be right in the middle of those who were ready to make a drastic move against the riders right away. But apparently Sam had not only grown older over the years since I had seen him last—he had grown wiser, too. I felt a tremendous sense of relief. Maybe things weren't as desperate as I thought. I could tell that in looking at the other ranchers he had been able to see how irrational was the wild plan for attack against the riders. That same irrationality had been in Sam himself earlier, but even since morning it had faded. I felt proud of him.

"As long as I'm in town I think I'll buy a few things I need," Sam said. "Becky's had her heart set on some cloth down in the general store for the longest time now, and I think I'll buy her some. I've got a few extra dollars right now, and it's been ages since she's had anything new." He started down the street, then turned. "Don't feel like you have to wait on me," he said. "Go on if you want. I'll just be a few minutes."

"I'm in no hurry. I'll wait," I responded.

I noticed a clump of men loitering around in front of the livery. Most of them were ranchers, apparently the residue of the meeting. Among them I recognized Luke McDonald. He stood in the center of the group, and though I could not hear his words he seemed to be delivering some sort of passionate tirade. I moved over and joined the group.

". . . and we can't afford to sit around and wait until something happens again. There's been one of us killed already. How many more might there be later? I'm disappointed in how this meetin' turned out—we should have made ourselves into a regular vigilante army and showed these riders that we ain't gonna take no more off of 'em. Now I figure that it's some big cattleman that's hired 'em out against us smaller ranchers. Some of 'em figure they should have the run of every inch of grazin' land in the territory, and when somebody throws up a fence it's like spittin' in their eye. And the local law ain't done one thing to check this out and I don't believe they're going to start. It's going to be us that has to protect our homes and land. And when I find out who's behind these riders I reckon that's gonna be the end of his hirin' any more guns, even if it takes killin' him and burnin' his ranch . . ."

With those words a cold chill shivered down my spine, like a winter wind coming from nowhere. Luke McDonald was not going to be content to punish merely the man behind the night riders—he would have to burn his home and probably threaten his family as well. And in this case Jennifer would be endangered. I wouldn't let him do it. I'd kill him first . . .

I felt a disgust for myself at that thought. Moments before I had been condemning McDonald and his kind, men who thought violent action was the way to correct all wrongs. And now I was ready to do exactly the same thing. The tension and anger inherent in this situation were beginning to get to me.

I looked around me at the dispersing men. All of them were family men, ones who would kill or die themselves to protect those they loved. Love. It was a frightening thing, in a way, for it could lead men to do things they wouldn't otherwise contemplate. Did I love Jennifer? I wasn't sure . . . or so I told myself. But in my heart I knew I would be just as irrational as Luke McDonald if it came to protecting Jennifer's safety.

Sam returned and headed back to the horses, and I followed. We rode to the ranch house with Sam carrying the cloth he had bought for Becky in a sack before him on the saddle. I felt slightly envious. I wished there was something I could do for Jennifer that would make her smile like Becky surely would when she saw that cloth. Jennifer had a pretty smile, prettier than any I had ever seen.

I thought of our planned meeting tomorrow. I was anxious to see her again, maybe this time for a bit longer than I had today. My feelings for her had sprung up uninvited, and they seemed to thrive and grow each time I thought of her.

She was on my mind when we reached the house, and she was still on my mind when I retired that evening. And when I slept I dreamed of her.

But at the borders of my mind I saw the image of Luke McDonald, standing with rifle in hand, and I tossed restlessly on my bed.

CHAPTER VII

❧

I arose early the next morning and enjoyed one of Becky's fine breakfasts once more. I was happy, not only because another night had passed without an attack by Guthrie's riders, but also because of the one o'clock appointment which I so eagerly anticipated. The morning would be long, a tantalizing wait until the time I could be with Jennifer again. The whole thing seemed unreal, like a dream. It was a dream I wanted more of.

Sam wasn't sharing my good spirits. He sat glumly through his breakfast, hardly speaking. I assumed he was still disgusted at the travesty of yesterday's meeting in Miles City.

I planned to spend the morning looking over land, so I asked Sam if he knew of any good areas nearby that were still available. I was surprised when he told me that much of the land between his own ranch and the Guthrie spread was still up for sale by the railroad. It was good grazing land, land used mostly by Guthrie, and it was because of his prestige, Sam figured, that people shied away from buying the property.

"I think I'll take a look at it," I said. "I might be just the one to buy it."

Sam looked at me as if I was a fool. "Don't you think that's a little risky, with Guthrie being right across the way with his riders?"

"I think I can take care of myself," I said. I was feeling cocky and proud this morning, more than I had a right to. But knowing that Jennifer was interested in me was puffing me up like a proud preacher at a camp meeting.

Sam looked at me and slowly shook his head, apparently sensing there was no point in trying to talk sense into me. He knew me well, and was quite closely acquainted with the stubborn streak that I had possessed since infancy.

After breakfast I rode out to the area we had talked about and looked it over. It was good land, level and rich, and a stream ran through the midst of it. In my mind I began mapping out a spread. I would put my house here, by the stream, a corral over there, a sod storage building there, a chicken coop yonder . . .

I began to feel an urgent excitement. I could sense that this time I would make it. The failures of the past were truly behind me now. This was a new land for me, and a new chance. Who knows? Maybe I would even have Jennifer with me.

I had to pull my thoughts up short. I tried to tell myself that notions of Jennifer and me getting married were just too premature to consider. Best to listen to reason instead of wild fantasies.

I rode in a wide circle around the area, trying to decide just how much of the land to buy. And I wondered how Guthrie would react when he found that some of his best grazing land was being taken over by the very fellow he ran off his property not long before.

I didn't worry about him. He had neglected to make any legal arrangements for this land, apparently counting on his prominent name to keep any settler off. Let him take the consequences of his negligence. It was his problem, not mine.

I saw a rider approaching from the south. I felt faintly apprehensive, but when he had approached within clear view I recognized him as Jack Tatum, the buffalo hunter. He had his rifle slung in a scabbard on the side of his saddle. He was riding a black.

"Howdy, Hartford," he said. "Didn't expect to run into you out here."

"Good to see you, Tatum. Your sorrel didn't make it, huh?"

He shook his head rather sadly. "Leg was just about broke clean through. Doc shot it for me."

"Sorry."

"Yeah. Got me another horse, though. It's a good one." He was right. The animal appeared spirited and strong.

Tatum glanced toward the east. "I reckon you heard about what happened over yonder last night, didn't you?"

I shook my head, tensing. "Over where?"

"Over them hills at the Guthrie ranch."

"No . . . what happened?"

"Some riders rode up on his house and fired a few shots. Nobody got hurt, I don't reckon. Killed his dog, though."

I felt weak. The image of Luke McDonald came immediately to mind.

"Some of the small ranchers? Fence-stringers?"

He nodded. "So I figure. I hear Guthrie's mad. There's been rumors that he's the man who hired the night riders. If he is then I think we can look for more trouble. He's not going to stand for folks attackin' his ranch like that. He ain't the kind to be patient and understandin'."

I felt almost sick. Luke McDonald—the old, simple-minded fool! He had done the very thing I hoped the enraged ranchers would avoid. And I doubted that he would be able to stand up to the consequences.

"You say nobody was hurt?" I asked.

"Not that I heard of."

"Good." A simple word, one totally insufficient to express my thankfulness that Jennifer was unhurt. But at the same time I wondered how she might feel toward me when she learned that my brother was a fence-stringer, and that soon I would be too, right on land her father used for grazing his herd. The prospect of buying the property seemed suddenly less appealing.

I talked for awhile to Tatum, then he moved on, heading north. I sat glumly in the saddle for several minutes, thinking of what he had said and wondering what would happen next. My spirits sank so low that not even the thought of my upcoming meeting with Jennifer was enough to lift them.

I arrived at the meeting place far ahead of time, trying to cheer myself up to meet her. It was no use. And when I saw her approaching there was something in her stance and stride that I didn't like.

She greeted me with a blank expression and great coldness. For a long and uncomfortable time she stood looking at me as if I were less than worthy of the honor.

"Jennifer, is something wrong?"

"Shut up. Don't open your mouth to me again. Why didn't you tell me what kind of business it was you were on yesterday? You stood up here sweet-talking me while your friends were down in my home accusing my father of being little more than a murderer. How could you do such a thing?"

Her words stung. I didn't know just how to respond, so I stood in appalled silence.

"I had heard of the fence-cutters before, but I never thought of them as anything less than trash. And that's how my father feels too, I can assure you. He would never give his support to such a thing as murder, no matter how many accusations you and your lying friends make.

"And now—after you do what you did—riders come *here* and shoot at the house. Innocent people could have been killed, Hartford. I could have been killed. Is that how you people take care of your worries about the riders? Pick a scapegoat and come shooting at his house under cover at night, not even being men enough to show your faces without masks?"

"Are you trying to accuse me of being one of the ones who . . ."

"I wouldn't be at all surprised. My father told me there is a rancher named Hartford west of here—is that your kin?"

"My brother."

"I figured you were tied in some way. You fence-stringers have ruined the range for my father and other ranchers like him. You disgust me. We will see each other no more, Mr. Hartford."

And with that she turned on her heel and began striding back down the slope toward the house. I watched her leave, my shock giving way to intense anger. I thought of all the things I could have told her, how I could have asked her to take a look in the hills behind her ranch if she doubted her father was involved with the night riders. I could also have told her how beyond those hills another "fence-stringer" would set up a ranch soon. In the course of hearing her berate me I had regained my desire to purchase the land I had viewed this morning. I wanted to show the haughty young lady that I would be scared away neither by harsh words nor night riders.

I would show her. I would prove that I didn't care what she thought of me.

Even though I did. I cared more than I wanted to admit.

That afternoon I visited the office of the railroad land agent and arranged to buy the land. He looked at me as if I was insane when I put my pen to the deal. But he smiled when I paid cash on the spot.

It was after nightfall when I returned to Sam's cabin. I was dejected, sullen. When I told him of buying the land he looked almost sad, but he said nothing. I realized that he was concerned about my safety, but still it irritated me.

When I lay down to sleep I found the rest would not come. I tossed fitfully, and the emotions that ran through me filled me with shame even then, more so later.

I was determined to show Jennifer that what she had said about me and my friends was foolish. I felt a childish desire to prove myself right and flaunt it in her face. I had grown to care so much for her, and she had returned that caring with scorn. And that hurt me very badly. I felt I could easily hate her right now. My mind said that I did.

My heart said I loved her.

I remained in bed for hardly more than an hour before I rose and dressed silently. Quietly I slipped out the door, my gun in my belt and my rifle in my hand; quietly I saddled my horse and moved off swift and silent in the night.

Reason had left me. No matter what the risk, I would learn more of the night riders. I would find some definite proof to link them to Luther Guthrie. I would see faces, learn names, gather evidence. I would ride right into their camp if need be, hiding myself nearby until they returned from the raid I was sure they were conducting tonight. I was a fool, and I knew it, but I didn't care. Jennifer's rejection had shaken me to the core, and I was acting completely against my usual reserved nature.

The plains were dark; the moon was obscured by clouds, and there was the feel of moisture in the air. A storm was brewing, and the low rumble of thunder shook the plains, echoing across the flat land like the distant, grumbling voice of some ancient god. I moved rapidly through the darkness, wanting to reach the hills where the riders made their camp, knowing I would have to reach them before they returned from their raid. I tried not to think of the other possibility—that they might be there when I arrived. If so it would probably be the end of Jim Hartford.

I reached the land I had purchased. My land. But it did not yet seem mine; I would have to take care of two matters before it seemed so. One was the night riders, the other my devastated relationship with Jennifer Guthrie.

The clouds were illuminated from within by magnificent bolts of lightning now; bolts leaped occasionally from cloud to cloud, lighting the plains as if it were noonday, showing in those instantaneous flashes the rolling grasslands, whipped by the rising wind, the weird and vast clouds tumbling through the heavens in anticipation of the wild storm to come, the barren hills rising before me, the scrubby trees and brush along their slopes thrashing in the wind. The air was damp with oncoming rain; in moments the plains would be drenched. Many women would rise the next morning to fill every spare cask and jar with water from the rain barrels for a temporary respite from the hard Montana waters. If the storm was to become as severe as this violent prelude threatened, then they would have a more than adequate supply.

I reached the base of the hills just as a tremendous bolt of electricity struck the earth far to the north, the yellow flash looking for all the world like a crack in the sky. The storm was moving this way; in only a short while it would be here. If the riders were out raiding tonight, the lightning might drive them back to their camp sooner than usual. And I would be waiting.

I led my horse by its reins around toward the south slope of the hills. I guessed that the riders camped right in the heart of the small chain of hills, for I had seen them enter through the narrow gap on the night I had followed them. I didn't want to be where they would find me, but yet I needed to be close to their camp in order to see them.

So far I had no reason to believe anyone was encamped in the hills at this moment, but nevertheless I proceeded carefully, circling the base of the hills. I came around to a rather rocky slope on the south, and I tied my horse to a tree as I searched for some sort of well-hidden route to the central portion of the hills. A blast of lightning ripped into the earth not more than a mile away, and I suddenly realized that I could not risk leaving my mount tied to a tree, which might serve as a natural lightning rod. I found a slight outcrop of rock under which I tethered the horse to a bush—not good protection but much better than before. Then I began climbing up the rather steep hillside with my rifle gripped close beside me. Lightning flashed, guiding my way.

I moved through a maze of small gulleys and around rocky hillsides, not having anything to guide me and always unsure of what I would encounter around the next turn. It was pitch black, and though the lightning came with enough regularity to let me see where I was going, the contrast between brilliant light and sudden blackness made it difficult to keep my bearings.

I stopped suddenly when ahead of me, visible through a small gap in the rocks, was the faint flicker of what could only be a campfire. Either that or a natural fire started by the lightning, but I had seen no bolts striking that closely. I crouched low and moved more carefully, then the light was blocked out suddenly by a figure moving between the fire and me, and I knew the riders were already in their camp.

I began to wish I was safe back on the straw tick at Sam's cabin, tucked away and sleeping. I realized suddenly just how dangerous my position was, and I debated whether or not to slip away and head home again.

But now that I was here it seemed pointless to not

at least try to see some face that I might later identify.
So I crept on, hoping I wouldn't make some unexpected noise and give away my presence. As I grew
nearer I could hear voices. I found a safe spot in a natural little nook overlooking the circular basin in which
they camped, and I began to watch and listen.

There were nine of them, some seated, a few walking about. One man was drinking coffee, and he was a
rugged-looking character, husky and with one eye covered with a patch. The rugged leather of his skin had
a pitted, scarred look. He wore faded denim, and a
scraggly beard covered his chin. There was something
wrong in his gaze, something distorted in the sallow
look of his single eye that flickered red in the firelight.
He lifted his tin coffee mug to his bearded lips and
took a long swallow, an amber stream running down
his throat to soak unnoticed into his faded blue shirt.

"I don't like this, Jess. It scares me." The speaker
was a thin man with a red beard and mustache that
drooped over his lips. He had a pale face, funeral-
parlor pale. And as he looked nervously toward the
sky it seemed to grow even whiter. "We're gonna get
struck, I tell you. Fried like bacon."

The one-eyed fellow—the one he called Jess—
didn't change his expression. He took another long
swallow of the coffee and belched. Then he tossed the
remainder of the beverage from his mug and said,
"Shut up, Jake. You'll be all right."

"I dunno, Jess. I had an uncle get struck once. He
bit his tongue in two like a razor had sliced it. It scares
me awful bad."

"For God's sake will you shut up?" came an exasperated voice from the midst of the group. "I'm hopin'
you do get struck just so you'll shut up."

"That ain't a nice thing to say, Horace. Not nice
at all."

I studied the group, looking at faces, trying to let
the features sink into my mind. I wanted to be able to
identify them readily, to know them by sight. I crept a

bit closer to the edge of the overhang upon which I lay, straining my eyes in the darkness. Thunder cracked and a drop of rain struck my arm, then more drops began pelting me. Angry curses rolled up from the men below me.

The one-eyed fellow stood. "I'm gettin' my poncho and stayin' in it 'til it's over. I hope I can keep my cigar dry." And at that moment my hand struck a piece of loose stone that clattered loudly down the slope to the camp below. My breath cut short and my heart pounded like a hammer on an anvil.

Just as the rain erupted in a drenching torrent every man in the camp was on his feet, all of them staring toward the spot where I lay hidden. I couldn't help but stare at the guns in their hands.

The leader spoke. "Get up there, Bill. Check it out."

A man moved toward me, gun in hand. I lay there, knowing full well I stood not a half a chance against the lot of them, and wondered if I should try to kill as many of them as possible before I took the inevitable bullet.

Then, with a tremendous roar and grating, skull-jarring shock, the world became an explosion of color and intense pain. I felt a sensation like I had never imagined possible, and every nerve in my body turned inside out.

CHAPTER VIII

❧

With an overwhelming jolt and a crushing sensation in my chest I was thrown backward, how far I could not tell. Then the world shimmered, faded away, returned, then began to fade again. I could hear voices growing steadily fainter as I lapsed toward unconsciousness.

"... nobody there ... Bill's hurt ... move ... forget about it ... to Guthrie's barn, now ..."

Then I was out, senseless.

I awoke to full morning light and a clear sky. All about me was water, almost over me at places. Everything was quiet. I tried to move, and it hurt.

For how long I lay there I did not know, for nothing seemed to make sense. I could not recall where I was, and at times even my own identity seemed a mystery. I lay confused and blinking, staring at the blue morning until the sun was high overhead. Then again I tried to move, and with considerable pain I managed to rise.

I was drenched, and the morning breeze was cold

against my body. I looked about me, trying to piece together the mystery of the immediate past, and as I came to vaguely realize my location, my memory started to return again.

I struggled to my feet and moved carefully over toward the place where the riders had camped. Through the bushes I looked, and there was nothing but the charred remains of their fire, some scattered and soaked articles of clothing, and bits and pieces of trash and broken branches. They were gone. The mention of Guthrie's barn returned to me.

I rubbed my head, trying to get rid of the horrid pounding there. Every muscle in me ached severely, as if the shock of the lightning had stretched them to the breaking point. Had I been struck directly? I looked about on the ground and found a large blackened spot not far from the campfire, and I realized that the lightning had struck the earth at that point, the electricity of the bolt traveling through the ground to reach me. If it had struck a few feet closer I might well be dead.

It seemed I could not stop shuddering. Partly it was because of the wind against my wet clothing, but it went beyond that. How much damage the lightning had done to me I could not tell, but I knew that I felt worse than I had ever felt before, and my head swam in a swirling sea of confusion and my stomach turned slowly over again and again, spasms of nausea welling through me each time.

I tried to remember where I had tethered my horse, and it took a long time. I found the animal standing drenched and impatient, and with an intense, gut-wrenching effort I managed to mount it. Then I turned toward home and headed across the plains with my body slumped forward, moving at a moderate speed.

The jolts of my horse's hooves were an endless pounding that kept me from going senseless again. Occasionally I managed to raise my head and look through bloodshot eyes across the land. The miles stretched to three times their normal length, and it seemed I would never reach the cabin. Then my sense of time slowly faded, and I dropped into a half-conscious swoon.

I was conscious only of Sam's hands helping me from the saddle, guiding me into the house, and helping me get out of my filthy clothing before I collapsed into the warmth of the straw tick and fell at once into a deep slumber.

I think that for many hours I did not dream as I lay there, but sometime later the fitful imaginations began, all of them disturbing, most confusing. Mostly it was images of faces—Sam, Becky, my parents—and others, too. One in particular kept returning; the face of the one-eyed man I had seen in the camp. There was something about him that I was supposed to recall . . . something . . . but what?

I woke long enough to see Sam's face above me, illuminated by the flickering light of a coal oil lamp. I said something to him, something I couldn't understand, then again I dropped into fitful slumber.

I awoke wet with sweat and very weary. It was light, I could tell that much, and the hurting in my brain was gone. Slowly I opened my eyes, and the light hurt them. I squinted and looked over toward my bedside. Sam was there.

"Hey there, brother!" he grinned. "I was gettin' a bit worried about you!"

I managed to smile. It was good to see my brother, the light, the cabin. I felt like a man who had just escaped some devilish torment.

"Sam . . . could I have some water?" He rose quickly and supplied me with a tin dipper brimming over with cold water. I think that until that time I never really appreciated how refreshing and delicious water could be.

"How long, Sam?"

He shrugged. "Long enough. Don't worry about it now. You still need a lot of rest."

I lay back, but I didn't close my eyes, for it was good to be awake and thinking once more. Perhaps I had been in a stupor for days. Apparently it had been for quite some time that I had been in this bed, or else Sam would not have evaded my question. I began to realize the seriousness of what might have happened. That had been a wicked jolt that had ripped through me. I was lucky to be alive, and I whispered a prayer of thanks.

Sam's eyes were tired and red-rimmed. He had sat up with me for many hours, I was sure. I realized with admiration what a good and strong man was my brother.

For a long time my mind did not return to thoughts of the riders or Luther Guthrie or Jennifer. The pain of Jennifer's last words to me was still with me, and I did not let myself think much about it. I think her scorn had burned even deeper than that powerful bolt of lightning.

But I did think of Luther Guthrie and his riders, particularly the pitted one, the one-eyed man that seemed to be giving the orders. From the first time I had seen him there had been something that stirred a hint of memory in me. I had seen him before—seen him, or perhaps heard of him. But where? Back in the valley in Tennessee? He looked like no one that I could recall from there. But still the conviction that he was in some way familiar lingered with me.

Becky's face appeared above me, in her hands a cup of steaming coffee. She helped me rise, then propped me up on pillows until I was almost sitting. I took the coffee gratefully. It was hot and delicious, and the warmness of the mug was pleasant on my hands.

It was only after several hours that Sam at last told me how long I had been in a stupor. Two days! I could hardly believe it. Becky told me of how Sam had ridden in search of the doctor as soon as I had arrived half-conscious back at the cabin, and of how he had been unable to find him. They had both lost much sleep, and Sam much work, caring for me. I felt a tremendous sense of gratitude.

I managed to make it to the table for supper that night. It was delicious—the first real food I had consumed in some time. I was thinner, and so weak that I trembled as I stood. But the meal put new strength in me.

Becky was cleaning up the dishes and I had just settled myself down in my bed when Sam came over to me. He sat on a stool beside my bed and leaned forward, speaking in a low whisper.

"Jim, tell me what you saw when you saw the riders. Faces, I mean." There was an urgency in his question that I could not understand.

"Well, I saw only one face clearly. There were nine of them in all, and it was only for a few moments that I was there. The one I saw was apparently the leader of the group. He was a one-eyed fellow, with marks on his face like he had once had smallpox or something. I heard one of the others call him Jess, I think."

Sam leaned back, frowning and looking somehow dissatisfied. I grew curious. "Sam, do you know him?"

He looked at me quickly, then shook his head. "No . . . I just wanted a description. I don't know anyone that looks like that." Then he stood quickly and moved away.

Now that was mighty strange, I thought. Why was Sam so curious about what I had seen? I could understand him wanting to know all he could about the riders that were threatening his life and property, but his question had a strange intensity and his expression was confusing.

I couldn't make sense of it, so I didn't try. I closed my eyes and settled back. The tick was soft, warm. Soon I was asleep.

In the days that followed I recovered rather slowly. Sam went back to his work, but he seemed always to be brooding about something. Several times in the evenings I would see him seated in a corner, a frown on his face.

For days there had been no trouble from the riding gunmen, nor any reports of such trouble from other ranchers, and that was to me a comfort. But I think Sam looked on it as a lull in the storm, a respite that was as impermanent as it was welcome.

I regained my strength and began helping Sam with his work. The sod building needed repair, and as we worked on it he struck a deal with me. If for this year I would work with him around the ranch and help him sell his stock, he would in turn help me build a cabin on my land, and next year would share his stock with me until my own herd could be built up. I liked the idea and quickly accepted. I needed some way of learning the ranching business before trying it myself, and working with Sam would be the ideal way.

And I would have time to build a good, solid cabin. I was determined to have a nice home, no matter how much work it took. Trees were not easy to come by in this country, but on Sam's spread was a creek lined by a good stand of trees, and there were several good trees on my own land, so I didn't worry. I spent an evening planning out the design of my cabin, as well as some smaller outbuildings, and the next day Sam and I set out for the creek, taking two good axes and some chains, along with my horse and his mule.

For a day we worked, chopping trees, trimming branches, then with the help of the horse, mule, and chains, snaking the logs to not far from Sam's cabin and laying them in a pile. The work was long and hard, but I was very well accustomed to gruelling labor, and before the day was through we had a good stack of logs. Not nearly enough for a cabin, but still a good supply.

The next day was spent in snaking the logs to my land, and in scouting out trees to be cut from my own property. I was happy, for idleness did not please me for very long, and it had been some time since I had done any real, satisfying labor. It was with real pride that I built up the stack of logs.

I gathered large, flat stones from the creek for use in the foundation. I planned on building a floor for my cabin, and designing the structure so that rooms could be added with no trouble. I found the work a challenge, a pleasure. It was with real sadness that I saw the day end, and Sam and I mounted and rode back to his cabin and another good supper of bacon, biscuits, and eggs.

The next day it rained again, all day. There was nothing to be done but make plans, and I was itching for work. But the water pounded incessantly on the roof without a minute's respite until sundown. Then the rain stopped, the sky cleared, and the stars shone down through cloudless heavens.

Sam, Becky, and I moved out into the yard in the evening, drawn by the beauty of the night. All was peaceful, still, calm.

We talked of quiet things, simple things. Becky had a look of contentment beyond any I had yet seen her show, and I smiled when I noticed her hand patting gently on her stomach, sending love to the young, developing life within. Sam saw it too, and a happy look came into his eye.

I talked to him of my cabin, and he gave me suggestions based on his experience with log buildings. Sam was an excellent craftsman, a fine builder, and I coveted his knowledge.

"Build your foundation high, Jim. I wish I had laid a good board floor in my own cabin, but in those days I hardly had the time to get a roof over our heads. That's why it's good you're working for me this year. You'll have time to build a home like it should be done. You've got enough money left over from buying that property to hold you for awhile, and what with vegetables from our garden and rabbits and such from hunting, you should be able to do just fine. You're lucky, brother. You'll make it good out here."

I hoped so. I hoped so with all my heart. I was happier here with what was left of my family than I had been in years, and I wanted that happiness to continue, even increase. Yet at heart there was an intense sadness, for I knew that Jennifer no longer cared for me. I had known her only days, yet in that time I had come to love her dearly, and knowing we were now together no more was intensely painful.

We sat there in the beautiful and clear night far beyond the time we normally retired, and it was only with reluctance that we at last rose and went to our beds. Soon, I thought, I would be sleeping in my own bed, in my own cabin, built by my own hands. It was a good thought. I rolled it over in my mind.

I laid down and slept, and in my dreams I was hewing logs, happily working, feeling the wood in my hands, moving my ax with careful and sure strokes, watching the wood chip away until the log was smooth and square. Then I cut notches, slanting dovetail notches, and with an auger drilled holes for pegs. It was a good dream. Soon it would be reality.

I woke to a sudden roar and the feeling of wood chips striking my face, stinging. I leaped up with a cry, and instinctively I dove for my rifle against the wall. Then I rolled over on my back and realized what was happening just as Becky cried out in the back room and Sam rushed to the door in his longjohns, his rifle in his hands, bullet pouch over his shoulder, and a wild expression on his face.

The roar came again, then another, then many others. The roars of rifles, the smacking of high-caliber slugs into the walls, and the shattering of shutters as the bullets tore through them to smash into the walls and shelves in the back of the room. One ripped right past Sam's head to embed itself in the wall of his bedroom.

"No!" he screamed, almost out of his mind in rage. "No more!"

"Sam, no . . ."

My cry did no good, for without hesitation or

thought to safety he threw open the door and dashed out into the night, firing and reloading as he ran, screaming in the darkness, weeping, cursing . . .

There were answering blasts from the riders, and even as I ran out after him I saw the dirt being torn up about his feet. Yet he made no effort to run, but stood fast, firing at the moving figures, all the while his voice crying out in desperation for them to stop.

He was firing too carelessly, too angry to realize that when his ammunition was gone he would be a helpless target. I moved behind the post of the cabin porch and fired two quick shots at the nearest rider. I didn't hit him, but I could tell my shots worried him, for he moved quickly away in the darkness.

"Sam! Come back! You're a clear target!"

He didn't hear, or didn't heed, at least. He continued his spasmodic fire at the dark figures that circled the cabin and rode in the fields directly before it. I shot at them, and I think it was only the peppering shots of my Winchester that kept them from drawing close enough to my brother to drop him where he stood.

I could hear Becky screaming in the room behind my, crying in hysteria as she looked over me where I crouched on the porch and saw her husband so insanely risking his life. I knew I had to get him and drag him back by sheer force if need be, before he was dropped by a slug in full view of his wife. I raised up from my crouched position and began to run.

The rider approached just as I darted forward, and the slug that ripped close by my head stopped me in my tracks. I saw him clearly, heading straight for Sam, a pistol aimed at his head, his finger ready to squeeze off the shot that would end Sam's life.

Sam's Sharps barked, and the figure was literally knocked into the air, flipping backwards over his saddle, landing with a loud grunt in the dirt while his horse wheeled and headed back into the night. And it seemed then that Sam's mind cleared of its rage, and he darted back toward the cabin. Together we moved back inside, Becky crying all the while, obviously profoundly grateful that her husband had returned to safety at least for the moment.

Sam slammed the heavy door shut, dropping the bar in place. Then he moved over to a place that somehow I had never noticed before—a place on the wall where a small opening was drilled, narrow from the outside, but flaring out wide on the inside to give a gunner a good sweep with his weapon. Sam had made the opening as a defense against Indians back in the earlier days, I guessed. I don't know why I had never noticed it.

I moved over to the window with the shattered shutter that had thrown splinters into my face while I lay sleeping. Carefully I peeped out toward the riders in the darkness.

They were moving, slowly, almost like phantoms, all in a line, and all deathly silent. They were coming toward the spot where their comrade lay dead on the ground, an ugly hole in his chest and his mouth and eyes open in a frightening, frozen expression of shock. They approached until they were right upon him, and I saw one of the group climb down from his horse to kneel beside the body. It was the one-eyed man I had noticed in the camp.

For a long time he knelt beside the body, then he stood and shook his head. He picked up the limp form and draped it over the saddle from which he had fallen when Sam's bullet struck him. Then he looked up at the cabin.

"You'll pay, damn you! You'll pay with your miserable lives!" He had a sort of rough voice, like gravels scraping together on a rusted shovel. And from his tone I could tell that he meant every word that he said.

Then he mounted and moved away with the rest of his men, riding openly and without any apparent fear of our weapons. I felt a murderous impulse to shoot them in the back, as many of them as I could hit before they moved out of range. But I fought off the feeling. Then Sam cried out with a loud voice and I jumped in surprise.

"Madison! Colonel Josiah Madison! It seems your murdering days aren't over yet, are they!"

One of the horses stopped suddenly, and a figure turned to stare back at the cabin. It was the one-eyed leader of the group. And at that moment I understood why his face had plagued me so. Stories came back to me, stories that Sam had told me, stories that had been the substance of many nightmares for many years.

"Sam, is that . . ."

"Yes, Jim, that man is Colonel Josiah Jefferson Madison, the very one who is wanted by the federal government for the atrocities that he committed when he was in charge of the Bryant Federal Detention Camp during the war. That was the man who took delight in seeing me and my friends tortured. He's a murderer, Jim, and now he has a grudge against me. Before this is over, someone is going to be dead."

He turned and strode back toward his bedroom, and I leaned my rifle against the wall and felt I might vomit.

CHAPTER IX

꿈

I couldn't believe what I had heard. I moved quickly back to where Sam leaned against the wall in the back room.

"Are they gone?" he asked.

"Yes. They rode off. But now I'm not sure they won't be back very soon. Especially if what you said is true."

"It's true. You can be sure of that."

I shook my head. "But Sam, how can you be so certain? You've only seen him across the distance in the dark. How do you know that it's Madison?"

"I know. You don't see a man torture your best friend to death and then not recognize him later. That's Madison, with an eye patch now, but still the same face. His eye was diseased during the war. It seems he must have lost it."

"Are you sure it was wise to let him know that you recognized him? He'll be after you for sure now. He's wanted, and anyone that can identify him he won't let live, and you know it."

"I know, Jim. But I promised myself all these years that if ever I saw Josiah Madison again I would not back down, I wouldn't try to hide from him. And I won't do that now."

I knew that there was no point in trying to convince him of anything. His mind was made up. And now we had a real problem, for no longer was this cabin the home of just another fence-stringer. It was the home of men that could identify a wanted man to the law.

Sam had told me many stories about Colonel Josiah Madison, and even from merely hearing about the horrors that went on in the prison camp that he controlled I had understood why Sam had such a hate for the man. A sudden thought struck me.

"Sam . . . you asked about the man just awhile after I woke up the other day. Why?"

"You were raving in your sleep, babbling about a man with smallpox scars and a bad eye. That made me think about Madison, and when I saw him just now I knew that's who it was."

Sam walked over to his bed and sat down. Becky was beside him, and she put her hand on his shoulder. "What now, Sam?"

"What I should have done the last time this happened. Listened to sense and fought back."

Those words chilled me. I saw the same madman rage burning in Sam that had been there several days ago. That rage had disappeared after the meeting with the other ranchers, but now it had revived again and with greater fervor. I began to fear that Sam would not react so reasonably this time.

"Just what does that mean, Sam?" I asked.

He looked at me sharply, almost in anger. "It means that tomorrow I'm taking Becky up the creek to the Ledbetter place and leaving her for safekeeping. Then I'm riding out to find Luke McDonald and tell him just who the leader of those riders is. And then you can probably guess what will happen."

I could. The ranchers would grow angry, arm themselves, and then there would be another attack on the Guthrie spread. And this time the occupants of that ranch might not come out alive. Jennifer . . .

At once a fiery rage welled up within me. Sam suddenly became my enemy, and I lashed out at him harshly.

"How can you do that? How can you become the very thing you're trying to fight? To shoot, murder . . ."

Sam looked at me coldly. My words did not cut him at all. He had determined his course, and nothing I could say would stop him.

I waited out the night on the front step of the house, my rifle across my knees and wild thoughts racing through my mind. When the morning came I again entered the house and glumly ate my breakfast. Sam and I said little to each other.

He left with Becky as soon as he had saddled his horse and hitched up the wagon for her. I watched them ride off, knowing full well that with the news Sam carried it would be only a few hours before a bloodthirsty army of ranchers would descend in force on Luther Guthrie's spread. I expected violence before the day was over.

I had to do something to keep Jennifer safe. I thought I didn't care for her anymore—perhaps I didn't—but still I would not let her be murdered. That I couldn't bear.

But what could I do? How could I get her away from the ranch? I certainly couldn't walk up and knock on the door and politely tell Luther Guthrie that a massacre was about to take place and I wanted to remove his daughter from the premises. And Jennifer would certainly not see me willingly even if I should manage to reach the house without being shot. No, there would have to be another way.

And the only way I could think of was to steal her away, to take her against her will and for her own good. That would be dangerous, for sure, but what other course was there? And with that thought I nodded my head firmly and moved back toward the cabin for my rifle.

I was out again quickly when I heard the noise of an oncoming horse. Who could be approaching the cabin at this early hour? I cocked my Winchester and cautiously stepped out to meet whoever it was.

It was Aaron McCuen, and from the looks of him he had been riding hard since before daylight. He was unshaven and bleary-eyed, and he rode almost up to the door at a full gallop.

Scarcely had I greeted him, laying my rifle aside, before he was talking at a fast pace. He was obviously worried, and very tense.

"Hartford, things are getting bad—real bad," he gasped. "There was more trouble from the riders last night, the first in days. And a little girl was shot when they fired at a cabin not too far up the river from here. It wasn't far past midnight when somebody came riding into town shouting the news. It woke up everyone. They fear the girl might die. People are worked up, Hartford, and there's blood about to be spilt. I can feel it. I didn't know how it will end. I felt like maybe we could do something, though I don't know what. I've heard that the sheriff is up in these parts, but I haven't been able to find him."

"It doesn't matter. What could the sheriff do? The riders were here last night, and they fired on us. We killed one of them."

McCuen's eyes grew large. "No! Are you sure you killed him?"

"I'm sure. But that's not the big news." I told him then about my trip out to the riders' camp and the man I had seen. And I told him of Sam's conviction that he was none other than the infamous Josiah Madison. McCuen shook his head as if the news was too much to take in one dose.

"If that's true, then those men will surely be out

for blood even more than they are now," he said. "I'm afraid that before the sun sets again there will be blood on the land around Luther Guthrie's ranch. A lot of it."

I had no trouble in agreeing with that conviction. "I've got to ride out there," I said. "I've got to get there before those ranchers have a chance to get organized." McCuen looked at me strangely. I felt a kind of embarrassment. How could I tell him my reason for wanting to go? How could I tell him how I felt about Jennifer Guthrie? I looked at him blankly.

"What do you plan to do when you get there?" he said. "What good will a trip out there do? I was thinking that you and I could . . ."

"I'm sorry. I can't explain, but I have to go. I have to. What are you going to do?"

McCuen rubbed his chin, and there was distress in his eyes. "I hoped to find some sort of lawman, but that hasn't worked out. I don't know what to do . . . I think I'll head for Bacon's ranch. He'll want to know about this. Can I meet you at Muster Creek?"

"Yes . . . meet me in the badlands straight across from Guthrie's ranch house," I said. "Up in the hills, the ones that look down on his spread. I don't know when I'll be there . . . if I'm not there when you arrive, then wait awhile. I'll wait for you if need be."

"Agreed. I can't imagine what any of us will do to stop this ridiculous business, but I'll meet you there. Maybe Bacon will be able to think of something."

"I hope so. I'll see you in a few hours."

McCuen left then, moving off swiftly, running his horse hard. The animal would be exhausted when it reached Bacon's ranch, no doubt. McCuen had already taxed the animal severely.

As I saddled my horse I felt helpless and fearful. This whole thing was beyond the control of any one person, and I suspected that no mind, not even one as keen as Jedediah Bacon's, could think of a way to stop the mindless slaughter that was approaching. And I for one was not particularly concerned with stopping it; there was no point in attempting the impossible. But one thing I did intend to do, and that was to get Jennifer safely out of the way before those enraged gunmen arrived to shoot up the ranch. I would force her away at gunpoint if I had to, I would kill anyone that stood in my way if it came to that. I would even die myself before I would see her harmed. I was surprised at the intensity of my feelings. For a long while I had thought very little of Jennifer, but now that she was in danger I found that my feelings were as strong as ever toward her. In haste I pulled the girth tight around my horse's belly and mounted.

I moved quickly across the land, now very familiar. There was a cool breeze blowing, and the wind felt good against my skin. But I could not enjoy the ride, for every second I worried that perhaps the ranchers might mobilize more quickly than I expected and reach the Guthrie ranch before I could get Jennifer away. It was ironic, being against my own brother in this, but I knew I could not do otherwise. Jennifer's safety was of paramount importance.

I slowed my horse down when I saw that the rapid pace was wearing him out. After a time I passed the area I had purchased for my ranch. Halfway I dreaded to look at my stack of logs, for I feared what the riders might have done to them. So I was mildly surprised and very pleased when I found them stacked in perfect shape, apparently untouched. It was the first pleasant discovery of the day. And maybe, I feared, the last.

Onward I moved, never stopping, never resting. Soon the hills loomed before me large, and I guided my horse to the south to cut around the same part of the hills where I had hidden not many nights before. If the riders were in those hills again I had no desire for them to see me. I passed around the south base of the slopes with no sign of life presenting itself.

I stopped, unsure of what to do. Were the riders hidden in the same area as before? Or had they moved down to the Guthrie ranch? I needed to know; it could be fatal to walk right into the midst of them. I tethered my horse to the same spot as before and crawled up into the same gully.

There was no sound, no movement anywhere before me. I crept slowly and carefully nonetheless, for it was possible, even likely, that if the riders were there they would be asleep. They had gone through a very busy night not long before.

But as I moved forward it all seemed utterly dead and empty. I carefully moved aside the brush that blocked my view into the little hollow where the riders' camp lay. I looked in. It was empty.

I stood and leaped down into the hollow. There were tracks, seemingly not too old, and the blackened remains of a fire. But there was no trace of any supplies, blankets, bags, or anything else to indicate that anyone now lived here. There were empty cans, old cigarette butts, and old chewed-out wads of tobacco, but nothing else. Obviously the riders had gone. I felt weak. There was nowhere else they could be but down there at the Guthrie ranch, just where the coming gunmen would expect them. That meant that the ranch itself would become a battleground, and with the riders down there with Jennifer, my chances for getting her safely away seemed remote.

It might be suicide to go down there. Was it worth it? Should I risk my life to save someone who would probably scorn my help and curse me even as I saved her?

Of course it was worth it. It was Jennifer. I didn't care what happened to Luther Guthrie or anyone else except to the extent that it concerned Jennifer. She was the only one I wanted to get away from that ranch before violence erupted. Of course, it bothered me to think of Sam being down there in the midst of the battle, but he was a grown man who had made his deci sion. He would be there by choice. Jennifer wasn't being given an option.

Getting her away from there was going to be a real problem, but that would come later. First I had to get down there to the ranch without being seen. And with the regular ranch hands there along with the riders, there were a lot of eyes to watch me approach. I had a lot of open ground to cover without being seen.

I moved toward the top of the slope that looked down on the house. I crouched down beside the trunk of a scraggly tree and looked over the terrain.

The house was not very far, but it was a long slope that I would have to descend. Many were the windows all along the back of the house, and the entire slope of the hill was in plain view of almost every point on the ranch.

I looked toward the south. The hill sloped down in that direction too, though not as steep. And I could descend it without being seen from the ranch or the house. But when I reached the base I would have to approach the house again, and I would be in clear view of the windows. But the house might hide me from the rest of the ranch grounds. I would have to count on my luck to ensure that I wouldn't be spotted from the house. It was the only way I could approach and have any hope of making it safely.

A man strode from a barn across the lot and toward the main house. I looked at him closely. Maybe he was one of the regular hands, maybe one of the riders. A realization came to me. If the riders were now openly living on the very ranch itself, then Jennifer would have proof that the accusations I and my friends had made toward her father were accurate. How she would react to that I could not guess.

I moved back down the slope again. I tried not to think too much about the tremendous task facing me. I had so far only come up with a plan to reach the house, and a weak plan at that. How I would get in

the house without being spotted, how I would find
Jennifer and convince her to leave without betraying
my presence . . . none of those matters had been
solved. I was a fool, and I knew it. No sane person
would try what I was about to do. Yet I felt I had no
choice.

I reached the place where my horse was tethered.
I loosened the halter and mounted. I certainly could
not ride around to the house, but I could tie my horse
a little closer to save some distance on the return trip.
That is, if there was a return trip.

I found a good place where my horse could graze
and remain hidden. Leaving it there, I hefted my Winchester close to me and headed around the base of the
slope.

I paused when I reached the point where I could
see the house. The rest of the ranch was hidden from
me, and that was comforting. If I were spotted, it
would be through the windows. If I was lucky, no
one would be looking.

I paused for a moment to gather my wits and
breathe a quick prayer. I knew that my best bet would
be to move as fast as I could toward the house and
hide directly beneath a window. The slower I moved
the longer I would be exposed to view. Taking a deep
breath, I darted from my hiding place and moved in a
crouch straight toward the log structure.

It couldn't have been for more than thirty seconds
that I ran, yet it seemed many minutes. And though I
tried to scurry along without much noise, I felt like a
crashing buffalo. I cast up all hope. Surely someone
had seen me, or at least heard me. Any minute there
would come cries, rifle fire, and I would be down and
bleeding.

But it never happened. I reached the house and
leaned panting up against the wall, sincerely surprised
and very pleased to find myself still breathing. I felt
like patting myself on the back. The first part of my
mission, at least, had been successful.

But now I had to get inside, and what's more, get inside without being seen. It bothered me to realize that when she laid eyes on me Jennifer would probably scream or call for her father, and all of my careful plans would be rendered pointless. But I had come this far, and I certainly couldn't stop now.

Which room would Jennifer be in? The very real possibility that she was not in the house at all occurred to me only then. That would be one fine mess—to risk my neck getting down here and pulling off the impossible feat of getting into the house only to discover that she was not even there. Were it not for the fact that I would probably get my head blown off, there would be something humorous in it.

There was a window beside me, and carefully I looked into it. It was my first real glimpse of the interior of Guthrie's home, and I was impressed with the fine way it was outfitted. Not the typical rancher's home, this place! There were real lace curtains on the windows, and paintings on the walls. The furniture was finely-made stuff, not the rough, knocked-together mess that one usually found in this part of the country. Guthrie's wife was dead, I knew, but apparently he had done his best during her lifetime to give her a home of which she could be proud. And now he was surely doing the same for Jennifer. I had to admire that in him. A man who cared for his family like he did could not be a totally bad man.

The room was empty. Maybe it would be worthwhile to try and get in through the window. Carefully I looked all about me, listening for the sound of approaching feet. There was only silence. All it would take to end the whole affair would be for someone to walk unexpectedly around the house.

Again I looked through the window. The room still was empty. I reached out to try the window, wondering if I could force it open. In the walkway past the open door of the room I saw a figure pass.

It was a man, I could tell, though I saw nothing

of his face. Luther Guthrie, perhaps? Possibly, though my short glance had given me the impression that this was a smaller fellow. I would have to be careful. He hadn't seen me, but my luck might not hold for long.

I tried the window, afraid to push hard for fear it would open suddenly and loudly, as stubborn windows are prone to do. Several times I pushed, but it was no use. The window would not budge.

There was another window to my right. I tried it also, but it too was either locked or jammed. It seemed that I wasn't going to get in at all from this side of the house.

Suddenly I heard it—a man whistling, moving toward this end of the house from across the ranch grounds. Had he not whistled I don't think I would have heard him at all.

There was nothing to do but dart around the back of the house. That I did, making far more noise than I would have liked, and becoming suddenly aware that I was in danger of discovery by the whistler.

What could I do . . . where could I go? There was someone in the house, but if I stayed outside I was certain to be found out. When I heard the whistling man turn the corner of the house and head toward the rear, I did the only thing possible.

I found a window, threw it open—this one, thank heavens, wasn't jammed—and half crawled, half leaped through. I hadn't even had time to see if the room I was entering was unoccupied. I turned and looked around me as I pulled my Winchester through the window after me.

Jennifer stood across the room, her hair disheveled and her eyes red and swollen as if she had been crying. I stared at her in surprise, not knowing what to say, and sensing that something was wrong here in this house. Something out of the ordinary was happening, and I had walked into the midst of it.

"Jennifer?" My voice sounded weak when I spoke her name.

"Jim!" Her words were choked, as if with fear. "Don't make any noise . . . there's a guard just outside the door, and if he finds you here, he'll kill you!"

CHAPTER X

For a long moment I stood staring at Jennifer with an open mouth. The sudden sight of her had startled me and left me speechless. The significance of what she had said did not sink in at once, but when it did I felt a chilling dread creep over me.

"Guard? But who . . ."

I could sense from the look in her eye that she couldn't figure out just why I was here. And also from her look I knew that somehow she didn't hate me anymore, and even in the midst of my tension and fear it came as an overwhelming relief to me.

"Jennifer, have the riders taken over this ranch? Are they the ones that are guarding this door?" I kept my voice at a low whisper, conscious of the sound of boots on the floor just outside the door. Jennifer answered with a tense nod.

"Yes . . . they rode in very early this morning and burst into the house. I didn't know what to think . . . I thought they were more of those same riders that attacked earlier. I had no idea that they were the so-called 'night-riders' that everyone has been talking about for weeks." She paused with obvious discomfort. "I . . . I owe you an apology, I guess. You were right, you and your friends. My father is the one who hired those men to terrorize the fence builders. I didn't know it until this morning. But he isn't in control of them anymore . . . they've taken over everything, and that horrible man that leads them is demanding that Father sign over the ranch to him."

"Sign over the ranch? You mean he wants control of the Muster Creek Cattle Company? But that's unbelievable!"

"Maybe so," she said, "but that's just what he wants. I heard it all . . . he came into the house this morning, even before it was light, and literally dragged my father from his bed. He said that one of his men had been killed, and that things were getting too dangerous for the pay my father was giving them. Father grew very angry, and demanded that he leave, saying that he no longer worked for him. The man just laughed, and it was a horrible laugh, just horrible. He said that unless my father signed over the ranch to him he would say that the murders he and his men had committed, murders my father did not order, Jim, had been carried out at Father's command. There was nothing my father could do. The man even . . . even threatened me . . ." Her voice choked off, and I felt a profound pity for her.

Yet deep inside I couldn't help but feel that Luther Guthrie's predicament was not undeserved. He had called in cruel men to spread fear among innocent people, and now that the situation was reversed it seemed nothing but just.

But still I knew that I would have to help him. Not for his own sake, but only for that of his daughter. And there was another reason, too: a man like Josiah Madison should not be running free in any civilized territory. His crimes deserved punishment, and I aimed to do my part to see that he received his just deserts.

It seemed that only then did Jennifer realize the strangeness of my presence and mode of entry. "Jim . . . just why is it that you came here? And why did you break in instead of just walking up to the door? I'm glad you didn't, for you would have been shot, but how did you know?"

"I came from the west and circled around the hills just behind us," I said. "I knew the riders were making camp in those hills, but when I checked they were gone. I knew they must have come here, so naturally I was careful. I didn't know you were in this room when I came in . . . I was just going through the first convenient entrance to avoid being seen by anyone. But I'm glad you're here. I came because everyone on this ranch is in great danger right now. There's going to be another attack in the next few hours, I believe. Those riders out there shot a young girl last night, and the whole territory is up in arms. Of course they believe your father was behind the whole thing, and there's no telling how much blood might be shed once they get here. I came to take you away." I wanted to explain about Madison, too, but there was not time. I was growing nervous, conscious that at almost any time the angry ranchers might arrive and the battle would begin. I had to get Jennifer away, and quickly. But how? With the ranch crawling with riders there was almost no way to escape unseen. And if she wanted me to help her father also, as I knew she did, then the task would be doubly difficult.

Jennifer's eyes filled with fear, and she spoke in a whisper of despair: "Jim, how can we escape? And how can we get Father away before they arrive? They'll kill him if we leave him behind."

I couldn't argue with that. Luther Guthrie would be one of the attacking group's primary targets. Protecting him from those angry ranchers, not to mention the riders controlling the ranch, was sure to be just short of impossible, and that was looking at it optimistically.

I let out an exasperated sigh. "Where is your father, Jennifer?"

"I'm not absolutely sure," she said. "I heard someone talking about the little log house on down the slope not long ago. I think that's where they're holding him. But there're guards all over this ranch, Jim. I'm sure that they'll have the house locked up and a man at the door with a gun."

My spirits sank as she talked. Not only would we have to get out of this house without being seen, we would also have to move across open land with guards everywhere, get into a locked building, and move out with Luther Guthrie and still hope to draw no attention. A conviction began to grow in me that this was the day I would die.

"My God, Jennifer, I can't work miracles! How can I get him away from here without getting all of us killed?" My voice was harsh, I realized, but now was not the time to dwell on niceties. But immediately I regretted my tone, for she again began to cry. I looked at her without knowing what to say.

"You mean you just want to leave him here to die? You think I can run out on my own father at a time like this?"

I sighed once more, and slowly shook my head. "Of course not, Jennifer. Of course not. Don't worry . . . we'll get your father away from here." I might as well have promised her the world in a burlap sack, for all the confidence I felt in what I was saying. But she looked up at me with an expression that somehow made it all worthwhile. I turned my thoughts to the immediate problem of escaping from the room.

The most obvious solution seemed to be to simply move on out the window in just the same way I had entered. If we could move quietly, then we should be able to do it without drawing the attention of the guard outside the door. I said as much to Jennifer, and she agreed.

But even as we moved toward the window a new thought came to me. The guard outside had a gun, one that would be turned against the ranchers when they arrived ... one that just might be turned against my own brother, perhaps. If I could eliminate the threat of that gun, then the odds of Sam's survival would be increased at least a small bit. I grasped Jennifer's arm.

"Wait. There might be a better way." I explained to her the idea that was forming in my mind. She looked troubled.

"But why take the risk? What if it doesn't work?"

I told her of Sam, and how I couldn't miss the chance to help him, even if I didn't agree with what he was doing. "I'll help out your father, Jennifer, but I can't ignore the safety of my own kin any more than you can ignore the safety of yours." That seemed to convince her, and as I took up a heavy bottle of some sort of cologne and hid against the wall beside the door, she moved to the doorway and cleared her throat before speaking in a clear, loud voice.

"Mister ... come in here. I need help."

There was the sound of movement just on the other side of the doorway, and a rough voice came back: "What? What's your problem?"

"Please ... I need help right now." Jennifer put a real tone of despair into her voice. She was doing a convincing bit of acting.

There was a moment of hesitation. "I don't know, miss ... the boss said ..."

"But mister, I need help ... please ..."

Again a time of hesitation. Then, "Oh, alright. Just a blasted minute." I heard the noise of his hands fumbling with the latch, and suddenly the door was opening and his head was poking through.

Down came the bottle, as hard as I could move it. The glass shattered, and with a groan and a shudder the man dropped to the floor. His eyes glazed over and closed, and for a moment I thought I had killed him. Jennifer stood back and stared down at him with a horrified expression.

I felt weak. I had never done such a thing to another human being before, and I didn't like it. But even then I knew it had been necessary, and I felt a kind of relief. "There's one that won't be giving anyone any trouble for quite awhile," I said.

We moved into the main room of the ranch house then, for there was no longer any need to sneak out the window. The guard had been alone in the house, so at the moment we were in no danger of detection. I headed for a window to look out over the grounds in hope of getting some sort of plan in mind about the rescue of Luther Guthrie. My hand bumped against the butt of my pistol thrust in my belt, and after a moment's thought I drew it out and handed it to Jennifer.

"Here. You might need this. Do you know how to use it?"

I think my question offended her, if the look on her face was any indication. She took the gun. "Of course I can use it. A girl doesn't grow up in this territory without knowing how to use a gun."

"That's good," I said. Then I looked out the window.

I saw two men moving back some distance from the corral, heading for the bunkhouse. Apparently they were holed up there. I wondered if any of the regular hired hands were being held prisoner, or if they had joined ranks with the riders. I asked Jennifer.

"I can't say for sure," she responded. "My father had many regular hands for many years, men that would remain loyal to him no matter what. But through the years they have drifted off, a couple have died, and so on. The men that work for him now are drifters, not the quality that he likes to work with. But he takes what he can get. I'm afraid that they might have joined up with the riders, as you call them. I wouldn't be able to say for sure, of course."

"I'd say you are probably right," I said. "We'll have to assume that they'll have sided against your father."

There was a large expanse of open ground between us and the log house where Jennifer suspected her father was being held. I noticed an armed man seated beside the door of the rough little building, and that served to convince me that Jennifer was right about where her father was.

The guard didn't look any too alert—he was nodding at his post—but still he presented a formidable obstacle to any plan I could dream up. I looked closely at the structure. There were no windows in the front nor on the side that I could see, and the door appeared to be of thick oak or some other strong wood. Looking closely I could see a padlock on the latch. The ground sloped up into a kind of hill behind the building, and the foundation was dug right into the hill, making the building appear to be sinking into the earth. I turned over plan after plan in my mind, only to reject each one in the light of logic. I shook my head. "Jennifer, I can't think of any way to reach that building, much less let out your father, without tipping our hand to the guard. He'll see us no matter what."

Jennifer looked at me with a firm expression. "Then the only thing to do is get rid of that guard." I looked at her in shock.

"What do you mean?"

She had a cold look in her eye that bothered me. "I mean if we're going to help my father, then we'll have to get rid of that guard outside. It's the only way."

I found myself shaking. I was still hardly over having to strike the other fellow in the head and now Jennifer was talking about something that sounded disturbingly like killing. I had never been a violent person, and quite frankly not a brave one either. My mind rebelled at the thought of having to actually try to kill someone. I couldn't do it.

"Jennifer, you mean we should *kill* that fellow out there? Is that what you mean?"

She hung her head a bit, but still she had the determined look in her eye. "Jim, those men won't hesitate to kill my father, and neither will your fencestringing friends that are coming. I don't like the idea of killing anyone, but what other way is there? I can't let my father die just because I couldn't bring myself to do something like that. You have to understand."

And though it bothered me to my very soul, I had to admit that she was right. If that was one of my kin locked away in that log shack, I wouldn't hesitate to do whatever was necessary to rescue him. And there was certainly no way we could get to Luther Guthrie if that guard was still alive.

"There's just one problem, though, Jennifer," I said. "How can we . . . how can we go about it? If we shoot him they'll hear us, and that would be the end of it all. And we can't just prance out there and knock him in the head."

I hoped that she could find no answer. But she pursed her lips and wrinkled her brow, and in a moment she spoke. "Jim, have you ever done any shooting with a bow and arrow?"

"Not much . . . why?"

"My father befriended a Cheyenne warrior at one time. He made a gift of a bow and a few arrows to my father. He's used it as a decoration in his room for years. It's old, but I think it is still strong. Maybe . . . maybe we could shoot that man from the house here and no one would know. It wouldn't make any noise . . ."

"That wouldn't keep the fellow from hollering if we were lucky enough to hit him from this distance," I said, glowering out the window. "And I'm not by any means a good shot with an arrow. I'm sorry. It just won't work."

Jennifer looked at me as if she were deeply disappointed. Then she looked out the window at the log shack and its lone guard. Then huge tears welled up in her eyes and rolled down her cheeks to splash onto her dress.

That did it. I couldn't stand to see her cry. "Jennifer . . . I'm sorry. Give me the bow. I'll do my best."

Jennifer hugged me then, and it made it seem worthwhile. But as she moved back to her father's room to get the weapon, I wondered if I was doing the right thing. I was risking my life to help a man who had hired riders to threaten the lives and welfare of my own friends and family, even of myself. Was I right? I didn't know. All I knew was that I wouldn't betray Jennifer. I would do for her whatever she wanted, even if I died in doing it. I hadn't even fully realized until then just how much I cared for her.

When she returned and put the bow in my hand I was ashamed of how badly I was shaking. I took an arrow with numb fingers and notched it on the bowstring. Jennifer watched me, and I know she could tell I was scared. And though she appeared calm, in her eyes I could see that she was as frightened as I was.

"Where should I shoot from?" I asked in a cracking voice. "The window?"

Jennifer shook her head. "I don't know . . . maybe the door would be better. Whatever you think." I clutched the bow tightly, feeling as if the whole thing was some sort of horrible dream. "I think I'll shoot from the door. I'll have more room."

I moved over to the front door and carefully opened the latch with a shaking hand. Slowly I opened it, trying to make sure that no one from the outside noticed. I opened it only as far as was necessary to give me a clear shot, then slowly I raised the bow. The man in front of the shack was rolling a cigarette. If I hit him he would never know what had happened. My arms wouldn't stop trembling.

Carefully I took aim and pulled back the string. I

was shaking so that I didn't think I could possibly hit the man.

"Jim . . ." Jennifer's voice was weak and shaking. "I can't ask you to do this . . . I'm sorry . . ."

"No," I said. "I'll do it."

And then I shot the arrow. I didn't realize until it was all over that my eyes had been shut when I released the string. As soon as I had fired my body went numb, and the bow dropped from my hands to clatter to my feet. Then I forced myself to look at what I had done.

The man was leaning forward, clutching at the arrow. It was stuck square through the middle of his chest. Even from across the distance I could tell he was dead. If I hadn't felt so numb I think I would have been sick.

Jennifer whispered in a voice with no expression. "You got him, Jim. You got him on the first shot."

Suddenly I knew I had to move. I had to run, to leave behind this building. Quickly I looked around. There was no sign of life anywhere on the ranch grounds. I grabbed up my Winchester in one hand and grasped Jennifer's arm with the other. "C'mon. Let's go."

We darted out of the house, moving at a dead run across the open land until we reached the log house. I tried not to look at the dead man, but somehow I couldn't take my eyes from him. He looked almost as if he were asleep, or maybe looking for something on the ground. I realized that he looked rather suspicious, so with great reluctance I pushed him back up to an upright position. His face was pale and his eyes were open and glazed. I looked away.

Jennifer was jerking on the padlock, pounding on the door. "Father . . . can you hear me? We're here to get you out!" Then I saw a figure walk around an outbuilding on down the slope, and by instinct I grabbed Jennifer and pulled her around to the side of the building and out of sight.

I could hear movement inside the shack, but there was no good chance to try to talk to Guthrie with the other man approaching. I wondered if he would notice how strangely quiet was the guard at the front door. I felt a chill of horror when the thought came that perhaps he was coming to relieve the man at watch. What would happen then?

But to my relief the man walked on past the shed, never even glancing toward us, and then he was gone. Jennifer and I scurried quickly around to the back of the shack, where we crouched low. I noticed then the small window just above us in the wall. Jennifer stood to a half-crouched position and looked inside.

"Father?"

Guthrie's voice sounded weak as he responded. "Jennifer . . . you'll get yourself killed!" It was quite apparent from the straining of his voice that he was in pain. I remembered then the stories I had heard from Sam about Madison's skill at torture, and I pitied Luther Guthrie for what he must have suffered.

"Father, we're going to get you out," she whispered. "I don't know how, but we're going to get you out."

"Jennifer, please be careful," he moaned. "Please . . . if they find you out here they'll kill you. I'm hurt bad . . . they made me sign over the ranch to them. There was nothing I could do . . ."

"I know, Father, I know," she said. "Can you push on the door? Maybe we can force the hinges apart."

My hand grabbed at Jennifer's arm. My voice failed me, and I pointed to the road that led down toward the main house.

On that road were riders, how many I could not tell. They were armed, and at their lead was a man who could be no other than Luke McDonald. And beside him was Sam.

This was it. The attack had begun, and we were caught right in the middle of it.

CHAPTER XI

∂

There was nothing to do but move and move quickly. I had resigned myself to whatever fate would befall me, and I was prepared to risk my very life to keep my word to Jennifer to save her father. Now, with the enraged ranchers on the verge of attack and the ranch just seconds away from becoming a battleground, the only thing I could do was expose myself, to throw secrecy to the wind and blast Guthrie out of that shack. Pushing Jennifer down to protect her from the gunfire I expected momentarily, I dashed around the front of the little building. I knew that I was seen by the ranchers, maybe the men in the bunkhouse too, but that didn't matter. I had but a few seconds to get Guthrie out, and there was only one way to do that. I threw the lever on my Winchester and sent a slug straight into the lock, blasting it open. I grabbed at the latch and threw open the heavy door. Luther Guthrie stared back at me, pale and scared.

I didn't waste time with explanations. I moved in just long enough to grab his arm and drag him back toward the door. I expected shooting to begin at any minute. When I pulled on Guthrie's arm, he winced as if in pain, and held back.

"You . . . what are you doing here? What are you trying to do?"

"I'm trying to get you out of here alive, along with your daughter, before this ranch turns into a bloodbath. Now shut up and run!"

But even as I pulled him out into the sunlight I knew that running was something that Luther Guthrie would not be able to do. I noticed a spot of blood on his thigh, and every time he put his weight on the injured leg he grimaced in pain. I didn't have to ask what—or who—had caused the wound. I knew it had been part of Josiah Madison's work on the man, a bit of his persuasive technique aimed at getting Guthrie to sign over his ranch.

"Why should I go with you . . . why should I trust you . . ."

A shot sounded and a bullet smacked into the wall just beside us, and Guthrie's complaints were cut short. The shot had come from the bunkhouse. It would be only moments before the battle was on.

"Move, Guthrie!" I commanded. "Your daughter is waiting, and I intend to get her away from here no matter what happens to you. Now get moving! Around the back of the building, then up the slope."

He obeyed then, moving as best he could on his injured leg. We rounded the back of the building as bullets began to smack close around us. Jennifer threw her arms around her father and kissed him. She looked with deep concern at the crimson spot on his thigh. "Father, did that man do this to you?"

"Yes . . . this and more. But I wouldn't sign the ranch over to him, Jennifer, not until he threatened you. Then I had no choice."

"Now isn't the time," I said. "Get up the slope! You run beside us, and keep yourself so that your father and I are between you and the bunkhouse. It's a long run up that slope, and they'll be shooting. I'll try to help you along, Guthrie."

Guthrie didn't ask why I was here at the ranch just as a battle was breaking out. He didn't ask how I had managed to get his daughter safely out of the house. He simply gritted his teeth, braced his hand against his wounded leg, and began to limp up the slope as fast as he could.

I tried to help him along, but his bad leg made progress slow. I glanced over my shoulder. The army of gunmen was riding down toward the ranch now, and from the bunkhouse men were running, some moving toward the main house, others positioning themselves behind whatever cover was available. It was going to be a massacre, I could tell. Right now the mounted men had the advantage, but they were not for the most part trained gunmen and fighters, as were the men riding with Madison. How the fight would wind up I could not guess.

It was to our advantage that the ranchers had picked this moment to attack, for the men holed up in the ranch buildings were so preoccupied with facing the threat they posed to take much notice of the three figures scurrying up the slope. But not entirely preoccupied, for bullets smacked around our feet and whizzed through the air above our heads. Although I couldn't be sure, I didn't think any of the shots were coming from the direction of Sam's group. Maybe Sam had been able to stop them from firing at us. But there was no way to be sure that even my own brother knew I was one of the three runners, for he did not know that I had come here, and he certainly would not expect me to be helping out Luther Guthrie.

The top of the slope seemed distant, and Guthrie was getting slower with each step. I could tell that his leg was paining him terribly. I suspected that Madison had put a bullet in this thigh to help motivate him to sign over the ranch. Or he might have worked on him with a knife. Whatever brutal method he had used, it had certainly done plenty of damage to the rancher's leg. And now, with Guthrie's injury slowing all of us down, I began to doubt that we would make it to safety before one or all of us was cut down by gunfire.

Jennifer had just opened her mouth to say something to her father when the bullet struck him. It struck him hard, square in the back, and passed all the way through his body. I saw him go suddenly weak, a shudder ripping through him, and his lips worked together as if he were trying to say something but couldn't get it out. We reached the top of the slope and found safety behind a large boulder seconds before he died.

I was amazed at the cold, objective way in which I watched Luther Guthrie die. In my own arms he died. And I, who had seen so little violence and had never even thought of killing a man until this day, could do nothing but stare at his limp form with a sort of numbness, a coldness within me. I looked first at his face, then at the ugly wound the bullet had made in his chest where it had come out of him, then at Jennifer. I expected tears, but in her eyes there was nothing but shock. I think the same coldness within me was also in her. We looked at each other for a long time and did not speak. The noise of gunfire from below came loud to our ears.

Gently I laid down the head of the man who we had tried so hard to save. His eyes were half open, and his lips were dry and coated with dust. It was strange to see him lying there, a moment ago alive, now as dead as the rock behind which we hid. I moved up on the boulder to look at the battle below, and Jennifer moved over to where I had been and took up the head of her father and laid it in her lap as if he were a sleeping baby. Still there were no words, no tears, only coldness. She stroked his hair gently, looking with no expression down into his face. Only then did the dull, throbbing ache begin in my heart. It was an ache of pity for the girl I loved, who had now lost the man who had raised her from the day she was born.

Below I could see the horsemen, most still unhurt, moving down hard on the main ranch house, the bunkhouse, the corral. Bursts of smoke would explode from the rifles of the fighters, then the sound would reach up to us a split second later. I saw a horseman—I think I even recognized him from some earlier time— bearing down on one of the men firing from the corral, and then he killed him. Even across the long distance between us I could see that the rancher's bullet struck the man in the head. I'm sure that he was dead even before the sound of the shot reached me.

I tried to pick out Sam's form among the riding gunmen, but such was the dust and confusion that I could not. Yet I knew he was down there somewhere. There were a few bodies scattered about here and there; some moved, others lay frighteningly still. Was Sam's body among them? I looked closely, trying to re- member what he had been wearing today. I couldn't recollect, and I began to worry.

The attackers were circling like Indians, their swiftly-moving horses making them difficult targets. Yet the same movement was making it difficult for them to get off any clear shots at the hidden gunmen holed up all over the ranch, and once those gunmen fired off their weapons they were in a position to get quickly under cover until they were ready to fire their next shot. The mounted fighters had no such advan- tage, and as the battle continued I could see that it was hurting them. All too often I saw bodies falling from the horses, and each time it happened I felt a jolt of pain deep inside. Was Sam to be the next to fall? I had picked out a man who I thought was him . . . yes! That was Sam! Still alive, still riding, still shooting. Thank God.

I followed his movements closely after I had lo- cated him, every breath a prayer for his safety. More and more riders were dropping from their horses, some to rise up clutching arms or legs to run to safety, others to land motionless in a cloud of dust. And always the continual crackle of gunfire, almost like the snapping of wood when a mighty oak strains to fall. How many men would die before this battle was finished? Was this the result that Sam and Luke McDonald wanted? Those men that lay still on the dirt down below would string no more barbed wire fences, herd no more cattle, put no more food on their families' tables. It was senseless. Senseless.

I looked back down at Jennifer again. Still she cradled her father's head in her arms, but she was looking at me. I could see that she had broken through her state of emotionless shock, for there were tears on her cheeks, flowing down profusely.

"I'm sorry, Jennifer," I said. "I'm so very sorry."

Very, very sadly she smiled. "We tried, Jim. We did our best. That was all we could do." Then she bowed her head and began to cry hard, her sobs shaking her and her tears falling on her father's cold face.

"Jim!" I recognized McCuen's voice. I had almost forgotten that he had agreed to meet me. I turned. He was approaching on horseback, and beside him was Jedediah Bacon and another man I didn't recognize. They rode up, and when he saw the dead body of Luther Guthrie, McCuen went pale.

"How, Jim? What happened?"

Briefly I told the story, and it seemed to hurt him to hear it. Jed Bacon's reaction was the same, and the unidentified man simply sat expressionless in his saddle. He had the look of a cowboy, and I figured him to be one of Bacon's employees.

"We're too late, I see," said Bacon. "Maybe it's just as well. There's not one blasted thing we could have done to stop this. It was inevitable."

"How are things going down there?" asked McCuen. I told him how things stood as far as I could see them, and then the three men crawled up beside me on the rock to watch for themselves. Jennifer gently lay down her father's head on a mound of moss and moved up beside me on my left. Her tears were gone, as if she had cried herself empty. I wished I could put my arms around her.

"My God, my God!" exclaimed Bacon, shaking his head. "It's all so foolish, all this fighting. The work of fools."

"That's the way it always winds up, Jed," said McCuen. "Men try to reason, to talk things out, and then impatience sets in and someone tries to settle things with a gun. And sometimes it works. But most of the time it just ends up that innocent folks die, and the problem is solved not because there's some sort of answer but because there's no one left alive to argue anymore. I've seen it a hundred times."

"This is one battle that won't solve any problems," said Bacon. "Settlers will keep on coming, barbed wire will keep on going up, and the old ways will keep on changing. That's for certain, and all the fence-cutting riders in the world won't be able to change it. If only people would learn."

I looked across at Jennifer. Her eyes were focused on the battle below, and they were very sad. I knew that McCuen and Bacon were probably both wondering what Luther Guthrie's daughter was doing up here with me. I think McCuen suspected that there was something beyond the ordinary in the way I felt about Jennifer. My strong insistence on coming to the ranch earlier today, along with her presence here with me now, were both evidence of something special in the way I thought of her. If there was any question still in his mind it was answered immediately, for I reached over and took Jennifer's hand in mine and held her delicate fingers in my own callused ones. McCuen looked silently at us for a moment, then looked back toward the battle again.

More bodies were strewn about, most of them those of dead ranchers. There would be much mourning tonight, for many men were dead and more would follow soon, I was certain. I looked furtively about for Sam.

There he was . . . on the ground. A tremendous nausea welled up within me. Sam was dead . . . no . . . he moved! He had been wounded, apparently, but he was still alive. How long he would remain that way would be hard to guess. I prayed for him.

It was getting toward dusk when at last the battle ended. It did not end at once. It more or less just faded out, growing steadily weaker and more sporadic, until at last it was over. The surviving ranchers rode off over the slope and left bodies littered behind them, Sam's among them. Then for a time there was no movement but the occasional stirrings of the men that lay wounded all around the ranch buildings. Then men moved out from the house, the bunkhouse, the out buildings, and picked up the wounded. Those that apparently were near death they shot, and it hurt me each time they pulled the triggers of their forty-fours. The ones not so bad off, Sam included, they carried back into the house. Hostages in case of another attack, I assumed.

"It's over," said Bacon. "There won't be another attack. I wonder how many men are dead."

"Too many, Jed. Way too many," said McCuen.

Then came a time of talk. I met the man that had rode in with Bacon. As I had guessed, he was one of Bacon's employees, a man named Loftis. I told of how Jennifer and I had tried to rescue Guthrie, of how he had been tortured into signing over the ranch, and how he had taken a fatal bullet within a few feet of safety.

"I'm very sorry for you, Miss Guthrie," said McCuen. "But you need not worry about the ranch going to Madison. That deed would never stand up once it was known that the signing was forced. And besides, no one like Madison would ever be able to run an operation like that openly. The law would grab him once his identity was known."

Jennifer looked confused. "What is all this 'Madison' talk? That's not what my father called the leader of those men . . . is that who you're talking about?"

I realized that Jennifer had not been told of the true identity of the one-eyed leader of the night riders. I filled her in, and she looked dazed. "Josiah Madison . . . I've heard of him. I can't believe a man like that would be tied in with my father. Father must not have known who he was."

"I'm sure he didn't, Jennifer," I said. "But no matter about that. That most definitely is Josiah Madison down there in that house, and now he has my brother again. If he recognizes him from the prison camp and knows that Sam can identify him, then that will be it for Sam." I thought of Becky.

"Let's get Miss Guthrie on back to town," said McCuen. "Jed, maybe Mr. Loftis can take her on back. And it would be a good idea if we got Mr. Guthrie's body on back, too. I know it will be unpleasant for you, Miss Guthrie, but . . ."

"Don't worry. I'm a grown lady. I can take it." Jennifer stood tall as she spoke, and I was proud of her.

I hugged her close before she mounted on McCuen's horse and rode off with Loftis. Luther Guthrie's body was laid across the back of Loftis' horse, the arms swinging with each step the animal took. There was no dignity in it at all, and Jennifer gained my sincere admiration for the way she rode proudly along in spite of the pain that must have been in her heart.

Then I was alone with McCuen and Bacon. "What should we do?" I asked. I could think of nothing but Sam. What might he be suffering right now at the hands of Josiah Madison?

Try as we would, we could think of no plan. And so we waited, for what we did not know, but still we waited. And then, when the moon was sailing high in a clear sky, the door of the Guthrie house opened, and the riders emerged. Quickly they saddled horses, and then they were gone, heading north. A deep depression settled over me. What had they done to Sam?

We moved down the slope at a run. The ranch seemed deserted. I passed over the bodies of horsemen that had fallen. One of them was Luke McDonald. I leaped over his body without even giving it more than a glance.

"Hartford . . . Jim . . . wait a minute," McCuen called out behind me. "Maybe I should go first. Maybe you should hold on before you go in . . . let me go first."

"He's right, Hartford," called Bacon.

I didn't listen. I had to know, and know right now, what had happened to Sam. I reached the door and burst in.

The place was a shambles. Furniture was knocked about, the walls were pockmarked with bullet holes. And there were bodies on the floor. I saw a man lying face down, and with a moment of hesitation I rolled him over on his back. I didn't recognize him. He was dead.

And then I saw Sam. He was crumpled in a corner, still and unbreathing. I felt my eyes begin to flood with tears. Slowly I moved over to him, conscious of Bacon and McCuen watching me silently. With trembling hands I rolled his body over so I could see his face.

It was Sam alright. And his throat was cut. I looked at him for a long time, then I stood and walked past McCuen and Bacon on out the door. I leaned up against the wall, weak and shaken, and felt I could die myself.

CHAPTER XII

❧

I was weary when we carried Sam's body, along with the other victims of the murdering night riders, back to Miles City. My body ached for sleep, yet my mind was darting wildly from one thought to another, alert and quick. I was horrified, almost devastated, by what had just happened, but what would come next was worse—the task of having to tell Becky of Sam's death. Becky, the quiet, gentle, loving wife that had stood by Sam through the hardest times—how would she be able to go on without him, especially with her child on the way?

We carried the bodies on crude moving conveyances made of two limbs, one on each side of our horses, with rope forming a crudely-woven support on which we strapped the bodies. The ends of the limbs dragged the ground, leaving little ruts in the dirt where the weight of the bodies pushed the wood into the earth. Bacon had learned how to construct the conveyances from an Indian friend, he said.

I had recovered my horse from the hills behind the

Guthrie ranch, and I rode numbly, dreading to reach Miles City, and then later to face Becky with the dreadful news. Part of me was restless, longing to go after Madison and his band of murderers, but yet I knew that right now I could not. That would come later, after preparations had been made.

Whether or not hatred is ever justified I do not know, but I learned at that moment what it was to truly hate a human being. I longed to see Madison dead, and to make sure that with his final breath he knew he was dying. Sam had lived with that kind of hate all of his life, for he knew Josiah Madison for what he was. And then he had died by his hand, and that was the cruelest thing about it. My desire for vengeance was powerful; I wanted to destroy Madison not only for what he had done to me, but also for the sake of Becky, and most of all for Sam. Whether my feelings were good or bad I cannot say; at that moment it didn't seem to matter. My rationality was gone, and I wanted only revenge.

We said little to each other as we rode. The hour was late when at last we reached Miles City; it would not be long 'til dawn. I had not asked McCuen or Bacon what they planned to do about pursuing Madison. It didn't really matter—I would go alone if it came to it, for such was my bitterness that I hardly cared what happened to me.

The undertaker was waiting for us when we rode down the main street of the town. He had heard of the battle, for many of the wounded had already been brought into town for treatment from the local doctor. He methodically took the bodies off the conveyances behind our horses and moved them inside. It hurt me when he took Sam's limp form away.

McCuen approached me as I removed the crude litter from the back of my horse. "What now, Jim?" he asked. He sounded weary.

"Come first light I'm going after them, McCuen," I said. "I have to do it." I halfway expected him to argue with me about it, but instead he simply nodded his head.

"I understand. May I go with you? And maybe Jed too, if he wants?"

I looked at him, rather surprised. From the look in his eye I could tell that he understood that this was my fight, my mission, and he seemed in no way inclined to look at it as anything else. Sadly I smiled at him. "Sure. I'll be needing some help, I would guess."

"Alright, then. I'll talk to Jed. I'm sure he will want to come along." He paused. "Jim, do you think we should bring the military into this? They would sure be interested in getting their hands on Josiah Madison."

Firmly I shook my head. "That would take too long," I said. "Madison already has a good jump on us, and by the time the army got into this he would be hidden away somewhere where they could never find him. Besides, this isn't an army affair to me now. It's personal. It's for me and Becky and Jennifer and all the others who have lost friends and family tonight. I've got no time for the military in this." I sounded rather rude, I fear, for I spoke with such force that it no doubt sounded as if I were angry at my friend. But he paid no heed, for he understood that my anger was not truly directed at him.

"You need sleep," he said. "I'm staying at the hotel. There's room for two if you would like to stay here for the rest of the night."

"I can't, McCuen. I've got to tell Becky what happened." I had tried not to think about it too much, for giving her the news was going to be the hardest thing I had ever done. It scared me.

McCuen shook his head. "If you want to get on Madison's trail at first light, then you'd best get some rest. You know that by now those survivors are back in their homes and Becky surely knows already that Sam was taken prisoner. I'll see to it that she hears the rest from someone who will break it to her in the right way . . . a preacher, maybe. But right now you're beat, and I think you better head for that hotel before you drop. You've got a big job waiting for you tomorrow."

Suddenly, I realized how very tired I really was. I had to sleep, or surely I would "drop," just as he had said. It was of infinite importance that I be able to trail Madison quickly and with accuracy, and Becky would surely rather have me on his trail than staying around just to spare her a little pain. I agreed to McCuen's proposition, and he looked pleased.

"Make sure Becky knows that I'm going to get Madison," I said. "Tell her that he won't go unpunished for what he's done."

"I will, Jim. Now go on to the hotel . . . I'll be there a bit later. You go ahead and take the bed; there's a good couch that I can sleep on. We only have a little while 'til first light as it is, so you'd best hurry."

He handed me the key to his room, and I headed for the hotel. I was so bone-tired that I never could remember crawling into the bed and dropping into a deep sleep. The next thing I knew it was morning, and I still was tired.

I raised up in the bed. McCuen stirred over on the couch but did not wake. I rose and walked to the window and looked out onto the street.

What kind of day would this be? Would I be lucky enough to find Madison, or would he have vanished into the wilderness as he had done so many times in the past? So far no one had been able to catch him, though many had tried. It seemed foolhardy to think that a simple Tennessee farmer could do what trained government agents had failed to do for many years.

But I was determined to try. Maybe those government agents did not have the motivation I did. Surely they had never lost a brother like I had, and seen a lifetime of dreams and hard work cut short by the cruel knife of a murderer. That was why I would succeed where they had failed—I had a powerful motivation, and I would not rest until I had settled with Madison.

The street was quiet; there was no movement to be seen but that of a lone dog that wandered down the boardwalk across the road. It was still early, but even though I was still very tired I was anxious to get underway. Madison would be many miles ahead already, and in the broad grasslands he would be difficult to trail.

I heard McCuen stir awake behind me. I turned to see him yawn and stretch. "Good lands, is it morning already?" he murmured. "It seems I just laid down. Morning, Jim."

"Good morning. Sleep good?"

"Fine, but there wasn't enough of it." He rubbed his eyes and looked at me seriously. "I rousted out a preacher after you came up here last night, and he agreed to tell Becky. I don't know how she took it, but I'm sure she knows by now."

I felt rather guilty. Maybe I should have been the one to tell her, instead of some preacher she didn't know. Nevertheless it seemed more important for me to be on Madison's trail than anything else. But still I couldn't shake the vague feeling of guilt. Had I done the right thing?

I glanced out at the street again. A wagon approached. I looked closely ... it was Becky. I felt a combination of relief and dread. I knew she had come to talk to me. Quickly I threw on my clothes and headed out of the room, telling McCuen of Becky's approach. He looked rather surprised.

I met Becky in the street. From the weary look on her face I could tell she had slept little, if at all. I didn't know what to say to her. Her eyes were red, and I could tell she had been crying. I couldn't blame her.

"I heard about your plan, Jim," she said. "The preacher told me you were going after Madison."

"That's right. It's what Sam would have done."

"Yes, it is. And it's for that same reason that Sam is dead today. He reacted the wrong way, and it killed him. He's gone now ... it's hard for me to believe, but it's true. Now you're going to be killed yourself if you go after Madison. I loved Sam with all my heart—you know that—and I would not say anything to slight his memory, but he was foolish to go up against Madison. He never had a decent chance, and he accomplished very little. Madison is alive, and Sam is dead. As far as I'm concerned, that means things are worse than before."

"But it was something Sam had to do, Becky," I responded. "I didn't understand that before, but I do now. A man can't stand aside while murderers like Madison run loose. It's his responsibility to see that justice is done to them. Madison has been murdering all his life. Who can say how many men he killed in that prison camp long before he ever set foot in this territory? We can't let him live any longer, especially after what he did to Sam. It's something I owe to my brother, Becky."

"And I think I owe it to my husband to make sure his brother doesn't get himself killed for nothing," Becky returned. "I don't want you to go, Jim."

I looked at her, not sure how to respond. "I'm sorry," I said at length. "I don't think I have any choice."

Her sad expression became a bit sadder, and she spoke softly. "Alright, then. I'll be going now." She turned away and climbed back into the wagon. I wanted to say something to her, but the words choked in my throat. I pitied her beyond all telling, and I knew there was nothing I could say that would lighten the burden she now bore.

I watched her drive away, then I turned again into the hotel. I found McCuen dressed and waiting for me. He still looked very tired, but also a bit more alert than before.

"Is everything alright?" he asked.

"As well as could be expected, I guess. Becky's a strong woman. Let's get some breakfast. Is Bacon coming?"

"Yes. I think he wants Madison almost as badly as

you. He blames him not only for all the deaths yesterday but also for the bad feeling between the various cattlemen. I suspect that he has a little personal stake in all this."

We had breakfast at the cafe as soon as the doors opened. My food seemed tasteless, and I ate it without enjoyment. All I could think of was the task that lay before me. When I had come to the Montana Territory I had anticipated nothing like this.

Bacon met us just outside of town a couple of hours later, after we had stocked up on supplies to last us for several days out on the open range. The three of us said little as we rode back toward the Guthrie ranch. I realized that Sam would be buried today, and I would not be there to see it. No matter. What I had to do was far more important.

The morning had a misty feel to it, a kind of freshness that at a happier time I would have found invigorating. My horse stepped along with great liveliness, obviously feeling rested and strong. As the morning passed we made good time, and reached the ranch more quickly than I had expected.

From looking over the place it seemed hard to imagine that only yesterday it had been a bloody battleground. The place looked serene and peaceful, and ruggedly beautiful. Horses still grazed nearby, and far away toward the east I could see the tiny forms of distant cattle grazing on the rich grasses.

We rode down toward the house, for what reason I am not sure, for we were looking for nothing in particular. We had seen the direction the riders had taken the night before, and I certainly expected to find no one about the place now. We rode down to the front door and dismounted.

The door was still standing open as it had been when we left it last night. The bodies were gone now, but there were tell-tale stains of blood about that made me feel weak. Try as I would I could not help staring at the spot where I had found Sam's body. I couldn't stand it. I turned and went outside again, McCuen following me.

"I'll kill him, McCuen. Kill him with my own hands if it comes to that. He tortured Sam for years in that prison camp, then he came back from the past to kill him. I won't let him live after doing that. I won't let him live." So violent were my emotions that my voice was choked. McCuen looked at me as if I frightened him a bit.

"Jim . . . it will be dangerous, and slow. And there's always the chance that Madison will get away where we'll never find him . . ."

"No! I'll tail him 'til his dying day or 'til he drops me," I said. "He'll not escape me, never." I think that at that moment I must have looked much as Sam did before the fateful battle. Certainly I was just as much the victim of violent hate and fear as he had been. I had lost my reason and was being driven only by the desire for vengeance.

Bacon walked up to us. "Well, we'll get nowhere just staying around here . . . whoa! What was that?"

I tensed at the tone of his voice. He was looking over toward the bunkhouse, his expression wary. I looked over and scanned the scene, but I saw nothing.

"What is it, Jed?" McCuen said, his hand creeping toward his sidearm. "Something over there?"

Bacon shook his head as if in indecision. "I'm not sure . . . I thought I saw a movement . . . hey, you over there! Freeze where you are or be shot!"

We had all seen him that time—a lanky man moving up on the other side of the building, peering around at us. I had seen something else, too: the flashing of sunlight on the barrel of a rifle. I mentioned it to McCuen.

There was no answer from the stranger for a moment, then a coarse voice called out: "Who are you? What are you doing here?"

"We might ask you the same thing, mister!" called out Bacon. "You'd best get rid of that rifle. There's three of us, and we might tend to shoot if we feel threatened. You understand me?"

Again there was a long pause, then a sudden clattering as the rifle was tossed out on the ground in our view. "The pistol, too!" called Bacon. A moment later it lay on the ground beside the rifle, and the lanky man approached with his hands high in the air. I had never seen him before.

"And who might you be?" asked Bacon, lowering his rifle after looking the fellow over. "Why are you around here today, especially after what happened yesterday?"

"The name's Bradley Sullivan," he said. "And I reckon I got a right to be here since this here ranch is where I work. I might wonder myself just who you are and why this place is deserted."

McCuen frowned, a bit confused. "You mean you weren't here yesterday? You don't know what happened?"

"Just got in this mornin'," he said. "I been on the trail for about a week, scoutin' out on the far ranges for Guthrie. Where is Guthrie, anyhow?" he asked, his eyes narrowing.

"He's dead," I said. "Shot by the riders he hired. This ranch is deeded over to the leader of those riders now—Josiah Madison."

He looked totally shocked. "Josiah Madi . . ." His voice failed him, trailing off to a whisper.

"This place was a battlefield yesterday," I continued. "There were a lot of men killed, and killed needlessly. Cattlemen, and your partners, too. Madison and his men rode out, and we're going after them. We aim to see him pay."

Sullivan shook his head. "Guthrie's dead—I can't believe it. It was a fool thing for him to hire those riders, and I told him so more than once. He wouldn't listen, though. Wouldn't listen."

Suddenly he looked up, a different look in his eye. "Men, I don't know who you are nor why you're interested in this, but if you're goin' after those riders I would sure like to go along. I'm good with a gun, and I'm one of the best trackers you ever seen. And I know folks all over this country that might have seen them scoundrels runnin'. What do you say? Am I with you?"

I didn't know how to respond to that. I cast a quick glance over at McCuen.

"I warned Guthrie about hiring them riders," Sullivan continued. "I knew it would come to something like this. I want to help out . . . please let me."

McCuen spoke up. "Alright, Sullivan, you're with us. It could get rough . . . I hope you know that."

Sullivan grinned, showing yellow teeth with plenty of wide gaps between them. "Rough is what I'm used to, mister. It's the way I like things."

I gave him back his gun, still a bit concerned about whether or not to trust him. He made no suspicious moves, though, and I relaxed a bit. Bacon mounted his horse, and we did the same. Sullivan moved over to the corral and chose a beautiful bay from the horses there.

"Always did take a shine to this animal," he said. "I guess now that Guthrie's dead he won't be needin' it none. C'mon, Sawbriar, let's get a saddle on you. You're mine now."

Sullivan was a strange character. He seemed to feel no real sadness about the slaughter that had taken place here, and he didn't seem at all concerned that many of his friends might have been among those who were killed. He grinned as if the danger involved was of no account. A very unique man, this Bradley Sullivan. I felt a vague dislike for him—maybe it was because of his beady black eyes or his unkempt clothes. Or maybe it was because of his general odor that hung like a black cloud all about him. For whatever reason, I knew he wasn't destined to become one of my close friends.

We moved off to the northeast, following the path the riders had taken the night before. Tracking was new to me, and I had no idea how we would find them. The land seemed so vast, so empty. They could lose themselves in so many places. The whole thing appeared hopeless.

But apparently Sullivan didn't share that feeling, for he moved out in the lead, keeping a close eye on the trail and leading us along with assurance. He seemed to have a keen eye for tracking, even better than Jed Bacon, for he hardly paused as he moved along, his eye picking up hints of the riders' path that I could not see. Even though I disliked him, I realized that it was fortunate that he was along.

We traveled for many hours, heading always north, until to the west hills broke through the flat grassland, rugged and tall. Bacon and Sullivan called a halt and peered at them.

"It looks like a likely spot, Sullivan," said Bacon. "They might hide in those hills a long time and not be found."

Sullivan shook his head. "They might be hidin' out there, but I know they ain't hidden entirely. I got a brother that tends sheep up in them hills. I ain't proud of it, but it's the truth. If they went into them hills he would know about it."

"How far is it to where he lives?" Bacon asked. Sullivan laughed.

"Well, sir, that depends on where he's livin' right now. He's got him a wagon that serves him for a house. He just rolls all over them hills and follers the sheep. I don't rightly know where he'd be at the moment."

McCuen rubbed his chin. "You think it would be worthwhile to find him, Sullivan? He might have seen them go by even if they didn't stop in the hills."

"I reckon you got a point," the cowpoke drawled. " 'Course, if them riders did hide up there, they might find us before we find him, if you get my drift."

I was getting his drift in more ways than one. I moved upwind from him and stopped beside McCuen.

"If they're hidden up there, then we'll have to go into the hills to get them anyway. It seems to me it's a risk we'll have to take."

The tall man looked thoughtful, then nodded. "I agree. What about you, Bacon?"

"I don't see we have much choice."

"In that case, men, let's go find my brother!" Sullivan's ever-present grin grew brighter, and he headed toward the hills at a gallop before the rest of us had even turned our horses. We took out after him, the hills growing larger as we approached.

I looked at them with apprehension. They appeared somehow threatening. I fancied we were being watched from their slopes even now.

But we had set our course and I intended to see it through. I pulled up beside McCuen as we slowed to a trot, and we rode silently together. The sun was moving toward the west. It would be dark when we reached the base of the hills.

CHAPTER XIII

McCuen was craving a cigar when we made camp at the base of the hills, but the fear that Madison's riders might be within eyeshot of us made it impossible for him to smoke. For a long while he sat grumbling in the darkness until at last the desire became overwhelming, and he lit up a long cigar, keeping the glowing ember at the end hidden inside his hat. Every time he lifted up the cigar to take a puff the hat's brim hid his face while billows of smoke poured out around the sweatband. I sat and laughed at him and Sullivan shook his head while digging into his pocket for a tobacco twist.

"You can have your cigars, fellers—I say I'll take a chew over a smoke anytime." He bit off a huge chunk and settled it into his jaw, then grinned like a gap-toothed tomcat on a nightly prowl. So that was why his teeth were so yellow.

Bacon was sitting silent, staring at the hills in the dim moonlight. "Do you think he's up there?" I asked.

The rancher shook his head slowly. "Don't know,

Hartford. It seems likely to me. We'll find out for sure tomorrow." Something in the way he said those words sent a chill down my spine.

McCuen extinguished his cigar and moved over beside us. I handed him a piece of jerky from my saddlebag and he began to eat.

"McCuen, there's a couple of things I haven't been able to figure out about this deal," I said. "Why would Josiah Madison do something like trying to take over ownership of Guthrie's ranch? It strikes me as ridiculous. It's like you told Jennifer . . . there's no way he could openly go into a legitimate business for fear of capture. I can't see why he wanted that ranch."

"I expect he didn't want it, Jim. Based on what I've heard about him over the years, I think the man is sick—mentally sick. Apparently he is a sadist of the worst sort, but one who seeks for some sort of pretext to justify his use of torture. Maybe it's guilt, I don't know. But during the war he justified his actions by virtue of the fact that his victims were war prisoners. I would guess that in the case of Guthrie he was torturing the man for no other reason than to satisfy his sadistic tendencies. The man probably had no desire for Guthrie's ranch—that was just an excuse, a justification for cruelty. Of course, I'm no expert on the human mind, but that's the way things appear to me."

It made sense. Madison had no doubt been infuriated by the death of the rider that Sam shot outside the cabin. Probably he took his fury out on Guthrie. It could have been Jennifer . . . thank God he had left her alone.

"Why did he kill Sam like he did, I wonder? He had taken him prisoner, I thought, to use as a hostage along with the others. But then he murdered them . . . they were no good to him dead, but he murdered them anyway. I can't really understand that."

But as soon as I had spoken I did understand. Madison must have recognized Sam from the prison camp. Even if he hadn't, he surely must have known him as the man who shot one of his underlings the night before. Sam had paid for that shooting with his life. I felt my stomach knotting within me. Madison was an animal, one that needed to be exterminated like a mad dog. I hated him, hated him with all that was in me. I looked up toward the hills, barren and dark in the moonlight. If he was up there we would find him. And though I dreaded the thought of the violence that would come, still I craved it back in some deeper portion of my mind.

It was insane, this mission of ours. Four men, none of us trained fighters, going up against a band of killers that outnumbered us greatly and that would as quickly kill us as look at us. Totally insane. But still we were doing it, and as I pondered that fact, I was filled with a sense of admiration for my two friends. Bacon and McCuen might well be killed on this mission, yet they were proceeding fearlessly by my side, and apparently not giving it a second thought. Even Sullivan earned some of my grudging admiration, for he had almost no reason to be here. Yet I couldn't help but feel a little cold toward the man, for my instinct told me that this death mission was nothing but a sport to him. I think he would just as quickly have teamed up with Madison's riders if the mood struck him. But he had been helpful so far, and for that I was indebted to him.

Sullivan had been sitting quietly for some time now, but suddenly he began to talk in a steady flow of rambling oration, as if he had decided at that moment to hook up his mouth to his brain and make his thoughts audible. And once he started he would not stop.

"No sir, I ain't got no use for the life of a sheep herder. I ain't a bit proud of havin' a brother that tends woolies, but let me tell you a little secret, boys . . . there was a time when I done the same thing myself. Yes sir . . . herded them devils myself." A huge wad of amber hit the ground with a splat to punctuate the remark.

"Couldn't take it for long, though, boys. Ain't nothin' but loneliness when you herd woolies. For days and days and days you just stand there and look over them fuzzy round backs and wish you wuz somewheres else, anywheres else. I did a lot of drinkin' in them days. 'Course, my brother was there with me, but that weren't no real help, since he never said nothin' but just stood off on the hill with that ugly dog of his and looked up at the sky and thought up poems. Yes sir, that's right . . . poems. He would think about 'em all day and write 'em down at night. I never read none of 'em—can't read, anyway—but he sure had a collection of 'em before I had my fill of herdin' woolies and took off on my own. And he would read all the time. Every time we would get into a town he wouldn't go off and get drunk like any sensible feller—he would head off and blow most of his cash on more books. I'd say that by now he has a durned wagonload of 'em. Reads 'em all the time and spouts pretty words to the sky. He's crazier than that Madison feller, boys, a lot crazier. Calls his dog a 'bosom companion' and a hoss a 'noble steed.' What in the livin' daylights that means I ain't got no idea. Like I say, though, he's crazy, so I guess it's to be expected . . ."

Forever the oration continued, boring and dreary, spoken in an irritating monotone and slurred voice. Sullivan looked at no one as he spoke, as if the words were as much for his own benefit as ours. After a time I rose and rolled out my bedroll and drifted off to sleep with Sullivan's voice droning in my ears. I awoke sometime later; I think I might have slept for close to an hour.

". . . and stupid, let me tell you they're stupid. They'd follow the leader of the flock right over the edge of a bluff if he went first. I ain't lyin'—I've seen it happen, They're skittish as can be, and sometimes it's all you can do to get them to head over the slope of a hill if'n they can't see what's across on the other side. Why, once it took me a good two hours just to get the flock to move on through a ..."

I groaned and rolled over, trying to cut out the sound of the cowboy's voice. That night I dreamed of sheep.

The next morning's breakfast was more jerky and a little water from our canteens. The sun lit the hills before us, making them sparkle as the dew reflected the light like a million diamonds scattered on the ground. My legs were stiff, and I walked around as I ate in an attempt to loosen them and ease the ache in my knees. Though the sunlight was warm I felt chilled clean through, and my clothes were damp.

In a short time we were riding into the hills. I was rather surprised to find myself unafraid, or so I thought, but when I noticed my hands trembling before me I realized that my nerves were on edge. I looked about me as I rode, fearing what I might see.

We encountered a flock of sheep after only a short ride, and Sullivan moved out into the lead, trying to see if his brother was anywhere near. I looked over to the north, and there he was, a lonely figure against the sky, a rifle in his hand and a dog beside him. The keen loneliness of such an existence became immediately clear to me, and I marveled that anyone could live like this, away from any human contact for months on end, with oftentimes even the isolated meetings that did take place short in duration and business-like in nature. Sullivan's tirade of the night before came back to me, and I suspected that while his brother might not be crazy, as he claimed, there were surely many other sheep herders that were. I was later to learn that my suspicions were true; the isolated life of the west had driven not only sheep herders but also ranchers and homesteaders literally out of their minds after a time. Often many people lived their whole lives with hardly any other companions but wind, toil, and rain. Life on the plains had a rough edge to it that often could cut right into a man or woman's mind and literally destroy them bit by bit, almost like an endless stream of water eroding a rock.

I pointed out the figure on the hillside to my partners. Sullivan squinted at the man, who was now coming down the slope with his dog running before him, and slowly he shook his head.

"It ain't my brother. I don't know this feller."

McCuen shrugged. "No matter. If he's friendly he might help us out anyway. If Madison came through here he's bound to have seen him."

The figure was close enough for me to see him well now. He was a red-bearded fellow with a wide-brimmed hat and clothes that apparently had not been washed in close to a year. His skin was ruddy and sunburned so deeply that I suspected that a year in a dark cave would not be sufficient to fade it out. He stopped well away from us and looked at us with no expression, though something like suspicion was visible in his eyes.

"Who are you?" he called at length.

"We came from Miles City," called Bacon. "We're looking for some folks you might have seen—a whole band of riders that might have come through here yesterday morning or thereabouts. The leader is a one-eyed fellow. You seen them?"

Obviously this fellow wasn't about to give out any information without first knowing the reason it was desired. He asked us our business. Sullivan answered him.

"I got a brother—Elijah Sullivan—tendin' sheep up here somewheres. You know him?" He said nothing of why we were looking for the band of riders, but apparently his mention of his brother distracted the wary sheep herder from his question. He moved a little closer to look at Sullivan, apparently trying to see if he bore any resemblance to the Elijah he had mentioned.

After a pause the sheep herder spoke. "I reckon you are 'Lij's brother . . . I can see it in your face. You'd be Bradley, I reckon."

He turned and waved toward the northwest. "Your brother's tendin' his sheep over yonder, not too far," he said. "There was a group of riders that come through here yesterday, headin' in that direction. And last night I heard what sounded like shootin' comin' from that way. Don't know if it had anything to do with 'Lij or them men, but I reckon they might have had some sort of ruckus." He dropped into silence then, and we thanked him for the information.

We rode off without hesitation. I pulled up beside McCuen.

"So he is here, after all." My voice sounded more choked than I would have liked. McCuen nodded.

"I guess so. And if I get my guess right, then we won't find Sullivan's brother alive."

Sullivan was riding in the lead, and though I could not see his face I sensed that he was concerned about what we had just been told. If Elijah Sullivan had in fact had a "ruckus" with Madison, then it was a sure bet that he had come out with the worst end of the deal.

We crossed two more hills before we at last came upon Elijah Sullivan's flock. It was smaller than the last one we had seen, and on the other side of the sea of wool that shifted and fluctuated as the sheep nipped at the grass was a wagon, the home of Bradley Sullivan's brother. There was no sign of any human presence in the little valley.

We paused at the crest of the hill and looked down into the valley. I glanced over at Sullivan. His brow was creased and in his eyes worry was reflected. I knew that he expected the worst, and in my heart I shared the feeling.

"Sullivan, what do you make of it?" Bacon asked. "Could he have left the flock alone for some reason?"

Sullivan shook his head. "No . . . he never has done nothin' like that before, and I don't reckon he would now. He should be here somewhere."

"Are you sure this is his flock?"

"Yeah ... that's his wagon over yonder. This is the right flock."

I felt a strange caution creeping through my mind, and a sudden impulse to turn back gripped me. Yet I was ashamed to mention it to my companions for fear they would think me a coward. So I sat still in the saddle and scanned the horizon, looking for I know not what.

"I'm goin' down there. I gotta see what happened to 'Lij," Sullivan said.

"We'll be right beside you," Bacon said.

Slowly we moved on down the slope. The sheep scattered around our horses, making a pathway for us to travel. Toward the sheepwagon we moved. All was silent. Silent like death.

We found Elijah Sullivan dead on the ground not ten feet from the wagon. It was a horrible sight to behold; he had been shot in the head, apparently with a high-caliber slug, and at very close range. In his hands was gripped a Sharps, cocked and ready to fire. All around on the earth were the prints of horse hooves, mixed with the smaller marks where the sheep had meandered about the body.

"My God," moaned Sullivan. "Elijah ... my God."

I noted another still, dead form close by. It was his dog, shot several times through the head and body, its brown fur matted with dried blood and its tongue hanging grotesquely from its dead jaws. Obviously the animal had tried to help its wounded master. Or had it been the other way around? Had Madison—for I was certain he was the man behind this little massacre—tried to hurt the dog, arousing Elijah Sullivan to try to protect it, thus getting both the dog and himself killed. That was a mystery that was to remain unanswered.

"I'm sorry, Sullivan," said McCuen. "It looks like Josiah Madison has done his work here, too."

"He'll die, Mr. McCuen. He'll die by my gun ...

or by my hands, if I can get them around his neck. Poor ol' Elijah . . . he never would have hurt nobody, not unless they were tryin' to hurt his sheep or his dog. There ain't no reason why this should have happened."

With those words there was a thudding sound, followed by a spurting geyser of blood erupting from Sullivan's suddenly shattered forehead. He pitched forward from the saddle just as the noise of rifle fire reached us, a fractional second slower than the bullet itself. Sullivan was dead beside his brother before any of us had made sense of the unexpected occurrence. There was the sound of lead whizzing past our heads and thumping into the ground around our horses' hooves, mixed with McCuen's voice exclaiming with astounding casualness.

"My Lord . . . we're being shot at."

He grunted then, and grabbed at his leg. I knew he had been hit, and I knew from where the shot had been fired, too, for I had seen the white puff of smoke that had materialized from behind a boulder on the ridge behind us only a second before the bullet and the noise of the shot reached us.

I yanked my Colt from its holster and fired in the general direction of the enemy—a futile gesture, for I could see no one, and the hope of hitting anyone at that distance with a pistol held in a numb and shaking hand was so small as to be nonexistent. But I emptied the cylinder with a mechanical action, firing slowly and regularly as if there was some purpose in doing it.

"Let's move!"

Bacon's voice was almost sufficient to pull me out of my dream world of surprise and shock into reality once more. I realized the danger we were in, and my heels dug into my horse's flesh, goading him forward after the others. I slipped my pistol back into the holster, alternately staring at the land before me and the thin trickle of red staining McCuen's trouser leg. His hand would grip the reins as he rode, then move down to rub the wounded leg, then back up to the reins again, over and over. I could hear gunfire continuing from the ridge, and lead whistled close by my head like the singing of some insect.

I crouched low in the saddle and moved swiftly, the wind whipping my face and roaring in my ears. I glanced back over my shoulder. Men had revealed themselves from behind rocks and brush on the ridge, firing steadily at us. But the shots were futile, for we had moved out of range. The men showed no inclination to pursue us. But we ran hard, just as if they were on our tails.

I was scared. More scared than I had ever been before, more scared than I had imagined possible. My breath came in short, shallow pants, fast, panicked. Before I had burned with a rage against Madison, yet now I felt no anger, none at all. In its place was only fear, blind, stomach-turning fear. I wanted nothing else but to be away from the hills, back on the grasslands, running as fast as my horse could carry me back to Miles City.

We ran for a long time until our mounts could carry us no further without a rest. There was still no sign of pursuit. Madison had apparently been satisfied by the death of Sullivan and the sight of our hasty retreat. We rested for a long time without words, letting the horrible events of the past moments play through our minds again and again.

McCuen's leg was bleeding badly, and he looked pale. Bacon examined his wound and pronounced it not too serious, but still it was something that could not be ignored.

"I'll have to dig it out, Aaron," he said. "You're lucky. If that bullet had entered an inch over it might have severed your artery. As it is I think you'll be all right once we get the slug out and get you back to Miles City."

"Do whatever you need to do, Jed. There's a bottle of whiskey in my saddlebag."

I fetched the whiskey, and Bacon poured a liberal portion right onto McCuen's wound. The man howled in pain as the alcohol made contact with the raw flesh, and with me holding McCuen down Bacon began to probe for the bullet. McCuen cried and sweated and gritted his teeth, and all the while I looked not at him but at the hills from which we had come, wondering if Madison's horsemen would show themselves and approach us before we could escape. I was shaking and weak.

When the operation was over McCuen was pale and clammy. It was clear he would require some rest before we could go on, yet it seemed dangerous to me to remain here, still so close to the hills and to Madison. I felt a hot anger against McCuen, irrational though it was. It was because of him that we were being forced to loiter here. If Madison pursued us, it would be because of this delay that he would find us and surely kill us. It was McCuen's fault, and I hated him for it.

The inhuman nature of my feelings struck me suddenly, sickening me. I was blaming an innocent man for something he could not help. I was letting my own panic steal my rationality, just like a scared rabbit that runs right into the jaws of a snake.

When at last we were again mounted and moving south toward Miles City, I lagged behind. I examined my mind, my feelings. And what I found made me intensely ashamed.

I was a coward. How else could I explain the way I had acted, the way I had cursed McCuen so unjustly? I had never suffered from the delusion that I was a brave man. I had never sought to be a hero. But a coward? Could it be that I was no more than a coward?

Never before in my life had such a feeling plagued me. Yet now it was tearing through me like a hungry rat eating away my insides, and nothing I could do could squelch it.

Coward. Coward. The word ran through my brain, as steady as a tune. After a time it ceased to be a suspicion and became a certainty.

I was a coward. A sniveling, scared coward. I could almost have wished I had stayed and starved back on the farm in Tennessee.

CHAPTER XIV

We rode steadily all day, until our horses were panting and dripping with sweat and lather. I think they could have not gone a mile farther when at last Miles City loomed up before us and we rode into the dusty streets. It was deep night; we had ridden far past sunset.

The doctor was asleep in his small room behind his upstairs office, but we roused him, and he went to work on McCuen, grumbling and wheezing all the while because his rest had been disturbed. I recalled that Sam had been unable to find this fellow when I was suffering from the effects of the lightning bolt; it was probably just as well . . . he would never have come all the way out to the cabin to look me over, if his attitude toward all his work was similar to the one he now was displaying. But still he did good work, giving McCuen medication to ease his pain and bring on sleep.

"He'll have to stay here for a while, maybe a couple of days," he said. "That leg don't look any too good. Infection might set in."

The news did nothing to lift my spirits, to say the least. I worried about McCuen; he had become over the past few days a very close friend who had proven himself worthy of comradeship and respect. The thought crossed my mind that he might have to lose that leg if worse came to worst. And all because he took a bullet while trying to help me revenge myself against Madison. Unselfish, this man. And immensely courageous.

Bacon and I were weary, almost exhausted, both physically and mentally. I took the liberty of taking McCuen's hotel key and heading for a warm bed. Bacon went along too, sleeping on the couch, for he was too tired to attempt to reach his ranch tonight.

We slept late the next morning. It was almost ten o'clock before I at last opened my eyes. I was groggy, as if I had been drugged. Dragging myself to the mirror, I looked at my reflection. My beard was scraggly and rough and my hair disheveled, and I looked at the world through bleary, bloodshot eyes. I looked like I had either been very sick or very drunk for about a week, or perhaps had crawled out of an undertaker's back room. Even after my long sleep my nerves were on edge. All of this was getting to be too much. Things couldn't go on like this much longer without me losing what little sanity I had left. My courage was gone already, I felt. Maybe it didn't really matter if I lost my mind too.

Bacon awoke, looking not much better than me. We said nothing to each other as we dragged ourselves about the room, doing what we could to get ready to face the world. I felt as if I were covered with grit and dried sweat, and I wanted the feeling of a sharp razor against my face and hot water and soap scrubbing my skin.

I treated myself to a hot bath downstairs, and basked in the luxury of the steaming water. My tensions eased a bit, and for the first time in two days I felt truly relaxed. Yet even then I sensed it was to be a short-lived relaxation, for there were still things to think about, to ponder. And one question that must be answered: was I in fact a coward, as I had become convinced yesterday?

With the thought I felt my muscles tensing and I began to worry once more. A vague sort of contempt for myself swept over me. Coward. Nothing could convince me otherwise. I felt a growing depression. I knew that today I must surely face Becky. After all of my grand declarations of my intention to capture Madison, all my lofty discourses on duty, how could I come crawling back to her like a whipped and frightened puppy?

I thought back on yesterday's nightmare out there in the hills. The horrible way that Sullivan's head had shattered after the bullet had struck it, the way that fear had gripped me, panicked me, the way we had run . . . it sent a thrill of terror through me, and shame. How could I look into Becky's eyes now—but even worse, how could I look into Jennifer's?

Jennifer. I had hardly thought of her, at least in my conscious mind, yet I think there had not been a moment when she had not been hovering somewhere below the surface of my thoughts, back in some deep corner of my brain. I had determined to get Madison primarily to revenge Sam's murder, yet also I had been acting on Jennifer's behalf. She had seen her father die by a bullet from Madison or one of his riders, and the pain it had caused her had been shared by me. And so this failure, this joke of a mission which we had botched so completely, would surely arouse her contempt. And justly so, I mused. I wondered if she would want to see me again after what had happened.

I rose up from the tub, the water now tepid, for I had lay there musing for a long while. I shook myself dry like a dog, then rubbed myself with a rough towel. Pulling on a clean pair of pants and a freshly-laundered shirt, I felt a good bit better. I stretched my muscles and enjoyed the feeling of it.

But now it was time to face the world once more, and I dreaded that prospect. Yet it must be done. I steeled myself for the task that lay before me, and walked outside determined to find Becky.

The day was clear and bright, and the air had a freshness to it that tasted good. The sky was brilliant blue, and high above floated massive, fluffy clouds that looked like heaps of wool piled up after a shearing. And all around was the land, the level, rolling land that was at places flat as a billiard table and at other spots smoothly rounded, rippling with low hills. And all so green, filled with the life of summer, waving in the breeze. This was a huge territory, a vast one. The buildings all around me appeared squatty and drab as I viewed the sky. But beautiful though it was, I could not appreciate it, for I was full of dread. I dropped my eyes from the clouds and looked across the street.

Jennifer was approaching. I gasped and went pale. I was not yet ready to see her, not yet. But on she came, dressed more beautifully than I had ever seen her before, her hair pinned back in a way that emphasized her loveliness. My Lord, she was more breathtaking than the scenery! I finger-combed my hair into place. As she approached me I managed to force out a smile.

"Hello, Jennifer." A dull greeting, to be sure, but I could manage nothing better.

"Hello, Jim. It . . . it's good to see you." She paused, searching for words, and I realized that she was every bit as uncomfortable as me.

"I heard . . . about what happened. I heard Mr. McCuen was injured. Is he alright?"

"He seemed to be doing well when we left him last night," I replied, avoiding her eyes. "He was shot in the leg—nothing too serious; I don't think he'll be laid up too long."

"I was very sorry to hear he had been hurt."

"Jennifer . . . there was a man killed, a man who

worked for your father. Perhaps you knew him ...
Bradley Sullivan."

She shook her head. "No. I had heard the name
mentioned a time or two, but I never really met the fellow. I don't think Father liked him too much."

There came a very unpleasant pause, then, and
both of us scuffled our feet in the dust and refused to
exchange even the smallest glance.

"Jennifer, I'm very sorry. I know that doesn't help,
but I'm sorry. There was just no way we could stand
up to them, not at the time. And when McCuen was
hurt we had to get back to Miles City for his sake. I
never intended for anything like that to happen ... I
didn't mean for Madison to escape."

Jennifer looked at me then, and her eyes were
faintly misted. "It's alright, Jim ... I worried about
you the whole time you were gone. I hate Madison as
much as you, but I don't know what to do about it.
Maybe it's best that we leave him alone ... let the authorities take care of him."

"The authorities have done nothing for years. He
has been wanted since Reconstruction for the things he
did at the prison camp during the war. But no one has
ever brought him in. Sometimes I think no one ever
will, unless it's someone like me that does it. But it
looks like I failed completely. I feared that you
wouldn't want to see me again, that you might feel
contemptuously toward me."

Jennifer looked at me tenderly. "No, Jim. I would
never do that. You are a brave man, and you need
never worry that I will ever think differently of you, no
matter where I might be."

How quickly did relief arise within me, and how
quickly again did it fade when I heard her last phrase!
There was something final in her tone, something that
hinted she wouldn't be around in the future. And that
was a prospect I couldn't bear to consider.

"Jennifer, what do you mean? Are you going somewhere?" I looked again at her fine dress and immacu-

lately styled hair, and suddenly I understood that she was not dressed in such a manner for no reason—she was preparing for a journey.

Rather sadly she shook her head. "I can't stay, Jim, I can't. After what happened with Father every building, every rock, every tree makes me think of him. This place holds too many bad memories. I just can't take it anymore . . . I have to get away, at least for a time, maybe permanently. I'm catching the train this afternoon."

I felt a growing coldness within my chest. Jennifer was leaving. It was unbelievable.

"Where, Jennifer? Where will you be?"

"Helena. I have an uncle, a widower, who is a merchant there. He's agreed to let me stay at his home for as long as I would like. I may go to work for him if I decide to make it permanent. I have to go, Jim. I hope you understand. I'm going to miss you. I . . . I really like you—I think maybe you knew that already."

I stood looking at her in silence. "Like," she had said. What an insignificant word, so utterly incapable of expressing even half of what I felt for her! Yet I could not tell her—the time was not right, and my voice was choked in my throat from the thought of being without her.

"May I see you to the train, Jennifer? I would like to do that very much." I tried to restrain the quiver in my voice, though with little success.

She smiled—it hurt somehow, knowing that I would see that smile no longer—and then she nodded. "I would like to have you along. I would find the company pleasant."

"Will you share a meal with me?"

"Certainly." She slipped her arm into mine, and together we walked over to the cafe. I relished every moment of her touch, and realized how fleeting were these final moments with her.

I could not keep my eyes from her as I ate my meal. We talked quietly, and with every tick of the clock standing in the corner I grew a bit sadder. The afternoon came quickly, and I found myself standing at the depot south of town, watching Jennifer's baggage being loaded onto the train.

Our parting was brief, for I could not stand to lengthen it. How I longed to kiss her! But I couldn't. Perhaps I never would.

I touched her hand as she boarded, and watched her through the window of the passenger coach. She looked back at me, and smiled, though I fancied there was something very sad in her look. The noise of the locomotive increased, and the air was filled with smoke, the smell of cinders, and faint sparks expelled by the smokestack to drift all around the train and sting sharply as they settled on the skin and clothing of nearby watchers. Then the train slowly chugged onward, increasing speed steadily. I watched it disappear, my eyes bloodshot and straining to hold back tears. When I reached the main portion of town again, there were many people going about their business, filling the street and stores. Yet the place seemed so very empty. She was gone.

It was with a heavy heart that I saddled and mounted my horse and headed back toward Sam's spread. Becky would be waiting there, I felt sure. I really couldn't anticipate how she would greet me. Even though she had spoken against my pursuing Madison, the very humbling nature of my return might draw her contempt nonetheless. No matter. With Jennifer suddenly gone it all seemed of little consequence. Let her think and say what she would.

I approached the cabin slowly, for there was nothing to inspire haste. I looked over the wide and rolling land, in the distance seeing a handful of cattle grazing lazily on a wide slope. I noticed the rich color of the grasses that grew thick on that low slope. It would be a good year for cattlemen—those that had lived through the fight at Muster Creek—and I felt I myself had a good future here, a good chance for success. Strange how that didn't seem to matter anymore.

The house looked strangely dark and empty as I approached. Puzzled, I dismounted and walked to the front of the cabin, looking for Becky. No sign of her. I wondered if she had gone down the creek to see one of her neighbors, maybe to share her grief with one of the other newly-widowed ladies in this country. After the battle at Guthrie's ranch there were about enough widows to make an army.

The interior of the cabin looked much the same as always, but I noticed some items were missing. I walked back into Sam and Becky's bedroom. The linens were stripped from the bed; the hand-made wardrobe was empty. Becky was gone.

I found a note left for me on the table in the main room.

Becky was gone east, the note said, back to her home in Duluth and her relatives that still lived there. With Sam gone there was nothing to hold her to the Montana plains. She wanted her baby to grow up amid more than wind and work, alone with a widowed bride who could never begin to take care of the ranch alone. The cattle and land were mine, she said, she herself requesting only half of the year's profits. She was gone to not return. Only after death would she make the trip back to Montana, to be buried beside Sam in the grave in the back yard, beneath a tree, deep in the land he had loved so dearly throughout his short life.

I cast the letter down and walked back outside and around to the grave. I had not seen it before.

The newness of the grave was obvious. Only a single wooden cross served as a marker, though rocks had been heaped upon the fresh dirt of the grave to keep out burrowing animals. On the cross were painted letters, letters that would rapidly fade away beneath sun and rain as the years went by. They said:

Here lies
Samuel Adams Hartford
Born 1844
Died 1884

I read the simple inscription over and over again until the tears blurred my vision and I could read it no more. I turned and went back into the cabin and wept like an abandoned child, images of Sam flashing through my mind—Sam and I together, as children, working, playing, laughing. It would never be again, never again.

The next two days were ones of profound loneliness. I stayed in the cabin not coming out, hardly eating, hardly wanting to live. My own fears of cowardice had faded when Jennifer had assured me she did not think of me as such, yet in my anguished mental state the same fears returned, growing to overwhelming proportions in my mind. All my waking hours were spent in pacing about the cabin, letting my fear of Josiah Madison grow and eat away at my self-respect, and my dreams were of him also. I saw him striking me, stabbing me, wounding me and those I love while I made no effort to stop him save for childish babbling. The dream recurred again and again, and each time I would wake up in a cold sweat.

On the morning of the third day I knew I had to escape the cabin or go mad. I had not shaved or cleaned myself since I had returned, and after I had taken care of that I felt much better. I dressed myself as neatly as I could and began riding back to Miles City again. I left the cabin behind me, dark and empty. I knew that no matter what I would never spend another night there. It had become almost a symbol of my own self-doubts. And also I understood in some obscure pocket of rationality hidden away in the back of my mind that if I remained there it would rob me of my sanity. As the miles dropped away behind me, I felt immensely better, almost happy.

I went into Miles City with no clear purpose. More than anything I was trying to escape the hours of self-condemnation the last two days had brought me. I wanted to do something—anything—just for the sake of doing it. McCuen crossed my mind. I did not know how well he was recovering from his wound, nor if the doctor had let him leave the bed in the back room of the office yet. I headed for the office to find out.

McCuen was still confined to the bed in the back room, and I was hardly through the door before he was declaring to me that there was absolutely no reason for it, he was fine, and the fool doctor only wanted to keep him there to run up a bigger bill. By heaven, he declared he was ready to pay him double just to let him escape. I sat and listened to his complaints, and it cheered me greatly. I smiled for the first time in two days, and it was like medicine for my darkened spirits.

McCuen continued his tirade for some time, then paused for breath. During the pause he looked at me, and a frown crossed his face, creating small wrinkles beneath the scruffy growth of beard on his jaws.

"Jim, you don't look too good. Way too pale. Has Becky been taking things rough, wearing you down a little?"

"Becky's gone," I said. "Gone back to Duluth and a sister that lives there. I've been alone."

He settled back down into the bed. "I can't say I blame her for wanting to get away. She's been through pure hell, there's no denying. Is she coming back?"

I shook my head. "I don't think so, McCuen. She left a letter and said as much. I believe her."

"What about Jennifer Guthrie? Have you seen her?"

I felt a pang of sorrow. "She's gone too, west to Helena. She has an uncle, a merchant of some sort, who is letting her live with him as long as she wants. Whether she will come back or not I don't know."

McCuen looked at me very seriously. He spoke in a quiet voice.

"You feel something pretty special for that girl, don't you, Jim," he said. "It's pretty apparent, if you don't mind me being so blunt."

I looked at my friend, and I could tell he understood my feelings. I was struck with a sudden desire to admit my love for Jennifer, for love it surely was. I was sick of keeping it to myself. I poured out my feelings, telling how I had met her, what had happened between us, how for two days I had been on the verge of losing my mind out of loneliness for her and the fear that I was a coward. It was a good feeling to let it all out.

"Love is a rough thing at times," McCuen said. "I was a married man at one time. She left me, and for a long time I did nothing but mourn and drink and cry. And I discovered something in all that—there's no pat answers, no tricks or gimmicks that can ease the pain that loving someone can cause. And there can be real pain, I can tell you, and you know that anyway. Loving someone is a bit like gambling—you lay your heart and feelings out before them, and sometimes you win. And sometimes you don't. And that can hurt. It's a gamble, for sure. You can't win without putting something on the line, without taking a risk.

"There's no reason to give up on Jennifer yet. She's been through a lot, and she needs time to think, just like you, just like all of us. If she cares for you she'll come back. If she doesn't . . . then you'll know you never really had any hold on her in the first place.

"And as for your feeling about being a coward— well, I'm not even going to try to answer that. I can't. That's something a man can only answer for himself, something only he can decide. But I will tell you this: I see no reason to think you are anything less than a brave man. And I think with time you'll realize that I'm right. But I'm not the sort to hand out advice very much, for there's not anything much more useless, and so I think I'll just shut up."

I wanted to say something to him, to thank him for his words, but I didn't get the chance, for the door opened and in walked Jed Bacon. With him was a stranger, a tall man with dark hair and eyes. Both of the men looked very serious.

CHAPTER XV

∽

The stranger's name was Nathan Thorne. Bacon informed us that Thorne was an agent of the United States Secret Service.

"I came to Mr. Bacon only last night," said Thorne. "As you might have already guessed, I'm coming to you in connection with Josiah Madison. I've been on his trail for years, along with half a dozen other government agents. He's evaded us all along, just like a slippery snake. From what I understand, you men have had the most recent contact with our friend Madison. I'm glad I found you here, Mr. Hartford. It makes things much more convenient."

"What can we tell you about Madison that you don't know already?" asked McCuen. "About the closest contact I've had with the man is when he or one of his men put this hole in my leg. I'll tell you everything I know, though."

Thorne produced a pad and pencil and sat down in the corner. McCuen told his version of the events of the recent past, then I did the same. Bacon had already talked to the man prior to their coming to the office. As Thorne took notes he nodded and frowned, grunting whenever something was said that he found particularly interesting. Something in his bearing made me careful of what I said, made me conscious of detail in the story, made me want to be as accurate as possible in every way. Thorne had a professional air about him, a no-nonsense approach to his work that let all of us know that he meant business when it came to capturing Josiah Madison.

That was a good thing to know. I was sincerely glad that someone was on the trail of the man who I loathed so much, not only for what he had done to my loved ones but also for making me look on myself as a coward. I looked at the tall, handsome Thorne. He was so unlike me, not the kind to turn his back on duty just because things got tight. I envied him.

I forced the thought away, reminding myself that I had just met Nathan Thorne; I had no evidence to prove that he was such a better man than me. It was only my depressed state that caused me to see him, and everyone else, as being my better. I felt a bit angry at myself. Self-condemnation had become a habit in the last two or three days, and I was growing weary of it, blasted weary.

"If you want to find Madison, look north of here," said Bacon. "I expect he's still in that general area. But I wouldn't advise you to go after him unless you're prepared to take on a little army single-handed. We were fools enough to go against him with only four men—there would be nothing to expect but death if you went after him alone."

Thorne stood and shook his head. "Don't worry. I have no intention of going against Madison alone. No intention at all."

"You have men with you?" McCuen asked.

Thorne responded with a look that conveyed its meaning perfectly: Official business—confidential. He pocketed his pad and pencil and shook each of our hands in turn.

"Thank you, gentlemen. You've been very helpful. I make it my business to talk to any person that has contact with Madison, no matter how slight. The information you have given me will go on record in Washington. I should tell you, I suppose, that if we manage to get Madison to trial you might be called to testify. He has a string of crimes to his name that couldn't be printed in a dozen books, and your wound, Mr. McCuen, is just a minor affair compared to what he has done to other men. He's a beast, and I plan to catch him. You will, of course, keep all we have said in confidence."

Thorne slammed his hand hard against his hip to punctuate his little speech, then turned on his heel and walked out of the room. If I hadn't been so overwhelmed by his rather pretentious bearing, I might have laughed at the almost military way in which he walked. But comical though some of his traits might be, I sensed that he was deadly serious in his intent to capture Madison. And if there was any man that could do it, it would surely be someone like Thorne.

"Well, there goes a character," said Bacon, moving over to the window. "But I guess it will take a man like that, dedicated to his work, to ever bring in Madison."

I moved over beside Bacon. Thorne was walking across the street toward the hotel, his shoulders straight and his head held high. He was wearing a light gray hat tipped to the side on his head. Very sharp.

"Pretty secretive about things, wasn't he," I commented. "I wonder how much he knows that we don't. He didn't seem too impressed when you told him to look to the north for Madison. Maybe the one-eyed devil has moved on."

"Could be," said Bacon. "He could have covered a lot of ground since we saw him last."

I asked McCuen if he minded my staying in his

hotel room until he was back on his feet. I would take care of expenses, of course. He seemed happy to agree.

"I've still got most of my stuff over there," he said. "Keep an eye on it, would you?"

After I left Bacon with McCuen I still felt the urge to roam. Being cooped up for the last two days inside Sam's little cabin had created a desire for open spaces and blue sky, and now seemed just the time to get a good dose of both. I headed south to the railroad depot and then eastward along the track. It felt good to walk and feel my blood pumping.

The air was fresh and pure, and it seemed to fill my lungs with an energy and vigor that then spread through my bloodstream. My legs grew slightly sore, for I had gotten little exercise in the past two days, yet it was a pleasant soreness, one that made me feel alive and well once more. I walked rapidly along the rails, taking in the scenery and remembering another time when I walked alongside the track—the time I met Jasper Maddux and then Jennifer.

The track appeared endless, stretching as far as my eye could see across the plains. Railroads fascinated me, and I had read of them as long as there had been talk of transcontinental rail service. Controversy had clouded their history from almost the earliest times, and greed had been the primary moving force that led to their creation. This particular line, the Northern Pacific, had only been complete since last year, but it had touched the whole nation in another way a decade before when a government loan had failed to come through to the financier of the line. The subsequent collapse of that financier had led the whole country into a five-year depression.

That had been about the same time that my own little farming empire in Tennessee had been steadily failing. Now, suddenly, there was hope once more. I had land now, even a herd of good cattle since Becky had left Sam's ranch in my hands. I hoped I could manage to give her more than half the profits. If I could simply get by this year I would be happy; she deserved much for what she had suffered.

With every step my mind grew clearer, my soul rose higher. Still the same fears plagued me—fears of cowardice, fear that I might lose Jennifer—but no longer did they overwhelm me. I felt something like happiness again.

It was then I saw, further down the track, a straggler, apparently very drunk, for he was weaving about as he stumbled along. He wore no hat and carried nothing with him. I stopped and watched him, debating whether or not to continue, for I had no desire to be hounded for money or a drink. He must have been *very* drunk, for it seemed it was almost impossible for him to stand at all. He would rise, then progress a few halting steps before collapsing onto his hands and knees, pushing himself up, then going through the same procedure again. As I drew nearer a suspicion began to plague me. Maybe this man wasn't drunk . . . maybe he was hurt in some way. It could be that he had fallen off the train. I knew from personal experience that such an occurrence could happen far more easily than most might think.

There was only one way to check out this character, and that was face to face. I trotted along quickly. I reached him only seconds after he fell for one last time, now apparently unable to push himself up at all. I knelt beside him and immediately saw what his problem was.

There was a tremendous knot on the back of his skull. This man had been struck by some very hard object, for the skin was laid open and blood trickled down the back of his neck. Gently I rolled him over onto his back. His eyes were still open, though they seemed quite dull and glazed. His tongue and lips were moving, as if he was trying to speak, but no words would form and only faint grunts emerged from his throat. This fellow was in bad shape, very bad.

"Easy, mister, easy," I said. "I'll get you into town

so the doctor can take care of you. First thing to do, though, is get you off this track. Can you stand up if I help you?"

I wasn't at all sure that he understood anything I said, but it seemed to me that he nodded slightly. So with great effort I pulled him to his feet. He leaned against me, moaning, and his feet seemed to be like weights of lead at the end of weak, quivering legs. Still, though, I managed to get him far off the track and into the shade of some low, scrubby bushes that grew on the crest of a little bank of dirt.

I made him as comfortable as possible, speaking words of comfort and trying to position him so that no pressure was placed against his ugly head wound. Obviously he had been either struck by some very vicious person, or else he had pounded his head against the track after a fall from the train. Either way, I felt absolutely no assurance that he would live for even the next few minutes.

I estimated I had walked about two miles from town. Obviously I could not carry this man back on my shoulders, and I had no horse or wagon. The only thing to do was to get to the road and try to wave down a passing wagon or buckboard and persuade the driver to carry this man into town.

Leaving him alone, I ran to the main road. There was no traffic for a long time, until at last a buggy approached. The driver was a very unpleasant-looking old man, and he ran right past me, cursing as I tried to wave him down. Angry, I kicked a stone after him as the buggy creaked on down the road.

There was no other passerby for almost an hour, and I began to worry about the wounded man, lying there alone on the hard ground. How long he had been wandering down the track I could not guess; he might be terribly thirsty and weak. I was just starting back to check on him when a wagon approached. This time the driver was not so crabby, and when I explained the situation to him he seemed glad to help.

Together we went to the wounded man and carried him carefully back to the wagon. We made him as comfortable a possible, laying him atop some empty cloth sacks and resting the back of his neck on a little pillow made with sacks stuffed inside a burlap bag. The driver urged the two horses on at full speed, and we reached Miles City in what I guessed was record time.

It took another thirty minutes to locate the doctor, who was drinking alone in the corner of a saloon. As I expected, he acted as if my request for him to treat the injured man was an intrusion into his privacy. But with considerable complaining he at last came along.

I think McCuen could have broken into a dance routine in spite of his wounded leg when the doctor informed him that he was going to at last be evicted from the bed in the office. Apparently the man I had brought in needed more immediate care than McCuen in the good doctor's opinion, so at last my friend was being set free from his upstairs prison. He wasted no time in getting across to the hotel for a bath and shave, smiling in spite of the soreness of his leg.

I loitered around the office long enough to hear the doctor's verdict.

"He took a hard blow. If my guess is right, it wasn't the result of falling off a train—that man was struck deliberately by someone who didn't care how much damage he did. But I don't think the man will die. He might be unconscious for a day or so, but then I expect he'll come around. He didn't have no wallet nor money nor name anywhere on him. I reckon if he does die I'll have to come to you for the bill."

Fool doctor, I thought. Blasted money-hoarding old billy goat. All he apparently thought of was hard cash. But he was the best the town had at the moment. I agreed to pay the bill if the man didn't survive, then left in a huff.

I saw Nathan Thorne emerging from the hotel just as I descended the stairs. He was dressed roughly, looking a good deal more like a cowboy than a government agent. For some reason I felt rather surprised to see him decked out as he was in denim pants, homespun shirt, vest, and gunbelt. In his hands was a bag, which I guessed held his possessions. He moved on across the street and toward the depot. The whistle of an approaching train carried across in the summer breeze, and I wondered if he was preparing to leave.

And where he was going must surely be where Madison was. I was intrigued. The train was approaching from the east, so surely Thorne was preparing to go west. Could Madison have moved in that direction? He had been on the run for days now. In that time he could have reached Billings, Bozeman, even—the thought brought me up short and sent a chill through me—even Helena. What if Madison had gone to Helena, the very place Jennifer now lived?

It didn't take much thought to realize the consequences such a move might entail. If Madison saw Jennifer he would surely try to kill her, for clearly he would want no one alive who could so readily identify him. If Madison had gone to Helena, Jennifer would have no knowledge of the danger she was in. Madison could reach her, even kill her, before she had any idea of what was happening.

Thorne was still moving toward the depot. On impulse I followed him. Maybe he wasn't going to catch the train after all. Maybe he was just going to meet someone. I prayed that it was true. If he boarded that train and headed west, then my fears would surely be confirmed. I tried to remind myself that there were many places west of Miles City other than Helena, and that there was no reason to suppose that Madison would pick out that particular spot among all the possibilities open to him. He might have gone into the mountains to avoid capture. But still . . .

I stayed out of view of Thorne until we reached the depot. There I loitered just around the corner from him, within earshot of his low whistling, and waited.

The train pulled up to a stop, and within minutes passengers began to emerge, while a handful of waiting people on the station porch gathered up bags and prepared to board. I breathed a little easier when I saw that Thorne was not among them.

A man dressed in dirty riding clothes stepped off the train and looked across the crowd. Upon seeing Thorne he moved quickly over to him. I tried not to breathe, wanting to hear what was said.

"Hello. Have you learned anything?" The man had a soft, whisper-like voice.

"A little. Nothing to really help. Here . . . take this and get rid of it in Billings. I'll leave tomorrow. Wait for me in Livingston.

"Something has come up, something I'll have to take care of. I thought our friend was out of the way, but I was wrong. They brought him into the doctor's office just awhile ago. It could be trouble for us if he talks. I'll have to eliminate that problem as soon as I can."

The shock that crept over me as I listened to those words was intense. Thorne was talking about the man I had carried into town, the one who might even now be dying in the doctor's office! Could it have been Thorne that opened up that hideous gash in the man's head? But why?

Thorne talked for a bit longer with the stranger, but the words were so quietly spoken that I could not hear enough to understand. My curiosity was aroused along with a feeling of repulsion. Judging from what Thorne had said I suspected that he had murder in mind. Murder! The thought was enough to make me shudder. I began to doubt the validity of Thorne's claim to work with the government. Something was going on here that I didn't understand. What secret did the man lying in the doctor's office hold that Thorne did not want revealed?

The man talking to Thorne boarded the train again, taking the bag with him. Thorne turned to walk around the corner and back to town, and I escaped detection only by slipping into a side doorway just as he passed. I watched him moving back toward town, and being careful to remain inconspicuous, I slipped out to follow him.

He walked past the doctor's office without stopping, though he glanced up the staircase. I fancied I could read the thoughts racing through his mind.

I had no idea what information the unidentified victim inside the office held, but I was determined to find out. Obviously there was some connection with Madison, and that made it of great interest to me. Thorne, whoever he might be, had come to Miles City impersonating an agent of the Secret Service, asked questions about Josiah Madison, putting on quite an act. Now, by sheer accident, I had discovered his involvement in what was at least attempted murder. And if his words to his strange companion at the depot were any indication, there would be another attempt later.

I paused on the street after Thorne again entered the hotel. What to do? Should I tell McCuen or Bacon what I had seen and heard? A dreadful possibility crossed my mind. What if Thorne was, as he claimed, a Secret Service agent? I had never thought that any government representative would ever sanction or take part in murder, but then I had no way to prove that conviction was accurate. Yet I could not shake the feeling that Thorne was an imposter. Anything I did would have to be based on that assumption.

I decided to let McCuen in on this, for I could think of no clear course of action. I climbed the stairs and found McCuen fumbling with his tie. He had only just finished bathing and dressing. With his beard gone and his hair washed and combed he looked like a new man.

When I told him what had happened he appeared a bit confused. The story sounded wild, I realized, yet I knew it to be accurate, for I had heard Thorne's conversation myself. McCuen sat down on the edge of his bed and frowned.

"This whole affair gets more unbelievable as things go on," he muttered. "But if what you say is true I think you are right in expecting something to happen. If Thorne plans to finish off the man you brought in I expect he would do it tonight. Things would be much too risky in the daylight. Let's get back over to the office and see how the man is. Maybe he's come around and can tell us something to give us a clue."

We crossed the street and climbed up the stairs. McCuen limped noticeably, though he tried to pretend his leg was alright. We met the doctor coming out as we reached the top of the stairs.

"Ain't no point in goin' in there," he said. "Your friend died a few minutes ago."

Now that was a shock. It threw everything into a new light. And it knocked out our chance to find out what Thorne was up to.

McCuen touched the doctor's shoulder. "Doc, if you don't mind, you could do us a mighty big favor. Are you heading out to get the undertaker?"

"Yes."

"I would rather you hold off on that right now. I have reason to believe that a murder attempt has been planned against the man in there."

"Murder attempt? But that ridiculous. He's dead already!"

"I know that, but the murderer does not. Doctor, I'm taking you into my confidence on this. I'm a Secret Service agent, and that man who just died was one of my partners. This is serious government business, Doctor, and we need your cooperation."

I almost laughed at the serious way in which McCuen bluffed the doctor, but apparently his story was believed, for the grizzled old fellow's eyes widened and his breath came quickly.

"No! Are you serious? You're a government agent?"

McCuen nodded. "Yes. And this is my partner. We're traveling anonymously, so we'll have to trust to your strict silence in this matter."

The doctor nodded and grinned. For the first time I noticed he didn't have any teeth.

"You got it, mister. What do you want me to do?"

McCuen pulled a few bills from his pocket and placed them in the man's hand. "Go over to the hotel and check into a room. Buy yourself a hot meal, a few drinks, anything you want. But leave the office just as it is. If there's to be any murder attempt we don't want the killer to know his victim is already dead. But remember—you must never say a word of this to anyone. Do you understand?"

The white-haired old man grinned and winked. "You betcha. Thanks a lot, partner." He started down the stairs, then turned suddenly. "What about the bill for that feller?" he asked. "You gonna pay it?"

It was my turn to bluff this time around. "You'll receive full payment and more from the federal government within two weeks," I said. That seemed to please him, for he grinned once more and headed on down the street to the nearest saloon. I expected he would blow most or all of what McCuen had given him on liquor.

"What now, McCuen?"

"We wait. And we watch. I expect that our friend Thorne will make his move tonight, if what you suspect about him is accurate. And I would be willing to bet that it is. I don't believe Thorne is any more a Secret Service agent than I am."

Chapter XVI

~

It happened largely as we expected. It was well after
dark when Thorne emerged from the hotel.
McCuen and I stood in the doorway of a deserted
building, nothing more than a rickety shack, and
watched him move slowly across toward the doctor's
office. Very calm he was, doing nothing that would
draw attention. He did not mount the stairs immediately, but instead stood at the end of the boardwalk,
smoking and watching people pass, listening to the
music from the saloons that lit up the street with the
glow spilling from their crowded interiors. Then, as if
he were doing nothing out of the ordinary, he crushed
out his cigar and slowly began moving up the stairs.
McCuen and I shifted our positions to make sure we
could see everything.

Thorne knocked on the door and waited, then
knocked again, this time with more force. When he
was satisfied that the doctor was not inside, he produced something from his vest pocket—though I was
too far away to be certain, I took it to be a file—and

began prying at the lock. In only moments he had forced the door open and was inside.

He must have remained in the office for no more than a minute before he again emerged, this time trotting down the steps gingerly, whistling a tune. It made me shudder, knowing that he rejoiced over the death of a man. I'm sure he had stabbed him before even checking to see if he was awake, for I noticed a large knife strapped to his belt. Obviously he had fired no shots, so the blade must have been the weapon. I doubted that he had noticed his victim was already dead.

He headed for the livery stable then, and within moments had emerged, mounted on a white horse. Where he had got the animal I couldn't guess; he had ridden the train into Miles City, I assumed. Probably he had bought the horse earlier today, maybe even stolen it. But wherever the animal had come from, it was rapidly carrying its rider out of town—toward the west, I noted.

It was what we had expected, and we were ready for it. We moved to where our own horses were hidden, already saddled and ready, and then we were after him, moving swiftly along his trail. McCuen was having a hard time of it, I could tell, for the jolts of his horse made his leg painful, but still he kept up with me, moving rapidly and surely. Where Nathan Thorne went we would go.

We left Miles City and the light of the saloons and brothels, and moved into the darker plains. It would be tricky, following Thorne in this darkness without drawing too near, but we managed to do it. Occasionally we would lose sight of his faint, small form far ahead of us on the grasslands, but always we would find him again. Where he was going I could not tell. I supposed that his main purpose was to simply get away from town to avoid suspicion in the death of the stranger in the doctor's office.

We were following the railroad, moving rapidly until we were well away from town. Then Thorne slowed, and we watched him move into an area of scrubby brush and low hills like shallow, rounded bumps on the land. And it was then that we lost him.

How he managed to disappear so totally I never was able to figure out. Partly it was an unexpected surge of darkness that came when clouds obscured the moon; partly it was because the man obviously was accustomed to life on the plains and knew very well how to take care of himself. I don't think he had any notion that he was being followed; probably he pulled whatever magical evasive action that had let him escape simply as a routine gesture. But one thing was beyond doubt: he was gone, and we would not find him.

"Well, if that doesn't beat all!" exclaimed McCuen. "All of this for nothing. But he is heading west, just like his partner earlier today. Madison must be in that area."

That was a conviction I shared. Again I reminded myself that just because he had moved west was no reason to believe he was going to wind up in Helena. But again there was always the possibility that he would. And then, what of Jennifer?

"Let's go back to Miles City," I said. "There's things I need to do."

"Don't tell me . . . you're going to Helena, aren't you."

"Yes. This time I'm not running from Madison. I'm tired of thinking of myself as a coward, and it's high time I proved to myself that I'm not. C'mon. We're wasting time."

There really was no hurry about our getting back, but I was filled with determination and wanted to get things underway. I would go to Helena and find Jennifer. If Madison showed up I would do whatever was necessary to protect her from him, and I would bring her back where she belonged. That was most important—to get her back with me again. And if she wouldn't return, then I was ready to throw my previous plans to the wind and live in Helena—anything to be close to her.

I got little sleep later that night, for I was gathering my possessions and preparing for the journey. It was really unnecessary; there would not even be a train through until the day after tomorrow. But I was too excited to wait. If I couldn't go tomorrow I could at least make preparations.

The next day seemed endless. All I could think of was Jennifer. I went to bed early to prepare myself. I would need all of my energy for the trip.

McCuen saw me to the station, and I was off for Helena. I rode third class.

The coach was full of every breed of humanity, all crowded into an oblong car and seated on rough, narrow benches. I looked over the group. Some were obviously cowboys and homesteaders, some ranchers making short-term trips. There were many stops all along the line, and the crowd, I knew, would fluctuate constantly. There were other persons on board that obviously were not part of the short-term traffic of the railroad. Some had a look about them that told they were in a strange land. I guessed them to be immigrants, from where I could not know. Maybe Ireland, Germany, almost any other place. I expected somehow that as the years went by there would only be more and more of them, coming from every part of the globe to try to make a success somewhere on the plains. I could easily imagine that what they saw out the windows of the car was not quite what they had expected. It was no promised land. Yet there was hope in the land, a chance for success. The railroads provided the means of travel and also much of the available land.

Yet in a sense the railroad was a barrier to the success of the immigrant, for land that had before been in the public domain, free for the taking, was now being held by the railroad as a result of the immense land grants given by the government to finance the building of the line. So the penniless and destitute couldn't make claims of free land as they could a few years ago. It was now a matter of paying anywhere from two to five dollars an acre for railroad property.

Many of those coming to Montana came, like me, to get into the cattle business. Others came to try their hand at farming the plains. I had considered that myself, but I knew enough to realize that it would take far more land to make a go of it in this country than it did in the east. A handful of farmers managed to eke out a living in the more fertile portions of the state, but in most of Montana it was cattle ranching that was the basis of the territory's economy.

The car was filled with smoke from numerous pipes and cigars, and most people were sitting silently, with a few obnoxious exceptions. Two women, one with a mouth well-stuffed with snuff and the other with a horrid-smelling pipeful of tobacco, sat talking in loud and coarse voices toward the front of the coach. Their language would have embarrassed a sailor, and I saw many young mothers holding the ears of their children beneath cupped palms to block out the voices. This, naturally, only made the children all the more interested in hearing what the old ladies were saying. As always, the forbidden fruit was the most desired.

The car rode roughly, rocking from side to side far more than I would have liked, and my palms were moist with sweat. I shifted constantly in my seat, for the hard wood of the bench was uncomfortable. At last a conductor came wandering down the aisle, selling small, straw-stuffed pillows at a ridiculously high price. Though it hurt me to do it, I bought one. It was a relief for awhile, but then the dry straw became matted and hard and I might as well have thrown the blasted thing out the window for all the good it was doing me. All the bad memories of my train ride to the Montana Territory came rushing back.

We stopped in Hathaway to pick up new passengers, and a few people got off. I was among them, for

I was very hungry, and I saw a lady hawking biscuits and ham on the station platform. I purchased three of the delights, along with a tin of milk (rather warm but still satisfying), and climbed back onto the train just in time. Engineers wasted little time at stops; they often did not give passengers more than twenty or thirty minutes to eat lunch.

I walked down the narrow aisle back toward my bench, doing my best to avoid trodding on feet that stuck out into the aisle while at the same time balancing my food and milk. I was taken aback when I discovered that one of the men who had just come aboard the train—a bearded man with very dark hair and a black suit and hat—had seated himself in the very spot I had vacated to buy my meal. I looked at him for a moment, unsure of whether or not I should ask him to move or simply look for a seat elsewhere.

"Oh, I beg your pardon—this was your seat, sir?" He was a polite enough fellow, at least.

"Well, yes . . . but keep it. I can sit over here."

"I think we might both have room if I move over . . . there. If you would like some company I would be glad to provide it. I know few people around here. It gets rather lonesome."

Whether or not I should trust the fellow I did not know, but after a moment's thought I gave a shrug and sat down. I said nothing as I began to munch my meat and biscuit and sip my milk. After a moment I noticed he was watching me eat from the corner of his eye. Letting out a sigh that was louder than I intended, I asked him if he would like one of the biscuits. Of course it was simply a polite gesture, and I knew he would not accept. Or thought I knew, for he smiled and grabbed the largest of the biscuits and began to gobble it down. I was greatly irritated, but tried not to show it. After all, I *had* offered it to him.

"Thank you so much, sir . . . I hadn't eaten since early yesterday evening." He extended a hand covered with biscuit crumbs, but before I could take it he withdrew it and began picking off the crumbs and popping them in his mouth. This fellow didn't intend to waste a bit of his free lunch.

"Barnabas Runyon," he said. "Man of the west, womanizer, occasional preacher, and mostly gambler—that's what I am. And you?"

I really didn't want to talk to Runyon, but I knew no way to get out of it. "Jim Hartford. I live north of Miles City."

"Ah, yes! Miles City is one of my favorite spots on God's green earth. I won over two thousand dollars there in one evening at a game of stud poker. If I hadn't stolen a horse and took off at top speed I would be moldering in a grave with rope burns around my neck. Folks don't often take kindly to losing all they own to a stranger. But that's how it goes, the way I look at it. Don't sit down at the table if you aren't willing to lose. Lord knows I've lost enough myself."

"That's how it goes." I had no desire to continue the conversation, and I did my best to end it. But no matter. Barnabas Runyon was in a mood to talk.

"I'm heading for Helena," he volunteered, and the news was not welcome. "Are you getting off there or going on through?"

"I'm getting off. I'll be looking up some friends there." I deliberately tried to sound glum and unfriendly, hoping he would realize that I was looking neither for conversation or companionship. It didn't work.

"Great! Perhaps we'll run into each other. If you spend any time in the saloons I'll guarantee you'll see me. I intend to leave Helena a wealthy man, Mr. Hartford. I'm broke down to my last dollar at the moment. That's why I'm riding a third-class immigrant coach instead of the first-class car. I've won many a dollar hustling the high and mighty that ride in the first-class coaches. If we were both sitting in one of them right now I wouldn't be telling you all this about myself. Instead I would be doing my best to get you into a friendly game of chance. And chances are I would walk away with every cent you had on you. Yes sir. I'm a gambler, and a fine one."

And a braggart and a loud mouth buffoon, I added mentally. This man was almost as irritating in his continual blabbing as was Bradley Sullivan when he talked about sheep herding. It was only with great effort that I managed to remain polite.

"Helena is a wonderful city in many ways, yet it can be a rough one, too. It started as a mining town, and after that it did nothing but grow and thrive, even after the gold ran out. But it didn't run out until nineteen million dollars' worth of the stuff had been dug out. Nineteen million! It's enough to make my mouth water. I got my hands on a little of it myself—not digging it out, mind you, but winning it off of miners at the poker table. Last Chance Gulch, they called it when it first opened up. It was the richest strike north of Virginia City. Helena was a wonderful town in those days.

"But a man had to watch his step mighty close, or he might wind up swinging from a tree limb somewhere. There wasn't any real law to speak of in the mining days, so folks pretty much had to provide their own. A man guilty of a crime didn't have much chance around Helena—nor an innocent one, if he stood too close to a guilty one. If in doubt, string 'em up. That was pretty much the way folks looked at it back then. Had a tree in town—the 'Hanging Tree,' they called it—and folks didn't waste much time on trials. Yes sir. A man had to watch his step in Helena."

Runyon talked some more, and after a while I quit listening. I nodded occasionally, and grunted every now and then as if I was listening closely to what he said, but on my mind was a face, a lovely face, the face of Jennifer. It made me feel warm inside to know that with every mile I grew closer to where she was.

I had come to the Montana Territory with a dream, a dream of success. Yet now it had changed, al-

ered somehow. It had divided in two, making room
for another besides myself. I looked past Runyon and
on out across the grassland. It was alien, a strange
world. But I could conquer it—me, a misplaced Tennessee farmer, if she was beside me. If she wasn't, then
I had no desire to even fight. Never, never had I met
anyone like her. Never before had I even imagined I
could feel about someone the way I felt about Jennifer.

My mind drifted to Madison. Where was he? All
the evidence indicated that he was in the western portion of the territory. But that was a large region, and
very rugged. Even if by chance Madison did come to
Helena, it would only be a slight possibility that he
would encounter either me or Jennifer. But something
was pulling me on—the desire to protect Jennifer even
against such a remote threat as Madison, the desire to
prove to myself that I would not run. I would not act
a coward this time if I should meet my enemy.

Runyon had talked himself to sleep, and for that I
was grateful. It was going to be hard to get any rest
on this hard bench, and with Runyon dozing beside me
I found it almost impossible to position myself into
anything resembling a comfortable position. I could
have shaken him awake and had him move, but I was
not about to do anything that might set that talking
machine in action again. So I shifted and turned, and
at last dozed off.

I awoke when the train lurched to a stop. We had
pulled up to one of the innumerable stations along the
way. Again there was a change in the population of
the coach, and then once more we were on our way.
The two foul-mouthed ladies got off at this stop,
which made me very happy, but Runyon came awake
again, and once more I was listening to a seemingly
endless discourse.

Night fell, and I traded seats with Runyon. I
wanted to look out across the vastness of Montana, to
see the rugged land, and mostly to dream of Jennifer.
And that I did, even after I had drifted off to sleep.

CHAPTER XVII

I stood on the street in Helena with my bag in m
hand, realizing that I did not even know the nan
of Jennifer's uncle nor where his store was locate
Runyon was beside me, grinning broadly and breath
ing in the fresh air with loud sniffs of satisfaction.

"Ah, Helena, you're even better than I remen
bered you!" he exclaimed. "You're a town of gold, an
I intend to take a good chunk of you away with me!

I found Runyon's cheerfulness to be a little irrita
ing, for I was pondering a problem. Where should
go? I looked at the row of stores and saloons lining t
street. Jennifer was probably in one of the those store
though I had no idea which one. All I knew what th
her uncle was a merchant, and that was a feeble clu
Only his relationship to the famous Luther Guthr
might help me find him.

"Well, are we going to stand here all day or a
we going to look for a place to stay?" Runyon sai
Apparently, I realized, he intended for us to stay t
gether. At first I started to protest, but then I thoug

better of it. I knew no one here. A companion who was familiar with Helena might come in handy, and Runyon might be able to help me find Jennifer's uncle.

"There's a hotel over there," I pointed out. "How about us checking in there?"

Runyon frowned. "You haven't seen their prices. They'll charge you an arm and leg for a bed and more for any extras. Down the street a little further is some other rooms—see the sign? Twenty-five cents a night. It isn't fancy, but it's cheap."

So to the little weatherboarded building we went. I didn't really like the look of the place, and when I entered the tiny room I was given I felt even more negatively inclined toward it. The bed was dusty, and I suspected several people had slept on the sheets now on it since it was last changed. I noticed the legs of the bed were sitting in little tins of some sort of liquid. I knelt down to smell it. Kerosene. I knew the purpose of it; this room was infested with bedbugs, and the containers of kerosene were there to keep them out of the bed. But when I plopped my bag down on the sagging mattress I saw one of the loathsome creatures scurry off to safety. I was almost itching already, just anticipating the night to come.

I was so hungry that I couldn't even think of beginning to look for Jennifer until I had eaten a good meal. I headed back outside to my companion, who had already dumped his few possessions in the next room.

"Well, Hartford, let's grab a meal somewhere. I'm as empty as a church house on Saturday night."

We found a pleasant-looking cafe immediately, and I turned to go inside. Runyon held back.

"I think I'll go on down a little further to the saloon. The food won't be too great, I expect, but maybe I can get into a little poker game and win some cash."

I nodded and went on in. The interior was dark and cool, and I removed my hat and enjoyed the coolness against my forehead. I sat down at a table and ordered a meal from the plump, friendly-looking woman who was hustling about the place, seemingly doing ten things at once. Let Runyon have his saloon and gambling table; I would stick to the simpler pleasures of a hot meal and a good cup of coffee.

I looked out into the street as I ate, watching people passing, wondering what it must have been like in the days when the strikes were pouring out gold like an endless stream. Surely there had been a tremendous excitement in those days—there must have been—an excitement that might never again be experienced in the history of the nation. To think of a town springing up within a few days in a spot that had before been only wilderness—Lord, that was something amazing. And it had happened all over the west, anywhere where some lonely prospector had turned up a chunk of shiny gold in his pan. Sam had been a part of that years before, back in Confederate Gulch, right after the war, when the rich deposits there turned out somewhere between ten and thirty million dollars' worth of gold. There had been a time when almost ten thousand people had swarmed around the region east of Helena, named Confederate Gulch in honor of the four men from Georgia that had first discovered the wealth buried in the land. It must have been quite a time! New towns rising up quickly to die as fast when the gold ran out or when fire ravaged the tinderbox buildings; men walking the streets with pockets heavy with gold dust; women calling out from tents and buildings along the way, offering themselves for that same gold; men like Runyon seated around tables in the saloons, trying to strike it rich in their own way without putting a hand to a pick or shovel. It must have been a time worth seeing. Certainly it was a time that would never come again.

I finished my meal and paid the bill. I moved back outside, squinting in the sunlight until my eyes adjusted to the brilliance. Runyon had gone into the saloon only a couple of doors down from the cafe. I decided I would find him and tell him who I was searching for. Obviously a man with a relative as famous as Luther Guthrie would be known to most of the people who had been around Helena for any length of time. Maybe Runyon could tell me just where to look.

I pushed my way into the saloon and glanced around until I saw Runyon seated at a corner table, studying his hand of cards. I headed toward him, then stopped suddenly in my tracks.

He was gambling with a man that looked terribly familiar, though I couldn't recall where I had seen him before. He was thin, with a red beard, and something about him filled me with caution. I stood transfixed for a moment, then the memory of a voice came back to me . . . a voice saying something about lightning striking and somebody's uncle biting his tongue in two.

Then I remembered. This was one of the fellows that had been hidden in the hills behind Guthrie's ranch that night, the night of the thunderstorm that had almost seared me with a flash of lightning. One of Madison's men, one of the riders. So they *were* here, they really had come to Helena, just as I feared. But where was Madison? He was not in the saloon, and the other man dealing cards with the red-bearded man and Runyon I had never seen before. I backed out through the door again, then peeped around the corner so I could keep an eye on the fellow. He was obviously unhappy about something; probably Runyon was cleaning him out with some sly deals.

That must have been the case, for suddenly the red-bearded man stood, his face growing so scarlet with apparent rage that I could hardly tell where the skin stopped and the beard began. He pushed his chair back violently and spoke in a loud voice.

"Why don't you try dealin' from the top of the deck, mister? I'm sick of your cheatin'—you'd best be prepared to take a lickin', 'cause I'm gonna take back my money right outta your skin."

The other man gambling with the pair backed away and headed out a back door. The bartender was watching Runyon and his challenger very closely, and the air in the room prickled as if with an electrical charge. Trouble not only was coming—it was here.

Runyon looked as cool as a trout in a frozen pond, never once blinking or looking frightened. Obviously this was no new game to him; he wasn't about to be taken by surprise by anything this fellow might pull. I recalled that Madison had called him Jake.

"When you accuse a man of cheating, it's a mighty serious charge," Runyon said calmly. "Some have died for less than that."

"And plenty have died for dealin' crooked cards, too," spit back Jake. "You'd best be prepared to tangle, 'cause nobody cheats Jake Crocker and gets away with it."

Runyon was up so fast that I couldn't tell what had happened until I saw Jake Crocker standing with a derringer aimed straight at his nose, the muzzle no more than two inches away from him. For a moment he and Runyon stood there in silence, and I wondered if my gambling companion was about to resort to murder.

"Get your tail outta my sight, and don't come around me again with your lies about cheating," growled Runyon. "I ought to shoot you, but you wouldn't be worth the wasted bullet. Now clear out."

I barely had time to step out of the way before the frightened man swept past me, not looking back one time. He mounted his horse and took off at a gallop, heading south. South. Maybe that was where Madison was holed up. If only I had a horse—I could follow Jake at a distance and find out for sure.

But that was impossible. He was out of sight quickly. I entered the saloon. Runyon was pouring a shot of whiskey and laughing for all he was worth. He raised his glass in greeting when he saw me enter.

"Mr. Hartford! You just missed the fun! Come and join me in a drink."

"No thanks. And you're wrong . . . I saw it all through the door. You do a pretty good job of taking care of yourself. But anyway, the reason I came in is I want to ask you a question. I'm looking for a local man, a merchant, who is related to Luther Guthrie. You know anyone like that?"

"Luther Guthrie . . . that's the cattleman, isn't it? I heard that he died a few days back."

"That's right. But do you know who that merchant might be?"

"I know, fella." It was the bartender speaking. "That would be Charles Cummins. He's a brother-in-law to Guthrie—Guthrie married his sister years and years ago. He runs a hardware store at the other end of town. Mighty pretty girl working with him now—Guthrie's daughter, I heard."

My heart leaped within me at the words. That was Jennifer he was talking about. She was alright, and soon I would see her.

"The other end of town—on this street?"

"No . . . next one over. You can't miss the store. It's two stories, painted white. The sign says 'Cummins Hardware.' "

I thanked the bartender and left him alone with Runyon. I headed down the street at a dead run, then turned the corner and headed toward the white building I could see at the other end of the street. I knew it was the hardware store even before I saw its sign. Halfway there I slowed, then stopped. Soon would come the meeting with Jennifer, and how she would react to my unexpected presence I had no idea. Steeling my nerves as best I could, I walked slowly toward the building.

It was a rather large place, two stories, with a multitude of plows, yokes, hoes, shovels, picks—all the things that were a part of the usual inventory of a western hardware store. And there were people about, too. Apparently Charles Cummins did a remarkable business. As I drew near I could see that the upstairs windows had lacy curtains, not the simple, functional ones like a business might have. I guessed that he lived above the store, and probably that was where Jennifer was staying.

My breath was coming rapidly as I mounted the porch, and I felt a cold sweat around my temples. Somehow I dreaded meeting Jennifer, yet I longed to see her. Probably I looked like an over-protective and over-anxious fool, running all the way from Miles City just to protect her from some vague threat, but now I knew that the move had been a wise one, for I had concrete evidence of Madison's presence in or near Helena. And besides that, I loved Jennifer, and I wanted to see her. And that, I emphasized to myself, was nothing to be ashamed of.

I looked inside before I entered, trying to find her. I didn't see anyone except a couple of men browsing about and looking over the stock of knives. A man in a canvas apron was behind the counter, figuring up a bill for a third customer. I took him to be Cummins. He finished his business and thanked the customer, then turned to greet me.

"Good day, sir. Anything I can do for you?"

Now this was a clumsy situation. I didn't know whether or not to try and explain who I was and why I was there, and for a moment I stammered unintelligibly, feeling a bit foolish.

"I beg your pardon?" he returned, frowning slightly.

"I'm looking for Jennifer Guthrie. Is she here?"

His face grew a bit cold then. He straightened up and inhaled audibly, eyeing me in quite a different manner than before.

"Why do you ask?"

I might have been offended at the question had

not understood the reason for it. Surely he knew about Madison and the threat he could pose to Jennifer should he ever find her, and his question was a protective measure.

"My name is Jim Hartford. I'm a . . . a friend of Jennifer from Miles City. Please—if she's here I'm sure she'll want to see me. May I speak to her?"

He looked doubtful, and for a time he said nothing. I felt embarrassed, but I could feel no anger toward him. Rather, I was glad that Jennifer was staying with someone who was so careful about her welfare. That's the way I wanted it.

"Sorry. There's no one here by that name. Now if there's nothing I can do for you, please excuse me. As you can see, there are customers I have to take care of."

That was that. I knew he would not let me see Jennifer no matter how persistent I might be. Feeling exasperated, I walked out of the store and back into the street.

I leaned up against the hitching post and thought the situation over. I knew Jennifer was somewhere in that store. She had not been downstairs, so obviously she must be in the upstairs living quarters. Now, if only I could get her attention somehow, without disturbing Cummins and maybe getting myself shot or run off at gunpoint . . .

I walked toward the alley between the store and the next building, a bakery. I ducked the window to avoid being spotted by Cummins, then rounded the back corner of the building.

There was a rough, brown, unpainted shed of weathered wood built up against the back wall of the store. The roof was of old shingles, and it sloped up slightly to meet with the wall of the main building. There was a window there, leading into the upstairs portion of the store. I looked at it doubtfully, not sure whether I should try the scheme that was formulating in my mind.

But I had to see Jennifer. I hadn't come all the way to Helena to be deprived of that privilege. Looking around, I found an old barrel, half filled with stagnant water, which I overturned and emptied. A miniature brown river swirled about my feet as I positioned the barrel at the corner of the shed and stepped on top.

I got a good grip on the roof of the shed and began to heave myself upward. It was surprisingly difficult; I felt much older than I had realized. But with much grunting and straining I managed to get one foot hung over the top of the shingled roof, then with a tremendous heave I rolled over on top.

I stood carefully and dusted myself off. The roof upon which I was standing didn't look any too strong, and it was with a trembling step that I moved forward. I could see only a few feet into the darkness of the window, and from what I could tell there was no sign of anyone being inside.

I inched over to the window, grimacing as the shingles snapped and creaked under my boots. When at last I reached the window I grabbed for the sill. I wanted to lean my weight against something besides the rotting roof that was giving way at least two inches beneath my feet. I shifted my weight onto my hands and looked through the dusty glass.

The window opened into something that looked like a large closet or storage room. There were old pieces of furniture stacked in it, along with a mop and broom and a few old buckets, as well as cobweb-covered rolls of cloth and piles of empty burlap sacks. I certainly would not find Jennifer in there.

Now I really didn't know what to do. I thought about trying to get the window open so I could crawl inside, but that seemed a bit criminal. If I were seen I might wind up in a cell instead of in Jennifer's arms. And anyway, I didn't want to startle her by popping up from nowhere. And to top it all off, the window was jammed.

Feeling rather ridiculous, I did the only thing possible—I tapped on the pane with my finger while softly calling Jennifer's name. If she happened to be anywhere near the storeroom she might hear me and let me inside. I wanted to call out more loudly, but I couldn't risk drawing the attention of anyone else.

For a long time I continued tapping and calling, but with no result. It was then that I heard above me a soft murmur, a kind of low, sustained hum that at first I could not identify. I glanced up.

There were two cats, both toms, and they were squaring off for battle right at the peak of the store's roof. Their voices blended into a kind of weird harmony as they looked closely at each other, every muscle stiff and tense, the only movement being the twitching of their whiskers and the back and forth movement of their tails. It looked like it was going to be a humdinger of a fight.

But I didn't have time to watch a couple of brawling animals, so I went back to tapping and calling for Jennifer. This time I did it a little more loudly, for obviously I was getting nowhere as it was. And at last I got results, for I saw the latch of the storeroom door slowly begin to turn, even as a sudden squalling above me heralded the commencement of war.

The door opened ever so slowly, and Jennifer's head peeked around it. I grinned broadly and waved, so glad to see her that I didn't even consider how strange the whole situation must have appeared to her.

She looked at me in obvious disbelief, and I saw her mouth forming my name. Then she smiled, her eyes brightening, and she threw open the door and moved to the window.

"Jim!" Her voice was slightly muffled through the glass. "What in the name of heaven are you doing here . . . and out on the roof at that?"

"I can't explain right now," I returned. "If you can get this blasted window open I'll come inside. Your uncle apparently didn't think I looked very trustworthy. He wouldn't let me see you."

"Oh, I'm so glad you're here—you can't imagine how glad!" She smiled and put her palm up against the glass. "Here . . . let me see if I can get this window open . . ."

She grasped the metal grips at the base of the window and gave a strong push while I did the same from the outside. The window creaked and groaned but did not open.

"It's jammed, Jim," she said.

"I know. But I think it gave a little. Try it one more time."

We did, and this time it opened. I stood face to face with Jennifer, and it all seemed too wonderful to be true. But she reached out her hand and touched me, and I knew that it was no fantasy. All around me ceased to exist—the roof, the window, the fighting cats above—and Jennifer became the sole reality in my universe. Her touch was warm and tingled against my skin like electricity. At once the whole world glowed with magic.

I hugged her close then, and suddenly I knew I had to kiss her. I would never have thought such a thing would even cross my mind, but so happy was I to see her that nothing in the world seemed too much to expect. I looked into her eyes and drew her close. Her breath quickened and her soft lips moved close to mine . . .

Two clawing, screaming, fighting balls of hot fur struck directly atop my head. I cried out in shock and threw myself backward, forgetting that I clutched Jennifer in my arms. Right through the open window she came, and when the rotting roof gave way beneath our combined weights, she, both cats, and I all tumbled through to land in one huge heap on the floor of the shed.

Jennifer uttered a word I had no idea she had even heard before, and the two cats made a sudden peace treaty and scampered off together. I lay stunned, watching the door of the shed open and staring up into the muzzle of a Sharps and on past it to the angry and flabbergasted face of Charles Cummins.

"Jennifer . . . what . . . how . . ." He lowered the rifle and stared at his disheveled niece, and I felt like crawling away like a miserable rat.

Chapter XVIII

It took quite a bit of time before Jennifer cooled down to the point she could convince her uncle that I wasn't a madman who had tried to carry her off. At last we got the whole confused mess cleared up, and I sat with a mug of hot coffee in my hand upstairs in Cummins' living quarters. He was seated across from me, apparently undecided about whether to like me, based on what Jennifer had told him, or to shoot me, based on what he had seen for himself. But no matter—at least he was accepting me. I had even received an invitation to move in with him and Jennifer, at least for a day or two. I would sleep on a pallet before the fireplace.

Cummins had closed the store when he heard that I had seen one of Madison's men in Helena. He had, of course, heard the story of our dealings with Madison from Jennifer, and he understood the danger the outlaw's presence posed to us. Jennifer was deeply concerned, and I myself felt quite apprehensive.

"This whole situation is hard to believe. Did that Crocker fellow see you?" Cummins asked.

"No. He was too worried about his own skin to notice."

Jennifer sighed. "What are we going to do, Jim? If Madison is in Helena, then we're as bad off as before. And if he lays eyes on either one of us . . . well, you know what might happen."

"I know, Jennifer. It isn't safe for either one of us here. I don't know what you'll think about this suggestion, but I believe that we should catch the first train back to Miles City. If Madison is here, I want to get you away. I ran from him once—I'll never do it again, not for my own sake. But I will take you away if it's necessary to keep you safe."

Cummins looked at me closely, his brow knit in thought.

"He's right, Jennifer. You know I love you and really am glad to have you here with me, but there's no point in staying if your life will be in danger. I think Miles City is the place for you. And anyway, you must realize that you own a large cattle ranch right now. You'll have to take care of it. You can't hide forever."

Jennifer turned on both of us, rage visible in her eyes.

"You don't understand—either one of you. I can't go back there, not until I've had time to think, to get used to the fact that Father is gone. The ranch is like a sort of hell to me now—I can't turn a corner or open my eyes in the morning without thinking of Father and the way he died. You don't know what it's like. You've never lost a father to a man like Josiah Madison."

I responded quietly. "But I've lost a brother. And I won't lose you."

Jennifer glared at me. "What do you mean, 'lose me'? Do you think I'm some possession of yours, something you own like a hat or a saddle? I think perhaps you'd better think again, Mr. Hartford!"

She turned and stalked out of the room, and I felt

my face turning red. Cummins stood watching me, and that made things not one bit easier.

I had presumed too much, it seemed. In the time I had been away from Jennifer I had come to idolize her, to look upon her as my own love. Now I was being forced to face the hard fact that it wasn't so. And that hurt pretty badly.

Cummins was obviously at a loss for words. The situation was a strange one for him. He had been dragged into it by chance, and he had at best only a sketchy knowledge of what was going on, in spite of the explanations he had heard from Jennifer. A sudden thought struck me: Cummins himself was not free from danger as long as Jennifer and I were near him.

"It will take her awhile to understand, Hartford," he said at length. "It must have been a hard blow, seeing her father die like he did. Luther Guthrie was not a gentle man, maybe even an unethical one, but he was always good to my sister and to Jennifer. I was truly sorry to hear of his death. I'm just glad that I was here. Jennifer needed someone to turn to."

I nodded and smiled at the man, but his words made me sad. How it would have thrilled me if Jennifer had turned to me in her time of grief! I would have loved to have been the one to dry her tears and comfort her. But that wasn't how it had been. Maybe I would just have to accept the fact that it would never be that way.

"I think we have one thing in our favor," said Cummins. "Madison has not seen either you or Jennifer around here, so obviously he won't be out looking for you. So as long as he doesn't know of your presence here you should be relatively safe."

"You said Jennifer wasn't here when I met you this afternoon," I said. "I assumed you were trying to protect her in case I was one of Madison's men. Am I right?"

"Yes, partly. I guess I just didn't like the idea of a stranger coming up unexpectedly and asking about her.

Of course, I had no idea then that Madison was in these parts. And she had mentioned your name to me several times, but for some reason it slipped my mind when you introduced yourself. Sorry."

"It's alright. I'm glad you're being careful with her. And I think it's good that you're keeping her up here away from the public eye. If Madison or one of his men came into town and saw her . . ."

"What about you? You could be just as easily recognized."

"I know. I'll have to keep a low profile too. I think we belong in Miles City instead of here, but until Jennifer's ready to go I don't plan to force her."

Cummins agreed. "I think you're right, Hartford. She'll go back when she's ready. Until then it will just be a matter of being careful."

That was for sure. We would have to be darned careful.

I waited until dark before I headed back to the room I had rented. I took up my pack and headed out gladly. The bedbugs could feed on someone else tonight; I was glad to have the pallet on the floor upstairs in Cummins' store. I was out in the street before I thought of Runyon. He would be gambling half the night, probably. But still I should leave him a note so he wouldn't think my possessions had been robbed. I scribbled one quickly on the back of an envelope and tacked it to his door. I didn't say where I was, for I didn't want to chance having the wrong eyes see it and get a little too much information.

I was out the door when the proprietor of the place called me down and demanded twenty-five cents for the room. I was aghast.

"I haven't even slept in it! I'm not paying you a cent!"

"I could have rented that room to another feller earlier today, but you was in it. You done cost me twenty-five cents, and I expect you to make it up. Hand it over!"

And rather than stand and argue with him, I did.

I felt cheated as I climbed the stairs to my sleeping quarters and lay down on the pallet. Cummins was softly snoring in his own bedroom, and I could hear Jennifer softly stirring about in hers. Strange it was to be this close to her. But there was still a distance between us that made me feel helpless and alone. Maybe time would close that distance. I certainly hoped so.

The next day was spent upstairs in the soft chair beside the fireplace. Jennifer stayed with me, and I found the company quite pleasant. Her anger had passed, though she gave no indication that her opinions had changed. It was clear that she cared for me at least a little—I had abundant evidence of that from past experience. But clearly my feelings for her went far beyond anything she felt for me—or at least beyond what she allowed herself to show.

Cummins had a good library, and lately I had read little, so now I did my best to make up for it. Learning had always been a passion of mine, and the one thing I liked least about the farming life I had always led was the lack of time to study and read. I had always managed to squeeze it in between chores, but never enough to really satisfy me.

Cummins had plenty of good volumes, both from European and American writers. I noticed several volumes by Twain on his shelf. I had been delighted by the work of that humorist many times over, and I picked up some of his books and began leafing through them. The day passed by slow and drowsy as I sat in that comfortable chair reading, and I felt a sense of lazy contentment.

I looked further into Cummins' book collection. Works by Shakespeare were there, along with a volume of popular modern poetry and a few of Paine's treatises. And of course there was the inevitable Bible. Most of the books were well-worn and dog-eared, showing that Cummins read as well as merely collected his books. And for that he gained my admiration, for

I respected men of learning. I hoped someday to be one myself.

Jennifer looked restless as she wandered about the place. I think the realization that we were pretty much prisoners here until the threat of Josiah Madison had passed was only just now beginning to strike her. Maybe she would see the sense in my suggestion of returning to Miles City, though I wasn't about to bring it up. Jennifer had suffered much, and I would force nothing on her unless I saw there was no other choice. So I leaned back once more and again started reading.

It was the middle of the afternoon when Cummins came back upstairs, looking rather weary.

"It's blasted busy down there today," he said. "I almost wish you two were working for me. You know, Hartford, I had Jennifer at work the first day she was here, but then I got to thinking I shouldn't have her out in public. It was just kind of an instinctive thing when I took her off work, but I'm glad I did.

"Anyway, I came up to deliver this to you. A railroad man brought it in a few minutes ago."

He handed me an envelope. I snatched it away quickly, intrigued. Who could be sending me mail here? And how did whoever it was know how to reach me?

The letter was from McCuen.

Dear Jim,

It took a lot of doing to find out where to reach you, but I have information I thought you would like to know. I hope this letter gets to you. I found out Mr. Cummins' name by asking around among local folks who know Guthrie's family.

As soon as you left for Helena I began thinking things through. Obviously we have not done a very effective job of taking care of Madison, so I did what I now think we should have done in the first place—I went to Fort Keogh and notified the

Army officials there about Madison, Thorne, and the whole business.

The reaction was predictable. While they were certainly glad to have the information, they were not at all pleased to be the last ones to find out about it. They did some checking on both Madison and Thorne. What they found out about our friend Nathan Thorne is worth knowing.

There is, in fact, a Nathan Thorne affiliated with the Secret Service. Madison's actions since the war have been considered subversive to the country, so the Secret Service has had Thorne and several other agents trying to trace the man down for years. And Thorne was scheduled to come to Miles City in response to the reports of Madison's presence here. The Fort Keogh staff knew he was coming, but his business here was unspecified to them.

The man you picked up on the railroad was checked over by the Fort Keogh doctor. Just as we thought, the man had been stabbed several times— after he was dead. And as you might suspect, checks by telegraph with Secret Service officials confirmed that the poor fellow matched the description of the true Nathan Thorne.

Which leaves some interesting questions. Why did our fraudulent Nathan Thorne take on the identity of a Secret Service agent and question us so closely about Josiah Madison? Why was he so dedicated to keeping his impersonation a secret that he was willing to murder the true Thorne? Does he have accomplices? If so, how many? Where does he get his information? Who was the man he met at the train station? And most of all, what is his interest in Josiah Madison?

There is something else you should know. Fort Ellis, near Bozeman, has received reports that a group of armed men matching the description of Madison and his riders has been spotted southeast of Helena. How the Army plans to deal with it I don't know, but I hope you and Jennifer will be careful. In my opinion you would be well advised to return to Miles City.

I hope you are enjoying your stay in Helena. Be careful of Madison. Please send my regards to Miss Guthrie, and I shall remain:

Yours truly,
Aaron McCuen

I folded the letter and sighed. Sometimes it was hard to believe all of this was real.

"Anything we should know?" quizzed Cummins.

"Yes, I think so." I filled him in on what McCuen had found out, explaining all the details that he didn't yet understand. He looked concerned, but at the same time he expressed hope.

"I'm glad the Army is into this," he said. "Maybe they will take care of that scoundrel before anyone else is hurt. This is the sort of thing for them, not for ranchers' daughters and Tennessee farmers and hardware merchants."

The day passed without further incident, and clouds began to gather in the heavens as the last light faded. I looked out the window at the rolling masses of dark clouds high above the buildings of Helena. The city appeared stark and small in comparison to the majesty of the violent sky. I felt small, insignificant.

The darkness fell, and the wind began whipping wildly, howling around the eves and corners of the buildings like a mournful, disembodied voice. I felt the desire to step outside and feel that wind, laden with the taste and smell of the coming rain, whipping against my face and hair.

I looked up and down the street. Deserted. Even the saloons did not have the steady in and out flow of customers that usually began at this time of day. The storm promised to be a wild, rough one, and apparently the threat of its impending explosion of lightning and rain was sufficient to drive everyone to shelter. But I had been cooped up all day; I wanted to taste that moist, moving air.

Surely it was safe. I could not see any sign of another human presence anywhere in the street. I headed out the door and down the stairs, then out onto the porch of the store. The lightning had begun, illuminating the dark clouds and the bare, exposed buildings with every flash, and the rumble of thunder was almost constant. A few scattered drops of rain struck my cheek, whipped beneath the sheltering porch by the moaning, wailing wind, a herald of the downpour to come.

I glanced up and down the street, still worried that someone might see me. Madison and his men might have come into town on a night like this, for even outlaws want shelter from lightning and rain. I thought back on the time I had watched them in the hollow of the hills behind Guthrie's ranch. If Jake Crocker was out there in the wilderness near Helena, surely he was worrying himself sick again, dreading the lightning. Let him worry—a long way from me and Jennifer.

Satisfied that I was truly alone, I sat down on the edge of the porch and watched the sky. Majestic, huge, unforgettable it was. A vastness filled with clouds and energy, lit with flashes of fire like the sparks from some heavenly anvil. I became engrossed in watching it.

A searing bolt of lightning leaped across the sky, followed a moment later by a tremendous jolt of thunder that shook the very ground. The noise faded slowly, like a low rumble, diminishing into nothingness.

And in the silence I heard a new sound, one that jerked my thoughts out of the clouds and lightning and sat them back down in the streets of Helena once more. It was a rider approaching.

The rider moved right down the middle of the street. He wore a dark, Mexican-style poncho, the hood pulled up for protection from wind and rain, and his horse plodded slowly. I could not see his face, though the glow of the burning tip of a cigarette cast a faint redness within the hood of the poncho. Whether or not he was watching me I could not tell.

It was Madison. I could sense it. Something in his stance in the saddle, the way he slumped, the way he gripped the reins . . .

He rode onward, not even glancing in my direction. The tip of the cigarette flared a brighter red as he inhaled a puff of smoke, then he was on past me, only his back visible. I shuddered.

Quickly I arose and moved back inside the building, then on up the stairs. How could I have been so foolish as to expose myself to him? I felt I should be shot.

I said nothing to Cummins or Jennifer about what had happened. They had been in the back room, not even knowing I had stepped outside, but they looked at me strangely when they reentered the room. I imagine I must have looked distressed.

Seated in the chair before the fireplace, I tried to convince myself that the man I had seen was not Madison. I hadn't even seen his face, and if he had noticed me at all he certainly hadn't shown it. It must have been some drifter passing through. I smiled to myself, relieved.

The rain had begun full force. I stood and went over to the window to watch it.

The streets were black like pitch, swept with rain. Upstairs in this secure building, warm and dry, I felt safe once more.

A lightning bolt ripped a jagged course through the sky, and for a moment the street was lit as if at noonday.

The rider was there, at the end of the street, facing the store. He sat like a statue, staring up at my window. Nothing more . . . just staring up at me as I watched him in the lightning's glow.

The light disappeared suddenly, and again the street was black. When the next flash came the rider was gone.

I cast myself down in the chair and stared at the dark window. A verse from the Book of Revelation played over and over through my mind:

". . . and I looked, and behold a pale horse: and his name that sat on him was Death, and Hell followed with him."

CHAPTER XIX

~

The next day I said nothing of what had happened to either Jennifer or her uncle. I didn't dare leave the security of my upstairs refuge, even though now hiding was almost pointless, and I felt like a tremendous fool for having so carelessly endangered myself and the others with me.

I spent much time staring out the window at the spot where I had seen Madison's shadowy figure the night before. It all seemed unreal; with a little self-argument I think I could have convinced myself that the whole thing had been merely a dream. But I couldn't afford to deceive myself. Josiah Madison now knew that I was here—he had obviously recognized me, and it seemed almost as certain that he would make some response to my presence.

I had never had any face-to-face contact with the man, though I had seen him indirectly more times than I liked. I could tell from his reaction to me last night that he knew me. I had been in Sam's cabin the night one of his riders had been shot, and I had been with

McCuen, Bacon, and Sullivan the day we were ambushed in the hills north of town. He might have even recognized me as the man who helped spring the ill-fated Luther Guthrie from his prison on the Guthrie ranch grounds. He had been given many opportunities to become familiar with my face.

I considered telling Cummins about the incident, but something kept me from doing so—something called pride. I found it impossible to admit that through my own carelessness I had put all of us in danger. Each time I thought of breaking down and confessing, my throat constricted and my heart pounded. I couldn't do it.

And the thought of again running from Josiah Madison was repulsive to me. I had determined in my mind that never, never again would I cower before him, and I was stubbornly set on keeping that determination. True, I had told Jennifer that I would run if it was necessary to keep her safe, but now that the situation had arisen I just couldn't make the move. The wisest thing we could do right now, I knew, would be to board the first train back to Miles City and put as much distance as possible between us and this place, but I shut the thought from my mind, deliberately not letting myself think of the possible consequences. I would not run. I would not run. Again and again I repeated the determination.

Jennifer must have noticed my anxiety, for she cast repeated covert glances at me all day, a puzzled expression on her face. I pretended I didn't notice.

"Jim," she said to me in the afternoon, "is something wrong? You haven't said two words all day."

"Nothing is wrong. Can't a man have a little peace without somebody jumping all over him about it?"

Immediately I regretted my unjustified rudeness, for I saw the hurt in her eyes. She lowered her gaze from my face and turned away. I felt immensely cruel

and even more foolish. I knew I should apologize, but
. . . well, maybe later.

I spent the rest of the day in the chair before the
window, looking out at the clouds rolling across the
sky. The town was still damp from the drenching it
had received the night before, but still the sky was free
of the ominous gray rain clouds that had lowered
around sunset yesterday, and in their place were huge,
billowed masses of snowy-white vapor floating high in
the heavens. It was beautiful, but I think thunder and
lightning would have better suited my mood.

I slept sporadically that night, every noise in the
walls and creaking in the joists making me jump. I
arose several times to go over to the window and look
out on the moonlit street, searching for some sign of
my enemy. Each time I returned to my pallet relieved,
for there was no sign of Madison, yet paradoxically
also perturbed, for the longer he waited to strike the
longer I had to endure the misery of dread.

The next morning I knew that I had to head out
to face the world or lose my mind. I had snapped at
Jennifer again, this time bringing tears which she tried
unsuccessfully to hide, and I felt the only thing that
would keep me from hurting her again would be a
good walk. After all, I reasoned, since Madison was already aware of my presence, was there any reason to
go on hiding? And with that bit of logic spurring me
onward, I picked up my hat and started out the door.

It was another beautiful day, and I enjoyed the
warmth of the sun against my face. Helena was busy
today, a general bustle going on in every store, wagons
and buggies moving in all directions, the drivers cursing and shouting at street stragglers and other drivers,
women stepping primly along the boardwalk. Children
splashed the contents out of remnants of puddles, and
lazy dogs basked in the sunlight, ignoring all around
them. Here in the bright glow of everyday reality,
Madison seemed only a vague and formless threat at

most. I stepped along with great vigor, whistling beneath my breath.

Leaned up against a hitching post, rolling a cigarette, I saw Runyon. I headed toward him, calling and waving. He lifted a finger for a moment, then licked the rice paper up and down its length before sealing it in place around the tobacco. He struck a match on the bottom of his boot, then lit the cigarette. A white cloud streamed from his nostrils to hang in the air and then be whisked away into nothingness by the draft from a passing buggy.

"Good day, Hartford! I haven't seen you around. How's Helena treating you?"

I shrugged and smiled, for that was a question I couldn't really answer. "I'm surprised to see you out in the morning. I would have figured you were dealing cards all night and sleeping in the day," I said.

"There are occasions when the day is just too beautiful to sleep away," he said. "And anyway, I only sleep when it's absolutely necessary. Too much of a bother, you know. By the way, I found the note you left for me. Nice of you. Where are you staying? The note didn't say."

I saw no harm in telling Runyon where I was. "I'm staying with a hardware merchant-friend of mine. I sleep on the floor, but it's free, so I'm not complaining."

Runyon gave a powerful drag on his cigarette that consumed at least a quarter of an inch of tobacco. "Don't reckon I'd gripe about that, either. Come over to the cafe with me and have something to drink."

"What are you doing drinking in a cafe? The strongest thing you'll get there is black coffee."

"In the morning that's plenty good for me. C'mon. I'll buy. I had a streak of luck last night—really cleaned out an old cowpoke."

We found a cafe and ordered coffee. It was strong enough to eat the rust off a crowbar, but it was good-tasting. I sipped it slowly, though, to avoid eating away my gullet.

"Well, what's been going on around here?' I asked idly. "I haven't heard much news lately."

"Only important thing I've heard is something folks were talking about around the table last night. There was some sort of vigilante action down south of town. Some soldiers from Fort Ellis found six or seven men strung up to a tree, like it had been a lynching party. I have no idea who it was. Folks were doing a lot of speculating, but in my book it doesn't amount to a hill of beans. I figure some rancher found some rustlers and just took care of them."

I looked away from Runyon, thinking. Six or seven men . . . south of town . . .

"You say you have no idea who they were?" I quizzed, perhaps a bit too eagerly. "No idea at all?"

Runyon grinned as if he were bemused a bit by my intense questioning. "You must be taking quite an interest in this, Hartford! No, I don't know who they were. Nobody else does either."

I was thinking of the man who had come to the doctor's office in Miles City claiming to be Nathan Thorne. If he had been working with others, as apparently he was, then possibly Madison's men had gotten to them and wiped them out. And of course, it might be just the opposite. Maybe one of the men hanging from a tree had been Josiah Madison, killed by the mysterious imposter of Nathan Thorne. And if that was true, then no longer was there any threat to Jennifer and me.

I stayed and talked to Runyon awhile longer, but it was only with real effort that I did so. I was almost trembling in excitement; maybe the danger now was over and I could again rest easily. I wanted to question Runyon further about the lynching, but I feared arousing his curiosity about my interest any further, so I let it go.

Runyon at last left to crawl into his twenty-five-cent-a-night bed, and I headed back to the store. I was back up the stairs in a flash, and I think that Jennifer immediately recognized a difference in my attitude. She smiled.

I apologized for my earlier rudeness, and she laughed it off. "I think something must have been bothering you," she said. "Is everything alright now?"

"Yes. I think maybe everything is just fine." I hugged her, not even worrying about how she would respond to such a forward gesture. To my surprise she hugged back.

I didn't tell her all that Runyon had told me for fear she would only be all the more disappointed if Madison turned out to be still living. But I did tell the story to Cummins when he came up after closing the store.

"That's good," he said. "But let's not get too over-confident until we know for sure that he's dead. If one of the lynched men is Madison, then there's no way that will be kept a secret."

"You're right. That's why I didn't tell Jennifer about it. No point in building up false hopes."

"Have you had any luck in convincing Jennifer to go back to Miles City?"

"No . . . but then I haven't really tried. I can't blame her for wanting to avoid that ranch. I have no fond memories of the place myself."

"Yes, but if she doesn't decide on her own in a day or so, I think I'm going to insist. I'm certainly glad to have you two here with me, but Jennifer can't afford to let the Muster Creek Cattle Company sit in limbo like this."

Cummins was right. After some thought I told him that if he decided soon to send Jennifer back to Miles City, even against her will, I would help him out.

Jennifer prepared a delicious supper of pork, beans, and sweet potatoes, topped by fat brown biscuits, and I ate far more than was good for me. After the dishes had been cleaned up I sat with her by the window.

"Jennifer, have you given any thought to the future? Do you plan to stay here permanently?"

"I don't know, Jim. I can't afford to neglect the ranch I've inherited. Father always expected that someday it would be in my hands, and he taught me what I need to know to run it. I expect that someday I'll go back, maybe even soon. Just don't pressure me."

"I'm sorry. Maybe it's not even my business. But I want you to let me help you in any way I can when the time comes. I hope you will."

Jennifer smiled, and her eyes looked so beautiful and soft that it was all I could do to keep from drawing her close and kissing those lovely lips. The fact that I couldn't do it made it only worse.

"You've already been plenty of help, Jim—more than you might realize. I hope you know I appreciate it."

I felt a warmth stealing over me. It was a good thing I wasn't wearing a hat—the way my head was swelling I think I would have burst the sweatband.

And I sensed that the time was right to clear the air about my ill-timed implication of romance between us that I had fostered after coming to Helena. "Jennifer ... I'm sorry about what I said the other day, that hint that there was something, well, special between us. I had no intention of being improper. I just thought, well ... I guess I was wrong."

She stood suddenly, moving toward her bedroom door. I felt like kicking myself in my own thick head. Clearly I had made another blunder ...

"Jim?"

"Yes?"

"You weren't wrong." And with that she closed her door, leaving me to sit in a daze.

I slept peacefully that night, and my dreams were serene.

It was very late when I awoke, gasping for breath.

My lungs were choked with hot, raw smoke. Unbearable heat struck me. In a moment it all sunk in, and I was up, calling, screaming Jennifer's name, trying to breathe, choking.

The heat was incredible, and smoke flooded every corner of the room. It was a searing, cutting smoke that ate into my lungs like hot acid. I staggered toward Jennifer's door, feeling increasingly weaker.

The latch was hot as if by a forger's flame, but I ignored the pain and threw open the door. Hot air and smoke struck me in the face like a hammer blow, and I fell back.

The air on the floor was clearer, and I gasped, filling my injured lungs with air. Then I crawled forward, through Jennifer's door, calling her name.

I could see her form crumpled before me on the floor, just beside her bed, a bed now roaring in flames. Every muscle straining, I inched toward her, the distance only a few feet, yet seemingly endless. With every movement I grew weaker, fainter.

My hand grasped hers, and I began dragging her limp body after me, moving back out into the main room again, so slowly that I thought the building would collapse about us before I made it to safety. Flames licked at the walls all around, and now even the air just above the floor was growing too hot and smoky to be breathable.

A door opened, the door to the landing and stairway that led down to the store. Cummins' voice reached me amid the sound of flaming timbers.

"Jim! Here is the door!"

I forced myself up to my feet, now not breathing at all, for the air was poison and hot. I grasped Jennifer, then lifted her up to my chest, covering her mouth and nose with my hand while struggling to see through the thick, flame-illuminated smoke that was everywhere.

I reached the landing, and Cummins was beside me.

"The stairs . . . the stairs are burning!"

He was right. Flames were shooting up the enclosed staircase, tongues of fire licking at us as if through an open door to hell.

I remembered the window, directly beside me. It was a second story window, but then it seemed the only escape.

"Hold Jennifer, quick!" I said to Cummins. He took her from me, his face red and lungs gasping.

With one kick of my bare foot the glass of the window shattered, and the flames roared up the stairs with increasing fervor. I pushed away the jagged edges of broken glass and moved my legs outside, sitting on the sill long enough to bark out an order:

"Toss her down! I'll catch her!"

Then I leaped. I struck the earth and rolled, and then I was conscious of others around me. Voices exploded all around as I struggled to my feet.

"Lord . . . here's one!"

"His pants are on fire . . . beat 'em out!"

"There's two others above . . ."

My strength faded suddenly, the world spinning and going dark. I collapsed into a senseless heap, my last thought being that Jennifer was still up there in the heat and flame, and I could not save her.

I awoke in a soft bed, a cool, damp cloth sponging my forehead. I looked up into the face of a middle-aged woman I had never seen before.

"There we are . . . back awake again. We were pretty worried about you."

"Where am I?" My mouth was filled with the taste of acrid smoke.

"You're safe, far away from the store."

"The others . . ."

"They're fine. The folks around caught Cummins and the girl when they jumped. They got out just before the stairway collapsed."

Jennifer was alright. With that assurance I drifted off to sleep, if the stupor into which I fell can justly be called that. I awoke again to brighter sunlight, feeling much stronger.

Jennifer was there, smiling down at me. She looked pale, though on her neck and arms there were red blisters. Some of her lovely auburn hair was singed, but still she was beautiful.

"Hello, Jim."

"Jennifer." I smiled, then grew solemn. "The store . . ."

"The store is burned down. We're at the home of Alex Murphy, another local merchant. And Jim . . ."

"Yes?"

"One man says he saw a fellow splashing coal oil on the porch of the store before the fire started. The witness was drunk and sleeping in an alley when he woke up and saw it."

I exhaled firmly. "Madison. He's the one, no doubt about it."

"Yes. I just wonder how he found us."

I stared at the ceiling, not answering. Then I looked again at her.

"Jennifer, we're leaving. We're going back to Miles City by the first train. Your uncle can come too, if he wants."

"He says he's staying. He says he won't let Madison beat him."

"Then you've already decided to leave?"

"Yes . . . what choice do we have?"

"It's settled, then. And Jennifer . . . we're not going to let Madison beat us, either."

CHAPTER XX

I felt intensely guilty when I saw Cummins again, for in one sense I was responsible for the loss of his store. It had been because of my carelessness that Madison had discovered my presence in Helena, and purely because of that that he had burned the hardware store. Of course, I had no proof that Madison had set the blaze, but I could think of no other culprit.

But Cummins did not know that Madison had seen me, thus he could not place the blame on me where it belonged. He simply looked on the whole thing as a mystery and let it go at that.

"I don't know how that devil found out you two were here," he said, "but I guess it isn't too surprising. Anyway, I'm just glad no one was seriously hurt. Mostly I'm grateful that we were able to get Jennifer out."

"Amen to that, Mr. Cummins," I said. "Have you checked on the railroad schedule?"

"Yes. There will be a train leaving at five this evening. I've already arranged for you and Jennifer to be on it."

Good, I thought. There won't be any wasted time. If Madison would go to the trouble of setting the fire, then surely he would check to see if his work had been completed. Once I discovered I had escaped the blaze he would surely try again.

There was little packing to be done, for most of our possessions had been destroyed, and we wore borrowed clothing. More than anything I regretted the loss of my pistol, for it had cost me good money and had been a fine firearm. And now I was pretty much defenseless should I encounter Madison. Perhaps it was just as well. I could never hope to stand up to him in a gunfight.

It hurt me to see the ruined shell of a building that was all remaining of the hardware store. Cummins had taken a tremendous loss. I promised myself that I would help him get back on his feet if it took every cent I made in the next ten years. It was my duty.

Jennifer bade her uncle good-bye when we reached the station that evening. The train awaited us a huge metal racing horse smoking and chugging and chomping at the bit. Jennifer had tears in her eyes as we looked out the window of the passenger coach and waved at Cummins.

"Do you think Madison will hurt him, Jim?"

I tried to sound confident as I assured her that her uncle would be alright. "Madison would have no reason to harm him," I said. "I don't really think h would even know him. It's me and you that he's after."

I wished I hadn't made that last statement as soon as I had done it. It didn't make Jennifer rest any easier—or me, for that matter. But it was true, and a long as we were in the same region as Madison w were in danger.

Cummins had gotten us seats in the second class section of the train, a slightly more luxurious ride tha the immigrant coach, though nothing spectacular. Bu at least Jennifer and I were on padded seats instead of rough wooden benches, and the cursing, swearing, uncleaned folk of the wilder side of the territory were not so close at hand. I realized that my desire to protect Jennifer from that aspect of life was pointless, for she had grown up on a rough-and-tumble cattle ranch and probably had seen much more than I ever would. But a man in love doesn't always think rationally, and if I was anything I was most definitely a man in love.

Jennifer sat close to me, and I loved every minute of it. I pretended to not notice, of course, and she did the same, and we both sat enjoying and acting as if we weren't as the miles rolled away behind us. I looked out across the hills and watched the day ending, the sun glowing brilliant red behind us.

I talked to her of the things I had seen, of Tennessee and my home near Cumberland Gap. I told her of the thousands who had traveled through the Gap when the first doors to the west were being opened. I told her of Gabriel Arthur, the young white servant captured by Indians and saved from death at the burning stake by a Tomahitan chief. I told her of Dr. Walker, who named the Gap, and of Daniel Boone, who in his life had become one of the most famous of all woodsmen. Jennifer listened closely, enthralled, for she had never been east in her life, nor south, and all of what I told her was pretty much new to her.

She talked too, telling me all she had learned during the years of watching her father develop his extensive cattle business. She told me the stories she had heard from him, how he had driven herds from Texas along the Chisholm Trail before settling in Montana. She talked of the coming of the railroad and how life was changing as a result. She spoke of the immense growth of the cattle business in the territory, and how it was becoming increasingly important for ranchers to cooperate on roundups, for the overcrowded range resulted in a huge mix-up of herds, with cattle of varied brands running alongside each other. I had never thought of ranching as anything other than hard labor, but now I could see that it had its own special sort of magic, and it could be a profession that could hook a man and not let him go. Suddenly I understood men like Luther Guthrie a little better. He had been in the territory for years; it was his land, his and other men like him. No wonder he had been reluctant to see his old way of life vanishing, fading away bit by bit.

The darkness came, and the train became a fiery serpent winding its way through dark hills. Here in the dimly lit coach, seated beside a protecting window and moving at high speed, the land outside seemed a bit eerie and unreal. As the trees whipped by like phantoms, I felt myself growing drowsy from the mesmerizing effect of it, and my chin began to drop down to my chest. Jennifer was already asleep, curled up against my shoulder.

I don't know how long I had slept when I felt a gentle nudge against my stomach, then another. I raised my head, confused and groggy, and forced my eyes open.

How can a man describe what it is like to look right into the face of death at a time when he expects it least? How can a man put in words what it feels like to know that what he has dreaded most is now a stark and immediate reality?

Madison sat across from me, grinning, evil, with his single dark eye glittering in the light of the flickering wall lamps. So intense was the shock that for a moment I sat stiffly and stared into his face, numb and wordless. Jennifer stirred beside me, and I heard her gasp when she, too, saw the apparition that had apparently materialized from nowhere, now grinning in a sort of evil triumph in the seat facing us. All hope drained from me.

"You know me." Madison's voice was low, almost inaudible.

"Yes. And you know me."

"I know you . . . and that you're the one behind

everything that has been happening. I know that you're
going to pay."

"You're going to kill us?" Jennifer's voice trembled, yet she spoke clearly and with courage.

"Of course. I can't let you live after what you've
done."

"And what have either of us done to you?"

Madison's face turned a deep crimson with rage,
and my heart pounded faster. "How can you look at
me and tell me you don't know what you've done?
You've been like a curse to me. Every time your ugly
face has turned up something has gone wrong. First
you show up and one of my men gets killed outside
that damn ranch cabin. You turn up at Guthrie's ranch
and my men almost get wiped out by those miserable
ranchers. You and your friends tail me and my men
into the hills. You put the Army on our tails. Carson
and his riders get to my men and wipe 'em out just at
the same time you show up in Helena. Everywhere I've
seen you there's been trouble. You're a curse, a jinx.
And you're gonna pay for it . . . you too, lady. I can't
have anybody like you around to identify me to the
law."

I knew his threat was not idle. But I suspected that
even Josiah Madison would hesitate to pull a trigger in
the midst of a filled railroad car where escape would
be difficult. No . . . he probably had something different in store for us.

I was confused by his reference to "Carson and his
riders," for that was a new name to me. But whoever
this mysterious Carson was, he had apparently massa-
cred Madison's men, though obviously Madison himself had escaped. So now the outlaw was alone.

Or so I thought. Something cold touched the back
of my neck, and I jumped. I twisted my head to look
at the man who so casually had touched the blade of
a knife to my skin. It was Jake Crocker, red beard, bad
smell, and all.

"Well, Jess," he said, calling Madison by his alias

rather then his true name, "it looks like we got 'em where we want 'em. What are you gonna do?"

Madison smiled in a way that made my blood run cold. "You stay here and make sure nobody goes out on the back platform," he said. "Me and my friends will be taking care of a little business back there. Now get up slow, you two, and move careful and easy."

I saw the glint of a small handgun in his grasp, and I knew it was useless to defy him. Slowly I stood, and Jennifer stood with me, clutching my hand.

"Now move on to the rear of the car. We're gonna go out and get a little fresh air."

We obeyed, trembling, not knowing what was coming, though expecting certain death. People watched us, no one knowing or caring about what was taking place.

We exited through the rear door of the car and stepped out onto the platform, Madison after us.

"Your name's Hartford, ain't it?" he said to me, grinning. "I reckon that was your brother whose throat I slit. I enjoyed that, you know—and I think the same will do for you."

His left hand whipped out a long and frightening knife in one deft motion. Grinning, he lunged out at me before I expected it. Only by throwing up my hand did I keep the blade from slashing my throat open. My hand took the worst part of the cut, and blood dripped from it onto the platform floor as I moved quickly to evade his next thrust.

"God! Jim, watch out!" Jennifer cried.

Madison was laughing insanely as he again stabbed out at me, this time ripping away a portion of my shirt and scratching my skin. I wanted to leap at him, but his pistol was still gripped in his other hand and pointed at me, and I couldn't risk taking a shot at such close range. And Jennifer was there, too, so a bullet might strike her even if by some miracle it missed me.

Jennifer moved unexpectedly, throwing her entire

weight against Madison, upsetting him. He fell back, cursing, and suddenly his gun hand was pinned to the wall. Jennifer held his wrist with both hands, crying out for me to grab the gun.

I saw the knife moving toward her, and at once I leaped. The blade passed deep into my thigh, and I cried out. Jennifer knocked Madison's hand hard against the wall, and the gun fell from his grasp. With one swift kick she knocked it from the platform to the ground at the foot of the grade.

Madison drew his knife back again and started to stab with it once more. But this time I managed to catch his arm and stop the blade from striking. Jennifer fell back, and Madison struggled to his feet, straining against my restraining arm, his free hand beating into my back and head.

I wrestled with his arm, but to no avail. His strength was incredible, and with the blood draining from the wound in my leg it was all but impossible to hold him back. My grip on his arm was weakening, and I knew it would be only a matter of moments before he broke free again.

"The ladder, Jennifer! Get up the ladder!"

It took her a moment to understand the meaning of my command. There was a brakeman's ladder running up the back of the coach, and now it seemed to be the only escape route for Jennifer. I expected that Madison would finish me off in only a moment, but at least Jennifer could run, even if to so poor a refuge as the top of the speeding train.

She was on the ladder, her knuckles white on the bone as she clung to it. The rumbling of the train made it difficult for her to climb, but she managed to work her way upward, until at last she disappeared from my sight, and I knew she was on top.

Madison shoved me backward, just as the rear door of the car opened and Crocker came out.

"You want me to shoot him, Jess? Should I shoot him?"

Madison said nothing, but instead lunged at me, knife blade extended. How I managed to evade the blade I never knew, but he grunted as he fell past me to the railing, striking his head. At that moment Crocker drew his pistol.

More out of desperation than anything else I lunged at him, knocking the pistol aside and making it impossible for him to aim at me. Madison was stunned from his fall against the railing, so for the moment at least he was not a threat. Crocker was taken by surprise by my tactic, and as he stood gaping, the breath knocked out of him, I swung a hard right against his jaw, the impact of my fist shattering the bone and sending him slumping to the platform floor.

Without hesitation I swung up onto the ladder and began to climb. I reached the top of the heaving, rolling train and looked across.

Jennifer crouched down at the other end of the car, a man beside her. For a moment I was shocked to see him there, but in the moonlight I saw a light glimmer, then a lantern was lit. It was the brakeman, the man who rode atop the train in almost all kinds of weather.

"Here now, who are you?" he called.

"It's alright—it's Jim!" Jennifer said.

"Well, where are them others, the ones who was botherin' you?" he asked. Then he spoke once more to me. "Well, come on up, if that's what you plan to do, and be quick about it. Let's have a look at you."

He was obviously confused by this strange situation, and he had a right to be. But apparently Jennifer had told him of what was happening, for he was clearly looking out for her, and wasn't going to let me near her until he was sure I wasn't one of the men seeking to harm her.

"I told you, he's alright. He's my friend, the one who was helping me. Don't hurt him!"

Gasping for breath, I pulled my body prone across the top of the rumbling car. "Madison is stunned. The other fellow too. Nowhere for us to run . . ." I panted until I had caught my breath. "You got a gun, mister?"

"No sir, I don't, and if I did I don't think I would give it to you. I don't like this business of fights and climbin' up here where you ain't supposed to be. So how about you two headin' on down where you should be . . . hey, now! Who are you?"

I stood quickly, wheeling around. Crocker's head was poking up over the edge of the car, blood streaming from his broken jaw. And before I had time to gather my wits, his right hand came up, gripping his pistol. I cursed myself for having not taken it from him just as he fired a quick shot that appeared to be aimed at no one in particular.

The brakeman was caught full in the chest, and he grunted loudly as he toppled from the speeding car to land in a rolling, contorted heap at the foot of the grade. His lantern lay on top of the car, rolling from side to side, the light flickering brightly.

I grabbed the lantern just as Crocker lifted his pistol once more, and before he could squeeze off the shot that would take off the top of my head, I swung the lantern square at his face.

The lantern shattered on impact, and suddenly the man was covered with flaming liquid, glaring in the darkness like a human torch. I saw the shocked, agonized expression on his face for only an instant before he let go his grip on the ladder and fell headlong from the train, his dying wail resounding.

Even after he had landed in a silent heap on the track I saw the flames licking at his dead body. And I knew that the next man up the ladder would be Madison.

I could think of nothing to do but try to get Jennifer as far away as possible from where he would be. It would be a one-on-one battle, one which I would surely lose. I had to get Jennifer away.

I grasped her hand and began moving toward the

front of the train. "C'mon!" I cried. "We're going to have to jump the cars!"

I found that running along the top of a moving train was something like riding a bucking bronco while standing on its back. But we both managed to keep our balance as we moved steadily forward, leaping from car to car, the smoke from the engine choking us, the smokestack showering us with sparks.

"If we can reach the engine—maybe we can get the attention of the engineer . . . he might have a gun . . ." I gasped out the words to Jennifer, though with the roaring of the engine and the singing of the wind in our ears I'm not sure that she heard me at all.

We were almost to the front car when I looked back over my shoulder. Madison was there, his knife gripped in his teeth, leaping over the gap between two cars, his single eye glittering with fury. I knew that in a moment he would be upon us. There was no time to try to get the engineer's attention.

"Jim! Look up ahead!"

Jennifer's cry was voiced with such urgency that I obeyed. And when I saw what had caused her to cry out I forced her down, my hand grabbing for anything at all to keep us from falling from the top of the train.

Before us on the track was a huge barricade of logs, completely across the track. The train had rounded a bend and illuminated the huge structure with its dim forward light far too late for the engineer to do anything about it.

The impact was beyond anything I had experienced in my life, and I thought my fingers would be torn from the roots as I grasped with one hand to the edge of the car and to Jennifer's arm with the other. For a long time there was a horrible commotion of loud cries, screeching wheels, burning smoke and ash, and flying, shredded wood.

Then as suddenly as it had come, it was over. The train was motionless, miraculously not derailed, and shattered, massive logs were everywhere. Screams came from the interiors of the passenger cars below us.

It was then that men emerged from the darkness of the forest, pistols, rifles, and torches gripped in their hands.

CHAPTER XXI

In the glowing torchlight I recognized the man who had come to Miles City claiming to be Nathan Thorne.

"Hartford! You alright up there?" He called out as if he was concerned for my safety, but at the same time he was brandishing a pistol in my direction. I simply stared back at him, then over to Jennifer. She was shaken up considerably, but not injured. I suddenly became conscious of the pain in my leg, and when I looked down I noticed my pants were deeply stained with blood, and I could feel a scab hardening where Madison had stabbed me. I felt thankful that an artery had not been severed.

People began to move out of the train, slowly, carefully, obviously frightened by the sudden jolting stop and the crowd of men awaiting them outside.

"Is this a holdup?" a man asked.

"No sir. You haven't got a thing we want," said Carson. "If everyone will cooperate there's no reason for anybody to be hurt. Men, start gathering pistols from these good passengers."

No one tried to stop them, no one pulled a gun except to hand it over. All of the men—some fifteen in number—were heavily armed.

Jennifer and I moved down a ladder on the side of the engine and joined the other train passengers who stood in a semicircle around the gunmen. Many were the cold stares, many the expressions of fear. But few words were spoken, for the realization that this was no robbery was beginning to spread. But if not a robbery . . . then what?

I thought of Madison, and turned. He approached, apparently unhurt by the collision, but two of the gunmen held guns pressed into his back. I looked over at the handsome, fraudulent Thorne. In his eyes was an expression of triumph.

He strode toward Madison, staring at him, laughing a bit beneath his breath in a way that was rather unnerving. The leader looked at the scowling outlaw with a mixture of hatred and delight. Madison returned the gaze with a blank stare, then he looked over at me with an expression of hatred. But there was something else in his expression, too, a childish questioning, asking me why this was happening, why once more my presence had brought him disaster. I had no answer. I drew Jennifer close to me, and realized that we were both trembling.

"Well, Carson, you've got me. What now?"

Carson . . . Madison had called him Carson! So that was the answer! It had been this man and his companions that had wiped out Madison's gang south of Helena. It had been this Carson who had impersonated Nathan Thorne in Miles City after attempting to kill the true Thorne on the train, and it had been him that had gone back into the doctor's office to finish the job he thought he had botched. Carson . . . who was he, and why was he doing all of this? I was intrigued.

"It's judgment day, Madison. It's your judgment

day at last. For all you have done to so many you are going to pay, for the sake of every life you've taken, every woman you've widowed, every son of the south you've tortured and maimed. It's time to make amends, after all these long years."

Madison smiled darkly. "And how do you propose to take care of me, Carson? How are you going to get your satisfaction?"

Carson wheeled around and faced the encircling train passengers, a crowd of mingled humanity from every level of western society. He stared at each of us in turn, and all mumbling faded, all shuffling about ceased. Every mind had its own questions about this, and clearly Carson was about to provide answers.

"Friends, you are not here to idly watch what will happen. You are witnesses of something that too often has escaped those who deserve it—justice. This, good people, is a trial. A trial of this man—Colonel Josiah Madison, the murderer of the Bryant's Fork prison camp, the creator of atrocities too numerous and too horrible to discuss in public. Yet they must be discussed, they must be brought to light. And most important of all, Josiah Madison must pay for them."

"Are you not goin' to rob us?" a man asked.

Carson laughed. "No sir. I have no need of any of your possessions. All I desire of you is one thing—that each of you witness what we are going to do, so you will know that justice has been done, and that what you see will not be idle murder. You should count this as a gift, the result of Providence. Beneath God's heaven, at last a sore is going to be healed. A debt is going to be paid. Justice is going to be done."

Jennifer leaned toward me and whispered, "He's obsessed, Jim. Almost like Madison himself." She was right. Carson didn't seem my idea of a sane man.

Since hearing the name Carson my mind had been working, straining to pull some item from my memory, some special significance connected with that name. But so far I had been unable to recall just what that significance was. It seemed, though, that Sam had mentioned the name at some point.

"The court to try Colonel Josiah Madison, formerly of the United States Army, is now in session," Carson said. "The defendant will be seated. Since he has no counsel he will be allowed to speak in his own defense, but only when given permission by the man who will serve as judge—Mr. Morgan Samuel." He gestured toward one of the gunmen, a one-armed man who handed his weapon to his neighbor and seated himself on a stone.

Morgan Samuel . . . another vaguely familiar name. Again the conviction that at some point I had heard Sam speak of him. It was beginning to make sense now . . .

"Madison, here is your jury. You will recall Mr. William Myers, Mr. Amos Hodge, Mr. Tom Bradlin, Mr. Ben Carrington . . ."

As he went through the list I suddenly remembered. Sam *had* mentioned these names before—when he talked of his days in the Bryant's Fork prison camp. Lord in Heaven, could it be? Had these men, these fellow prisoners of Sam, pursued Madison all of these years? Did they hate him so much that they had followed him for all this time just for the pleasure of giving him the same hell he had given them? The evidence stood before me.

"Friends, seat yourselves where you are. You shall be our witnesses, you shall watch as Josiah Madison pays for his crimes." Carson wheeled and strolled back and forth, his hand rubbing his chin, as two gunmen wrestled Madison to the earth and forced him to sit. Clearly, Carson was going to be the prosecutor in this farce of a trial. And who was in doubt about what the verdict would be? Madison was as good as dead, and he knew it.

Since the name of Josiah Madison had been spoken, the crowd behind me had whispered among itself and stared at the man. The name was infamous, the subject of many legends, and to actually see the man in the flesh, being tried by a court of his victims, was something beyond the wildest fantasies of any of them.

The trial got going at full swing, the list of charges being lengthy. Specific atrocities were enumerated in gory detail, and I saw many women and not a few men go pale and cover their faces with trembling hands. But still Carson continued, listing the crimes from memory without a single stammer or moment of hesitation. He had clearly gone over that list many times, pounding it into his memory until it could be called forth with ease. For almost half an hour he continued, and when he mentioned the crimes committed against the men now sitting in judgment against the defendant, shirts were pulled down and sleeves rolled up to reveal scars that served as evidence of the truth of the charges. The "judge" Morgan Samuel revealed the stump of his arm as Carson described the way Madison had chopped it off, and I felt ill. Many in the crowd seemed on the verge of fainting or losing their suppers.

Madison sat like a statue, seemingly unmoved by it all, but his fists were clenched and his arm trembled slightly. He stared at Carson throughout the oration, the moonlight and torchglow bathing the whole scene in an eerie light.

The jury looked like a congregation of phantoms, sitting very still, their faces stony. I noticed for the first time that some of them were dressed in the ragged remnants of Confederate uniforms, covered with patches and very dirty. I think it must have been somewhat of a symbolic gesture, and the effect apparently did not go unnoticed by the silent defendant, for occasionally he would cast a glance at the silent group, covering his fear with a veneer of calmness that looked increasingly thin.

Carson finished his list of charges and dropped into sudden silence, during which he looked first at Madison, then at each of the jurors, if the group deserved such a title. At last he turned again to Madison.

"How do you plead, sir? Do you deny the truth of these charges? If so, then speak your defense."

Madison stared at him, and his lip trembled slightly. But he said nothing.

"Speak, devil! Speak or let your silence serve as a guilty plea!"

Still no words.

Carson stomped his foot like an impatient child. "Speak! Or we'll pronounce sentence right now!"

Madison seemed to swell with sudden rage. And with unexpected suddenness he lurched forward and spit into Carson's face.

The man responded with a ringing slap across Madison's face. Then he backed away, pulling a handkerchief from his pocket to wipe the spittle from his face. "Judge, let the court pronounce its verdict."

The pseudo-judge turned to the line of men sitting in jury. Looking at the first he said, "Carrington?"

"Guilty." No hesitation, no change of expression. Just the dully sounded word that fell dead into the night.

"Myers?"

"Guilty."

"Bradlin?"

"Guilty."

"Hodge?"

"Guilty."

And on down the line it went, the answers predictably the same, each sounded with the same dull expression, each responded to by Madison with a desperate, almost pitiful flashing of his eye and flaring of his nostrils. He was doomed. All knew it. He knew it.

When at last the verdict was in, Carson turned to the man sitting in judgment. The very silence seemed to ring in my ears, and Jennifer moved closer to me.

"You have heard the verdict, Your Honor. What is the court's sentence?"

The "judge" stood and looked toward Madison.

He looked straight into his face and said in a clear voice, "Death. By hanging, at sunrise."

The crowd seemed to break through its stupor then, and angry voices were heard, protesting the insanity of it all, horrified by all that had occurred and fearful of what was to come.

"Here, now—I won't be a witness to murder!"

"This is absurd—I insist that this man be taken to the authorities for a real trial . . ."

"This is preposterous!"

Carson whirled about, a pistol flashing torchlight in his grasp. "Shut up! All of you! There has been a trial and a verdict, and the sentence will be carried out! Ben, get a rope—it isn't long 'til dawn."

I heard a sudden rustling behind me. A lady, dressed in a fashionable and highly starched dress, had fainted into the arms of a seedy cowboy who looked at a loss as to what to do with her. I couldn't blame her for passing out, for I had no desire to see what was coming any more than she did. I almost envied her.

Strange how I found it hard to hate Madison now. I knew that he deserved exactly what he was getting, but still . . .

I looked at Carson and his men. Obsessed, maddened men, forever warped by the horrors they had seen in the war. Their lives had known one central purpose all of these years—to find and destroy Josiah Madison. And when he at last was finished, what then would they live for?

Carson. A man so obsessed with justice that he would commit any injustice to attain it. So hateful for Madison that he became just like him to destroy him. There was an irony in it I was sure he would never himself see.

A noose was tied and strung across a limb, and as it dangled menacingly in the fading night there were many murmurs of dissent. But no one could lift a finger to stop the execution, for several of the gunmen had turned their weapons on the crowd, apparently in a deliberate effort to dispel any thoughts of trying to stop what was happening.

In the east the sky lightened into a gold touched with violet, then the colors faded into the yellow of the last morning Josiah Madison would ever see.

Carson looked over at the pitiful outlaw, who now had lost his air of defiance and trembled like a whipped child. "Tie him up," Carson ordered.

The order was carried out, thongs being tied roughly around Madison's wrists behind his back. I could tell that the bonds were too tight, for Madison winced as they pulled them into hard knots that constricted his wrists so tightly that his hands reddened and seemed to swell.

Other men were dragging crates from the train and emptying the contents on the ground. Three of the large crates were dragged over to the tree and stacked atop each other beneath the rope. It was a rickety platform—and deliberately so. A ladder also taken from the train was leaned against the tree beside the crates.

"Up the ladder, Madison. Move, man! The time has come!"

Madison broke down, screaming horribly, weeping, cursing Carson and those with him. But nonetheless he was shoved forward, moved toward the makeshift gallows that stood silently in the early morning light, the noose casting an ominous shadow on the trunk of the tree.

Madison was forced up the ladder and out onto the platform of crates, and the noose was adjusted tightly around his neck. And then he was left alone on his perch, the ladder kicked away, Carson's men moving aside.

"Jim, I can't watch this . . . I can't," Jennifer said, turning and burying her face in my shoulder. I wanted to turn away too, but something kept me from doing so. I felt strangely obliged to watch what was happening.

Carson moved forward, smiling up at the doomed man on the crates.

"Josiah Madison, for crimes against innumerable innocent victims throughout the course of your miserable life, I hereby do carry out the sentence of this court. Pray, if you know how, for your life is now ending."

Madison lifted his eye to the sky as Carson moved forward, and tears streamed down his cheeks. Just as Carson's foot kicked away the bottom crate the outlaw wailed out a cry, the words indiscernible, the pitiful wailing cut sickeningly short as the rope jerked and separated the bones in Madison's neck. For a moment the body twitched, then the eye glazed, and it was over. Behind me I heard the sound of someone vomiting.

Josiah Madison was dead.

Carson's men made no noise, gave no cheer. They moved forward and grouped themselves around the silent, hanging body, staring at it almost like worshippers at a shrine. Carson's face showed at first a sort of satisfaction that then faded into a look of emptiness.

I couldn't stand to watch anymore, and I turned away. Jennifer was weeping, and I pulled her close to me. In all my life I had never felt so mortal, so aware of death.

Chapter XXII

The sun drove away the morning mist, and Carson and his riders vanished with it.

The body of Madison was cut down and placed in an empty crate from the train. With the swinging, limp form gone from the tree, it was hard to think of what had occurred as more than a dream.

To my surprise the train's engine was not too damaged to continue, and after the tracks were cleared and minor readjustments were completed the passengers boarded and the trip resumed almost as if nothing had happened. Jennifer and I sat clinging to each other, though, finding it hard to believe that it was all finally over.

After a time of silence we began to talk about what had happened. "How did Carson know Madison would be aboard that train?" she asked.

"I don't fully know," I said. "But I suspect one of his men spotted Madison in Helena, saw him board the train, and wired the information on the telegraph. Carson probably had a wiretap set up. It amazes me to see the extent to which he and his men worked just to get their hands on Madison. How could any human being hate another that much?"

Jennifer made no attempt to answer that question. I drew her close to me, and her presence strengthened me. In that strength I found the ability to ask the question that had nagged at my mind almost since I had first met Jennifer that first day in Montana. And the answer she gave filled me with joy.

I met McCuen in the streets of Miles City the following day. He was laughing, shaking his head in disbelief.

"Marriage! That astounds me, Hartford! It's not exactly what you expected when you came to Montana, is it?"

"Not by a long shot. But I'm grateful it's happened. And I want you to come to the ceremony, of course."

"I'll be there. I wouldn't miss this for the world. And I've got just the present for you . . ."

"What's that?"

"A few rolls of barbed wire, of course."

"Thanks . . . I'll be needing it. With Sam's spread, as well as my land and that legally owned by the Muster Creek Company, we'll be stringing a lot of fences."

And so ends the story of how I came as a destitute farmer from Powell's Valley, Tennessee and married the daughter of the richest cattle baron in the Montana Territory.

ABOUT THE AUTHOR

Cameron Judd is at the forefront of today's new generation of western writers. Marked by a love for the land and the men and women who died upon it, his writing is authentic, entertaining, and bursting with the spirit of the old west. Hailing from Tennessee, he has just finished a historical novel about Daniel Boone.